RICKY'S HAND

Also by David Quantick
and available from Titan Books

All My Colors
Night Train

RICKY'S HAND

DAVID QUANTICK

TITAN BOOKS

Ricky's Hand
Print edition ISBN: 9781803360461
E-book edition ISBN: 9781803360478

Published by Titan Books
A division of Titan Publishing Group Ltd
144 Southwark Street, London SE1 0UP
www.titanbooks.com

First edition: August 2022
10 9 8 7 6 5 4 3 2 1

This is a work of fiction. All of the characters, organizations, and events
portrayed in this novel are either products of the author's imagination or
are used fictitiously. Any resemblance to actual persons, living or dead
(except for satirical purposes), is entirely coincidental.

A CIP catalogue record for this title is available from the British Library.

Printed and bound in the UK by CPI Group (UK) Ltd.

To Matthew

ONE

One morning Ricky Smart looked down at his hand and screamed.

Ricky thought of himself as an observant guy. It went with the job, which was taking photographs of people who didn't know he was taking photographs of them. Ricky called himself a paparazzi, although the right word was *paparazzo*, and everyone else just called him a creep. But he made money selling the pictures to websites and newspapers, although it wasn't a lot of money because nobody cared about quality anymore and any clown could take a picture of a celebrity with their phone.

It wasn't much of a living, but it was a life. Until the day he looked down at his hand and screamed.

He woke up that morning without a hangover, which was a bonus. Ricky checked all the things in his head that he might need to know before he got up: where was he, had he done anything last night he needed to be worried about, would he fall over if he got up, and so on. The list complete – *in my own bed, no, probably not* – he opened his eyes and lifted his arm to look at his watch. His eyes were still gummy from sleep and dehydration, so for a moment it was hard to focus, but after he screwed up his eyes and blinked, Ricky could see that his watch was not on his wrist.

This was odd. Ricky was very much someone who slept with his watch on. Not only was it practical, it also saved messing with the complexities of a strap while drunk. Also, Ricky had no memory of taking the watch off. True, he had no memory of a lot of things – including all of July 2009 – but taking his watch off was something he would have remembered, if only because last night had been so dull that taking off his watch would have been a high point. And yet there it was. No watch.

Ricky lifted his hand to look more closely at the place where his watch should be – and then he froze.

There was something wrong. It was his hand.

It was different.

Ricky rotated his wrist to examine it more closely. His hand looked perfectly OK as hands go. Four fingers, a thumb, all the nails, everything present and correct.

But it wasn't *right*.

First, it was the wrong weight. Ricky had no idea how much his hands weighed, because they'd never been detached from his arms and put on a set of scales, but he would have said they were probably the same weight as each other. But this hand seemed to be a little heavier than the other. All his life, Ricky had felt fairly balanced in the matter of hands, but now he felt like someone had stuck two large and differently sized vegetables on the ends of his wrists.

Second, there was the shape. This hand seemed to be a bit *stockier* than the other one, like it was the hand of someone who worked outdoors, or lifted weights, or some physical shit like that.

And third, there were some scars that he had definitely never seen before. Not new scars, either, but the kind of whitened, hard scars that time had worked on.

"What the hell?" Ricky mumbled to himself. The whole thing was stupid. People didn't wake up with new hands like Frankenstein or something. They woke up with their old hands and the only thing that ever changed was that the hands got older. It must be his eyes, or the light, or some stupid thing.

He rolled off the bed, dislodging his watch and its broken strap – *there it is*, he thought – and made his way into the bathroom. Ricky wasn't a fat man, not exactly, but he was a little busty and his navel stuck out of his hairy stomach like a whale's eye. He flip-flopped his way across the tiled floor, turned on the light above the bathroom mirror, and lifted his hands up like he was about to surrender.

Now Ricky could see that his hands weren't the same as each other. The right hand was entirely familiar to him – the skin quite soft, almost downy, the nails badly manicured – even down to the small, sickle-shaped scar on his palm that he'd got in a fight with a girl as a teenager. But the left hand – the left hand was different somehow. The skin seemed more weather-beaten, harder and maybe even tougher. The nails were small and ground-down. And the fingers were chunky, the knuckles like nuggets of bone under the skin.

Ricky brought his hand (the *new* hand, as he was trying

not to call it) closer to his face; and then he saw it. At first he couldn't understand why he hadn't seen it right away. Maybe it had been the light, or maybe he just hadn't looked properly. All he could do, once he'd realized fully what he was looking at, was stare.

On the knuckles of his right hand, carved in faded but deep ink and written in a shaky, just-legible hand, were four letters.

F U C K

Ricky had never seen the letters before. He hadn't put them there. But someone had. The person that the hand belonged to.

And that was when he screamed.

Ricky screamed so hard he stepped backwards and fell over. He grabbed at the bathtub but too late to stop his fall, and went over like a toppled penguin.

"Oww!" he shouted as his head slammed into the hard floor. He lost consciousness for a moment, and when he came round a few seconds later couldn't remember where he was or even who he was. He gazed up at the ceiling, groaned, and pulled himself upright with his other hand on the side of the toilet.

Ricky sat on the side of the bath for a few minutes, feeling the new bump on the back of his head.

"What a crappy start to the day," he said out loud to himself.

He frowned. Something had happened. Something to do with his—

He looked down. There it was again.

F U C K

"Fuck," said Ricky, agreeing with his hand.

He stood up, went over to the basin, turned on the water and put his hand under the stream. It gushed out nearly boiling but

Ricky didn't care. As the water scalded his hands, he rubbed at his knuckles with soap. *I'm gonna wash that fuck right offa my hand,* he hummed to himself.

Ricky looked down. Nothing had changed. He reached under the sink for a bottle of bleach, its neck encrusted blue, and poured some onto an old nail brush. Ricky winced as he scrubbed at his knuckles. The writing wasn't coming off, but quite a bit of skin was. He stopped. All he was doing was hurting himself. He rinsed the bleach off his burning skin, gently dabbed his hand dry with a towel, and went back into the bedroom. He sat down on the bed and tried to think.

Ricky had read something once about the five stages of denial. They were, he vaguely remembered, something like denial, anger, depression, acceptance, and lust. After a moment's thought, he shortened the list to four by excluding lust. After a few more moments' thought, he decided that he was passing through denial quite quickly – it was hard for him to deny the existence of something as solid as a fucking hand, after all – but he was still a long way off acceptance. Anger, then, was his current state and, Ricky mused as he stared at the fleshy interloper on his wrist, who could blame him?

He looked around for his phone and found it plugged into the charger by some miracle. Picking it up, Ricky jabbed at the home screen, but with no luck. The words *"Fingerprint not recognized"* appeared on the screen.

"Shit the fuck!" Ricky shouted. "Shit the fuck this and piss on it!"

He smashed his new hand into the wall, remembering too late that, while it might not be his hand, it was still attached to

13

his muscles and nerve endings. The pain was quite considerable, and made it even harder to type in his old security password with his new fingers.

A few moments later he had the number he needed, and he dialed it.

"Fuck you," said a woman's voice.

"That's no way to talk to your brother."

"Says you."

"Listen, I wouldn't normally call—"

"Then don't. Bye."

"Wait! This is a fucking crisis."

Ricky's sister sighed.

"It's always a fucking crisis with you," she said, and rang off.

Ricky swore for a while, then called the hospital.

"Mount Ararat Medical Center," said the voice at the other end of the line. "Which department do you require?"

"Hi," said Ricky, and stopped. What department *did* he require?

"I need the emergency room," he said finally.

"If it's an emergency, you'll need to come in yourself. Unless you're unable to, of course."

Ricky waggled his fingers.

"Nope," he said, "I can come in."

Ricky put a plastic glove on his hand, the kind they give out in a chicken restaurant where the food is extra greasy, and took a shower. He didn't know why he had put on the glove, but it seemed like a good idea. *Maybe it's infectious,* he thought, and an image came into his head of touching his dick and his dick turning into something else. He tried to shake the picture out of his head and concentrate on being a regular person just taking a shower. But the image would not go away. Ricky's hand on Ricky's dick. Ricky's *new* hand on Ricky's old dick.

New dicks for old! thought Ricky. He remembered a story about a king called Midas, who made everything turn to gold when he touched it, and wondered if Midas had ever touched his own dick in the shower.

Ricky hurriedly finished his ablutions, dried himself and got dressed (he rarely shaved, believing – wrongly – that his stubbly cheeks were alluring to women). Then, because deep down he was a practical man, he made himself a bowl of cereal and ate it hurriedly, Cheerios spilling from his milky mouth.

He took off the plastic glove, wiped his mouth, picked his coat up from off the floor, checked for his car keys and, after a moment's thought, went to a drawer full of mismatched socks, old underwear, balaclavas, and gloves. Ricky took out his favorite pair of gloves, but the right glove didn't fit. Swearing a little, he found a second, woolen pair that fit both hands fine. Ricky pulled them on and left the house.

Ricky's car was parked right outside his apartment. It was a yellow Pontiac Aztek, which Ricky had chosen because it was cheap and inconspicuous, or at least it had been before Ricky had filled it with Burger King debris. It also had a tent in the back that folded out, which Ricky was sure might be useful on a long stakeout, but so far had not been. He checked the location of the hospital on his phone and started the engine.

Twenty minutes later, Ricky was crossing the Mount Ararat parking lot to the emergency room.

"Hi," he told the receptionist, a portly man called Steven, "I called earlier."

"Yeah," Steven replied. "We don't really do bookings. Take a ticket."

Ricky sat down. The room was half full with people who seemed to have been stabbed, cut or just battered with varying degrees of success. He was sure people were staring at him and noting with disapproval his apparent lack of flesh wounds.

After some time, his name was called and he went into a small room with a large window, where a cheerful-looking woman in her forties introduced herself as Nurse Mike.

"Don't I get a doctor?" Ricky asked.

"This is the emergency room. You get Nurse Mike," said Nurse Mike.

Ricky worked in the entertainment industry, so he was used to people referring to themselves in the third person. He said, "OK. But this might be something for a doctor."

"And you might be hurting my feelings," Nurse Mike replied. "Now please, shit or get off the pot."

Ricky took off his gloves, first the left, then the right. He thrust his hands out at Nurse Mike.

"You see it?" he asked.

"See what?" answered Nurse Mike.

"My hands," said Ricky.

"I see your hands," Nurse Mike agreed. "What about them?"

"They're different!"

Nurse Mike smiled. "Everyone's hands are different," she said. "I mean, a little bit. Look at mine."

"I don't want to look at your hands," said Ricky. "I want you to look at my hands."

"Oh," said Nurse Mike. "I get it now. They are different."

"Finally," Ricky said.

"You've got that offensive tattoo on your right hand."

"What?"

"Right there," Nurse Mike said. "The F word."

She gave Ricky a friendly, understanding look.

"But this is the emergency room," she said. "We don't do laser removals here. You need—"

"It's not the tattoo," said Ricky. "It's the whole hand."

"You want the hand removed?"

"No!" Ricky said. "I mean, maybe... I don't know."

Nurse Mike shook her head.

"If this is a body image thing, I sympathize. We had a guy in here, wanted his leg off. But again, this is the—"

Ricky shouted, "It's not my hand!"

"Excuse me?"

"This! My hand! It's not my hand!"

Nurse Mike frowned.

"It's not your hand?" she repeated.

"No," said Ricky. "I woke up this morning and this fucking thing was where my hand should be."

Nurse Mike leaned in.

"It does look a little different," she admitted. "But that could be for any number of reasons."

"Like what?"

"Allergy, bee sting, animal bite, various kinds of infection... all of those would make it swell up."

"Yeah, but none of those would make a tattoo appear on my hand."

"Listen, pal," said Nurse Mike, sitting upright. "Maybe you

got bit by something, you freaked out, got drunk, had a tattoo done for some reason, I don't know. But whatever it is, it's not an emergency, and this—" she said, getting up and opening the door, "—is the emergency room."

After sitting in the Aztek for a few minutes and banging his head on the steering wheel, Ricky considered his options. He could ask to be admitted to the correct department, but he had no idea what the correct department was. He could forget the whole thing, which was hard to do when he had this fucking hand. Or he could just take a few deep breaths, make an appointment with a doctor, and in the meantime get back to work. Ricky decided this was the best option. If nothing else, he still had to eat.

Ricky lifted up his hand and addressed it directly.

"I don't know who you are or what the fuck is going on," he told it. "But I have a full day ahead of me and you are not going to mess with it."

The hand did not reply so Ricky drove home.

Once back at the apartment, Ricky went into his bedroom and opened his tiny closet, most of which was taken up by a bulky safe. Ricky's safe was his number two prized possession. Ricky's number one prized possession was inside the safe. He jabbed at the electronic display until it beeped at him and the small but hefty metal door swung open. He crouched down and was about to reach inside when he remembered his hand and put the plastic glove back on. He was almost sure that touching the contents of his safe with the hand would be alright, but better to be cautious; besides, the glove was opaque so he didn't have to keep looking at what was written on his knuckles. He reached into the safe with his other hand and took out a large black case with a strap. Closing the safe, he placed the case on a table and opened it.

Inside was Ricky's camera, a slightly scratched but impressive-looking Olympus. Ricky stroked its smooth black casing: he and the Olympus had been in a few tight spots together, and almost always come out on top. He checked that the camera was fully charged and ready to go, slung it over his T-shirt (*MILEY CYRUS LIVE 2010*), picked up the camera bag, and headed out the door.

Ricky got into the Aztek, pushed out several burger wrappers, placed the camera bag delicately in the passenger footwell, took out his cell phone and looked at his schedule.

9AM LEGALLY BLONDE IV SCRNG was the first entry. Ricky looked at his watch: 9.40. Ricky shrugged: nobody went to screenings.

10.30 REGALITY HOTEL SCALA JAQ. This was more like it – if it was true. Ricky's contact at the Regality did a little too much coke for Ricky's liking and had a tendency to spin gold from bullshit. Scala Jaq – singer, actress, and influencer – *could* be checking into the Regality at 10.30, but equally Ricky could be getting scammed for a hundred bucks.

Ricky shrugged again. He had nothing to lose, and if Coke Boy was right, it was going to be a nice payday. He turned on the engine and pointed the Aztek toward the city.

Ricky grew up in Miami Beach and so, being Ricky, he had always lived in Miami Beach. When his parents died, Ricky bought an apartment on the outskirts of town, and that was the only thing that had changed about his life. That, and the job.

Growing up where he did, Ricky had seen so many celebrities that they seemed to be part of the scenery, in the same way that the tourists, the retired people, and the homeless were part of the scenery, with the difference that none of the homeless, the retired, and the tourists were always stepping out of limousines, walking into clubs, dining at fancy restaurants, staying at beautiful Art Deco hotels – or being photographed.

Unlike many people, Ricky knew that he would become a celebrity only by killing someone or being killed by someone. He was not photogenic, had no screen presence, and whatever "it" was, Ricky had never had. But he did belong to a Camera Club, for the simple reason that he was lonely and he had a camera (his dad's) and, after a local nature photographer came to Ricky's club and revealed his actual source of income, Ricky evolved a career plan.

Since then, Ricky could be seen most mornings, afternoons, and nights hanging around outside hotels, bars, and clubs, camera round his neck, trying to get famous people to move a little to the left or the right, so that he could take their picture and then sell it to someone else for anything up to ten thousand dollars. Most of the time he just got a middle finger or a blurred head turning away, but occasionally (like with Miley Cyrus back in 2010), he hit the jackpot.

It was a tough life, by Ricky's standards anyway. He was outdoors most of the time, competing with other, more ruthless, paps, and he was always at the mercy of cops, rentacops, private security, angry fans, and jealous stalkers. Nevertheless, Ricky thought of himself as a Zen-like patient fisherman, prepared to wait for hours for the perfect time to cast his rod and reel in a big catch. Of course, very few fishermen ever got punched in the face, but so it went. Ricky was a pap now, and that was all there was to it. He made a living, he sometimes took vacations, and one day he was going to hit the motherlode.

But for now he was taking the Aztek at a moderate speed toward a hotel that was right on South Beach itself, on a tip that might be solid gold and might equally be bullshit. He had a full tank of gas, a reliable camera, and the whole day ahead of him.

And someone else's hand on the end of his wrist.

TWO

Ricky didn't want to think about the hand, but he supposed he had to. And he was enough of a pragmatist to know that if he ignored it, it wouldn't go away. So he forced himself to think about the hand.

One, it was at least a hand. Whatever malevolent force – and he was sure it was malevolent – was after him had at least given him a hand in the place where a hand should be, and not a claw, or a foot or (*a dick*) something worse. It looked like a hand and – from all the evidence so far – it acted like a hand. Ricky could hold things with it, open doors with it, drive a car with it, and (he checked) scratch his ear with it.

Two, it wasn't actually harming him. Despite being clearly not his, the hand didn't hurt, throb, or ache. It didn't lunge at him or try to gouge his eyes out. It wasn't attempting to drive the car or write Satanic messages. It was just a hand.

Three, it was fucking weird. This was Ricky's main issue with the hand. No way was there supposed to be someone else's hand on the end of his arm. It was technically possible that he might have had a new hand sewn onto him, but that would be something that would take time – the sawing, the sewing, the arrangement of muscles and nerves and so on – and Ricky was pretty sure he hadn't lost three days of his life and forgotten about it. Last night he had been a man with both his hands in the right place, and now he wasn't.

Four, which was still part of three, it didn't hurt. At all. Not only was there no Frankenstein-style ring of stitches around his wrist, but his new hand just felt... normal. It was completely ordinary in the way it just sat there at the end of his wrist and, basically, did hand stuff. Even if it had been surgically added in some mysterious surgical process that Ricky could not remember, it surely ought to throb, or at least itch a little; but it felt fine.

Five – and five was the summary of all the other points, the grand total after adding them all up – Ricky's hand was completely impossible. This was the conclusion Ricky was reluctant to make. He could cope – just – with the hand being not his. He could live, more or less, with the hand acting like nothing was off, and hands were always just appearing on people's wrists. What he couldn't cope with, however, was the idea of the thing.

Hands don't do this, thought Ricky, watching the hand that was not his hand flick up the turn indicator.

He realized that he was nearly at the Regality. There was a small crowd outside that might have been there for Scala Jaq or might not have been. Either way, it was enough to make Ricky forgot about the hand for five minutes and focus instead on finding somewhere to park.

The Regality was one of the oldest hotels on South Beach, and had for many years also been one of the most run-down. In 2007 it was bought by a new conglomerate and given an extensive makeover that removed most of the original features but retained the ocean front; it was thus the only hotel in Florida that looked better from behind.

Which was where Ricky found himself after parking the Aztek and hurrying to the front of the hotel, where the hardcore paps had gathered, along with the TV crews and the legit journalists. Sent on his way for not having the right pass, Ricky had simply gone around the back of the hotel and – at a nod from Coke Boy, keen to get more dollars – had skipped in through the bar and was now lurking behind a tall baggage cart, cramming a flash unit onto the body of his Olympus. A tag flapped in his face and he was about to flick it away when he saw the name scrawled on it:

SCALA JAQ.

Ricky couldn't believe his luck. Coke Boy had come through! Scala Jaq was staying here. He looked at his watch. 10.30. If she was on time—

"Take this to the Tangerine Suite," said a voice, and for a microsecond Ricky thought it was talking to him.

"Yes, sir," a bellboy replied, and the trolley began to move.

Ricky thought fast. He took a baseball cap and a pair of sunglasses from his pocket, dropped the camera bag onto the cart, and followed the bellboy into the elevator, thus negating any need for a key card.

The bellboy swiped his own key card and, looking uncertainly at Ricky, asked:

"What floor please, sir?"

Ricky knew the layout of the Regality like (*the back of his...*) he knew his own name.

"Tenth," he said, because in his clothes "Penthouse" would have aroused suspicion.

"Very good, sir," said the bellboy and pressed 10 before pressing P.

They rode in silence, Ricky recovering his camera bag from the cart.

"Thanks," he said as the door opened onto the tenth floor.

He stepped out, waited for the elevator to go on up, and made his way to the service stairs.

Arriving out of breath on the Penthouse Floor, Ricky leaned against the wall for a moment, then, satisfied he wasn't going to die, sat down at the top of the stairs. He wasn't going to do anything dumb like walk up to the Tangerine Suite and shout, "Room service!" because Ricky's job was a waiting game. He looked at his watch again, sat down on the stairs, took out his phone, and waited.

Half an hour later he had just finished his tenth game of Snake when he heard the elevator doors open. Ricky opened the fire door, stepped out, and flattened himself into an alcove containing a large fire extinguisher.

He could hear voices now.

"I'm not doing it." A woman's voice, young.

"Scala, it's ten minutes." An older man.

"It's never ten minutes, Jonty. Is the room ready? I need to lie down."

"You just got here."

"I don't feel great. Is that OK? Or do I need to clear it with you first?"

"These people have been waiting for hours."

"Then they won't mind waiting a few more. Just give me a half hour."

"It's never a half hour."

"Touché, you shot me down. OK, a half hour."

"A real half hour."

"Alright."

Ricky heard the elevator doors close. He gingerly poked his head out of the alcove. The woman beeped her key card at the door.

In videos and on posters, Scala Jaq shone, her dark skin accentuated by jewelry, expensive clothes and the retoucher's art. In person, wearing an olive-green flight jacket and a cheap baseball cap, she still possessed – Ricky had to admit – some kind of glow, as if stardom came from within. It was an interesting thought, but not one Ricky had time for. He reached for his camera, then restrained himself. She might hear him, and besides, who would pay for a photo of someone opening a door?

Ricky had no plan but he was a born improviser, which was another way of saying that he had no idea what he was doing. Seconds later his patience was rewarded as Scala Jaq unzipped her jacket and took out – *a bottle? a baggie? a gun?* – a small dog. It was scrawny and had fur the way an ageing rock star has hair.

Ricky fired off a few shots. They weren't much, and Scala was dressed like she was about to fly a helicopter – that jacket, combat pants, leather gloves for God's sake – but it was a candid shot and the agency liked candid shots.

"Be quiet now, Jonas," she told the dog. The dog snuffled rebelliously but did not bark. Scala opened the door, put the dog down, and closed the door behind her.

Ricky checked the images on his camera. *WHAT'S SCALA HIDING?* would be a good headline, he decided, although the dipsticks at the agency never took his suggestions. The shots were OK, maybe a few hundred dollars, but there was no jackpot here.

Ricky thought about the kind of shots he needed. *Exclusive* was a word that came to mind. *Intimate* was another.

He wondered if he could get into the room.

• • •

Jonas scurried about the suite, his claws clattering like a maniac typing on a keyboard. He sniffed the couch, ran into the kitchenette, and barked at a decorative cat made of wire.

"It's not real, Jonas," said Scala. "This is a hotel, remember? None of it's real."

Like many people who had worked in the entertainment industry for much of their lives, Scala had gone through naivety (*they love me!*) and past cynicism (*I'm just a cash cow*) to an understanding of what it was to be a star in the modern era. She knew that, while millions downloaded her videos, watched her feeds, and sang along to her songs, she was not so much a product as the spokesperson for that product. And she was also aware, as many artists are not, that her life could be much, much worse.

Scala had begun her career in a kids' show on a streaming

network, where she'd been first a dancer, then a backing singer, and finally, at the age of fifteen, a featured performer. With a cute image and a couple of movies under her Hello Kitty belt, Scala was launched onto the teen market. She was a huge success with family audiences and even made a Christmas album. Then at seventeen she discovered she could write songs, and the second phase of her career began, in which she at least gave the impression of taking control, as both her songs and her new image suggested that here was a new, more mature adult artist who would not be doing anything cute or Christmassy.

And now here she was, in a very nice hotel with a dog that couldn't tell real from fake and a few minutes to herself. Her luggage had been unpacked, and her tablet placed on a low black marble table. She switched it on and opened her official fan account. It was the usual geyser blast of caps-lock sycophancy, unhinged love, and veiled threats (her management had weeded out the actual threats, and police in several states were on constant alert for the real nutjobs). But a few crazies and stans got through and Scala liked to make sure she knew who they were.

Next she typed her own name into the big search engines, just to see what people thought she was up to right now. Most of it was officially sanctioned drivel: boys she was supposed to be seeing, events she had attended, movies and albums she was making, and so on. But some of it was half-deranged rumor. Her membership of a satanic coven had apparently been confirmed, as well as her sexual relationships with a congressman, a WWF wrestler and two K-Pop stars. Oh, and she had had her lips both made bigger and made smaller, which seemed rather a waste of money.

Finally, she opened her email account. This was encrypted to almost secret service levels, with three constantly changed computer-generated passwords, and so far had evaded the hacking skills of several hundred freaks and weirdoes living in their moms' basements. Ignoring the slew of emails from family members, record company staff and management, she began to type in a name that autofill completed for her and wrote:

Hey.

A few seconds later she got a reply:

Oh, hey! Or "hey stranger," I should say. Where have you been?

Scala typed again:

Sorry, been in transit.

That's OK, the reply came, *I had things to do as well. So – where are you?*

South Beach, some dumb hotel.

I bet it's nice.

Yeah, Jonas likes it.

She looked round. Jonas was staring at the cat sculpture, teeth bared.

Listen, she wrote, *I'm still not good.*

Is it worse?

No, the same. But it's freaking me out.

Seconds went past. Scala could hear the buzz of the aircon in the room. Then:

OK. Time to do this. You ready?

She thought for a moment, then typed:

I'm ready.

. . .

"Excuse me, sir?"

Ricky woke up. He was sitting on the stairs. A large man with a huge face was standing over him. *Shit.*

"Yes?" he said.

"Is this yours?"

The man was holding Ricky's camera bag. He opened it and saw it contained a charger and a flash unit.

"Not mine, no," said Ricky. He stood up, which only brought him closer to the huge face.

The man stared at Ricky. It was like being stared at by the full moon.

"If you don't mind, I need to search you," he said.

"I do mind," Ricky said, but the man patted him down anyway.

"It's a form of words," he said.

He found nothing, and seemed disappointed.

"If this isn't yours," he said, "I'll hand it in at the front desk."

Shit.

"No skin off my nose," said Ricky.

"This is a restricted-access floor," said the man. "You shouldn't be here."

"I'm gone," Ricky replied, and started back down the stairs, the huge face watching him.

Three flights down, Ricky heard the fire door close. He crept back up, retrieved his camera from a windowsill, and went down to the lobby.

Coke Boy was there with his hand literally out.

"Not now," Ricky said.

"Aw, man," said Coke Boy.

"When I get the shot," Ricky said.

Coke Boy said nothing, just sniffed dolefully.

Ricky walked out the front entrance, sat on a wall, and called the agency, who were keen to see the corridor shots of Scala.

Ricky was down a flash gun and a charger, but up a thousand dollars. Not bad for an hour's work.

He looked down at his hand.

"OK," he said. "Now we can go see a doctor."

THREE

Ricky didn't like doctors for two reasons. One, they cost money. And two, they never had a good word to say about him. Every time it was the same: the doctor would make him take off his shirt, which he was never happy about, and then they'd stick things in him, and make him run on a treadmill, or tell him to cough while they cradled his nuts, and at the end of it they'd just look at him and tell him he was fucked. Fucked, and he needed to cut down on his drinking, and his smoking, and his eating, or something: although these days it wasn't something, it was everything.

Ricky didn't like doctors, and he didn't like going to the doctor's. So today was special because even though he wasn't coughing up goo, or sweating out vodka, or breathing like a busted whoopee cushion, Ricky was going to the doctor of his own accord, like he enjoyed going to the doctor.

The doctor he was seeing today was called Doctor Martinez and she was a pain in the ass.

"I see from your records," said Martinez, not even asking

Ricky how he was, "that you continue to smoke and drink and eat junk food even though it is having a highly deleterious effect on your health."

Ricky liked the word "deleterious" because it made Doctor Martinez sound drunk when she said it, but he didn't like the way the doctor was saying it, so he played his ace.

"I'm not here about any of that, doc," he said, almost defiantly.

Doctor Martinez gave him a look best described as "you're a fucking idiot then."

"Why are you here then, Mister Smart?"

Ricky removed the bag from his hand.

"Because," he said triumphantly, "of this."

Doctor Martinez frowned.

"Because of what?" she asked.

"My hand," said Ricky.

"What about your hand?" said Doctor Martinez.

Jesus, thought Ricky, *is she simple?*

"Look at it," he said.

"I am looking at it," Martinez said. "Four fingers, one thumb, everything where it should be."

"It's not right," said Ricky.

"It looks fine to me," said Doctor Martinez. She frowned. "When you say it's not right—"

When I say it's not right, I mean it's not my fucking hand, Ricky wanted to say. Instead he said:

"I mean it feels wrong."

"Go on," said Doctor Martinez, in a different tone of voice. Ricky hated that "go on." It sounded interested, and it meant he'd gone from *crazy asshole* to *interesting crazy asshole*.

"You wouldn't understand," he said, sulkily.

"No," said Doctor Martinez. "I mean, I might."

Ricky took a deep breath. "It doesn't feel like my hand," he began. "It just feels like—"

Like someone's else's hand. Which it is. It's someone else's hand.

"—like it's not mine," he finished.

"Is it numb at all?" asked Doctor Martinez. "Does it feel strange to the touch? Is it painful?"

Ricky shook his head.

"There's a condition called body dysmorphia," Martinez said. "People sometimes feel that their arms, or legs, are wrong in some way. In extreme cases, they arrange for them to be amputated. Is that how you feel?"

Ricky stared at her.

"I don't want my hand amputated," he said. "Because then I wouldn't have a hand."

"Alright," said Martinez, hurt. "I'm just going through the options here."

"Look at it!" Ricky repeated. He thrust his hand at her.

Martinez took his hand.

"It's not the same as the other one," Ricky added, weakly.

"No," Martinez agreed, "it's not."

"You can see that?"

"Oh yes," Martinez replied, and Ricky felt a twinge of hope. "But that's pretty common. The human body, as I'm sure you know, isn't entirely symmetrical. One side may look like the mirror image of the other, but that's not the case – which is why our reflections seem odd to us."

"But this hand," said Ricky. "It's not just a little bit different, it's a lot different."

"Of course it is," Martinez said. "Unless you're one hundred percent ambidextrous, one hand is always going to be stronger than the other, or more developed, depending on whether you use it for writing, or manual labor or—"

"It's a different *color*!" Ricky said, agitated.

Doctor Martinez smiled implacably, the undefeated mind chess champion of Miami Beach.

"Ever rest your arm on the door frame when you're driving?" she asked. "You can get a tan on one hand doing that."

Ricky got up.

"Thanks for your time," he mumbled, and left.

Outside in the parking lot, Ricky sat in the Aztek and punched the dashboard repeatedly.

"Fuck!" he shouted. "Fuck!"

The writing on his hand agreed with him.

Ricky sat in the parking lot, watching the patients and the medical staff come and go. He wondered how many of them were having a good day, and how many were having a bad day. He tried to guess which people had just been given terrible news, and which had just got the all-clear for something. He wondered how it would feel to have an illness where the doctor said, "No problem, lots of people have this, and we cured it years ago," and filled out a form so the patients could get their pills and get well again.

Ricky wondered if that could be him, looked at his hand, and shook his head.

Not a fucking hope, he thought, and turned on the engine.

He had no idea what was going to happen next but, if his life so far had been any indicator, it would involve money.

Time to go back to work.

Ricky accelerated out of the parking lot toward the beach, because the money and the work were both staying at the Regality, in the Tangerine Suite.

• • •

Ricky walked into the lobby and Coke Boy was already there, his red nose twitching like he was a neon rabbit.

"I want my money," he said.

"Get me into the suite first," Ricky replied.

"I'm not fucking doing that," said Coke Boy. "Anyway, she's not in the suite."

Ricky gave him a long look.

"What?" said Coke Boy.

"Where. Is. She. Then?" Ricky said as slowly as possible.

"Oh, got it. She's on the roof."

"The roof?"

"Yeah, they got a new pool up there."

"She doing a shoot?"

"No!" Coke Boy smiled. It was more of a leer than a smile, and more of a hideous gurn than a leer. "She's doin' laps."

Ricky, whose experience of doin' laps was mostly confined to strip clubs, didn't know what Coke Boy meant for a moment. Then he got it.

"She's swimming? You mean, like a workout?"

Coke Boy shrugged.

"I think she likes swimming," he said.

Ricky shook his head. Celebs were weird, there was no doubt about it.

He went up to the roof in the service elevator. Coke Boy had refused to get him a staff outfit, but Ricky had kept a name badge he'd filched on a previous visit and that would have to do. Pushing a cleaning cart, he acted like he was keeping his eyes to himself, looking down at the ground as much as possible so any security on the roof wouldn't get antsy and think he was spying.

But when he got out onto the roof terrace, ignoring the raw sheet of sun bearing down on him, Ricky couldn't see any security. In fact, he couldn't see anyone at all. He took a spray gun from the cart and sprayed cleaning fluid on the surface of the poolside bar, all the while trying to look around without raising his head.

Above the faraway roar of the cars down below and the tinny pulse of reggaetón coming from the bar's speakers, he heard the slow splash of someone swimming.

She's up here on her own? Ricky thought. Disbelief turned to excitement as the realization crept into his head. He crouched down behind the bar, fumbled the camera from its bag, and nearly dropped it in his haste to turn it on.

Like a sniper in a trench, Ricky raised his head over the bar top. He could just see an arm curving out of the water like a shark's fin. He frowned. This was a terrible vantage point, and besides, he'd get nothing usable while she was still in the water. Slinging the camera round his neck, Ricky used the cleaner's cart as cover to move nearer to the pool. Then he crouched down, waiting for Scala to emerge from the water.

This could be the greatest shot of my career, he thought, training the lens on the pool's steps. He began to imagine tabloid front covers, viral images on social media, the envy of other paps, the money…

"What are you doing?" said a voice behind him. A woman's voice.

Ricky tried to wrench the camera from round his neck and succeeded only in half-throttling himself. He came out of his crouch and stood up.

Behind him was Scala Jaq, looking furious in a fluffy white robe. Ricky just had time to look back at the pool and see a middle-aged skinny guy climb out of the pool before Scala yanked at his camera strap, which broke, grabbed his camera, and tossed it into the pool.

"That's my property!" he yelped.

"Eye for an eye," Scala said. "Now fuck off out of here before I call security."

Ricky frowned.

"You're not going to call the police?" he asked.

Scala thrust her hands deeper into the pockets of the robe.

"If you want me to," she said, sounding uncertain.

"I get it," said Ricky. "You didn't tell anyone you were up here."

"I don't have to tell people where I am," said Scala, angrily.

"Yeah, you do," said Ricky. "If anything happens to you, they're in deep shit. You're a star. You're an *asset*."

"And you're an ass*hole*," Scala said. "Now get out of here."

Ricky looked at his camera, which had now sunk to the bottom of the pool.

"You better get rid of that," he said.

"I'll keep it as a souvenir of our meeting," Scala replied.

Ricky almost smiled at that.

"Now fuck off," said Scala.

Ricky fucked off.

Down in the lobby, he strode past Coke Boy and into the street. He took out his phone and angrily scrolled through his schedule, before remembering that he didn't have a fucking camera anymore. Ricky drove to the used camera store, winced at the price of a decent Olympus, bought it anyway, and drove home again to charge it up.

Back in his apartment, Ricky remembered his hand. He was still furious with Doctor Martinez, who, he was now sure, had pretty much been laughing at him the whole time he was with her.

After watching the orange light on the charger blink away for a few minutes, Ricky went into what he called his office – a small room with a tiny desk and an even tinier window high up – and woke up his computer. He thought for a moment before opening a search engine and typing in *someone else's hand*. A slew of links appeared. Most of them involved suggestions as to what he could do with someone else's hand. Ricky deleted the search terms and wrote *not my hand*. This brought up nothing of use. He tried *different hand*, then *a hand that isn't mine*, and then, after a moment's thought, *this is not my hand*. Nothing useful came up.

Refine your terms, Ricky thought, and typed in: *I woke up yesterday and discovered that my hand had been replaced with someone else's hand.*

Nothing again.

Think.

He typed:

I have a body part that doesn't belong to me. It's like—

It's like—

Ricky thought.

It's like some kind of transference.

He deleted the words, wrote:

Body part transference.

And stared in disbelief at what came up on his screen.

· · ·

Scala went back to her room. She thought about calling security and telling them about the pap, but decided she'd scared him off herself. She sat down at her laptop, went into her messages, and typed:

Hi.

Hi! How's it going?

OK, I guess.

You ready for tonight?

Not really. Yes. No. I don't know. I'm terrified.

I can understand that. My first time was – difficult.

This won't be your first time?

No. I'm sorry, I thought I told you that.

Scala sat back on the couch. She made a mental note to scroll back through her emails.

I'm pretty sure you said this would be your first time, she typed.

OK. I must have meant my first time here. *Like I've been to others, but not in South Beach.*

There are others?

Oh sure. You think we're the only ones? There's one in every city.

I didn't know.

There was a knock at the door. More of a tap, really.

I have to go.

Sure. Are you mad at me?

Scala hesitated for a moment, then typed:

No.

Yeah you are. It's OK. I should have been clearer. And it's a tough time for you.

You got that right.

OK, go. I'll see you tonight.

The tap returned. It was definitely a knock now. Scala ignored it and typed:

How will I know you?

She waited. There was no answer.

"Scala!" her manager called through the door.

"I heard you!" she shouted back and closed the laptop.

"What?" she said to Jonty as she opened the door.

He walked in right past her, which was something she hated, and sat on the couch, right by her laptop.

"Playing games?" he said.

"Ugh, no, I hate games," said Scala. "Creepy gamers always talking about how they'd like to nail some famous woman."

"Better that than they're on the streets," said Jonty. He took an apple from the fruit bowl on the table and smelled it.

"Why are you here, Jonty?" asked Scala.

"You know that producer we like?" Jonty replied, as he put down the apple and picked up a kiwi fruit instead.

"Stop smelling my fruit. What producer?"

"$enziMila. With a Z and a dollar sign for the S. The Colombian guy."

"Puerto Rican. And you like him, not me."

"He's in town this week and he wants to meet up."

"Great. Another VIP room."

"He wants to meet at his studio. Tonight."

Scala shook her head.

"Can't do tonight."

"Why not? What else you got planned?"

She shook her head.

"Private stuff."

Jonty put down the kiwi fruit and gave her a look. Scala knew he thought it was his "don't mess with me" look, but the way he did it, it always came out more like it was his "I just soiled myself badly" look.

"Scala," said Jonty. "I checked your schedule. There's nothing tonight."

"That's because it's private stuff," she said, feeling embarrassed without knowing why she should feel embarrassed.

"Is it a boy?"

"No," Scala said, feeling even hotter. "It's not a boy. You know I consult with you before dating."

Jonty nodded, relieved.

"Family stuff, then?" he asked.

Scala shook her head.

"Dad's not talking to me right now and Mom's in Europe. And my brother's a lawyer, so he's always fine."

Jonty shrugged.

"Maybe you have cousins I don't know about."

"Jonty, I don't have bathroom breaks you don't know about."

Jonty looked conflicted, pleased on the one hand to have his authority confirmed, vexed on the other that the same authority was in some way being undermined.

"Then what?"

Scala went to the door and opened it.

"MYFB," she said.

Jonty got up.

"Let me guess," he all-but-sighed.

"That's right," said Scala. "Mind your fucking business."

Jonty tapped his brow in mock salute.

"Have a great time," he said. Then, "Could you at least let me know what part of town you'll be at?"

"I'll wear my ankle tag," said Scala, and pushed him out the door.

Scala closed the door and sat down with her laptop again. She looked at the screen.

How will I know you?

No reply.

FOUR

*B*ODY PART TRANSFERENCE: THE FACTS.
     YOU AND BODY PART TRANSFERENCE.

Ricky just kept scrolling and scrolling.

BODY PART TRANSFERENCE; YOU ARE NOT ALONE!

Ricky bookmarked that one.

I NEED TO TALK TO SOMEONE ABOUT BODY PART TRANSFERENCE!

He stopped, clicked on the link.

All over America (he read) *thousands of people are in the grip of what's being called "body part transference." They wake up one day convinced that their body is no longer their own, that their ear, their finger, even their hand* (Ricky stopped at this, gulped, and carried on) *are not their own – that, in fact, they are someone else's.*

Doctors mock and scientists say that body part transference is impossible but still they come. The worried, the concerned, the panic-stricken – the fearful – all looking for someone to understand. Which is why—

Ricky's phone began to ring. Coke Boy. After his money,

for sure. Annoyed, he turned the phone off and returned to his computer.

Which is why some of us – the sympathetic, the understanding – are trying to help. In every city in America, in the world, people are suffering. And we can help, or try to. We're setting up meetings where anyone can come by and talk. There's a list below.

If you have issues with body part transference, come and see us.

Ricky scrolled down. There was an address on 18th Street, and a time, and a date. He looked at his watch, trying as ever to ignore the fact that the skin on one side of the watch was his, and the skin on the other wasn't: the date was today's and the time was two hours from now – plenty of time to get to wherever this place was. He could even stop at a Denny's on the way for dinner.

Ricky's charger beeped: the light had turned green. Ricky unplugged the new camera and put it in his camera bag. Then, without really thinking, he hooked the bag over his shoulder as he headed for the door.

His Denny's experience was disappointing but Ricky put this down to nerves; that, and maybe he shouldn't have ordered a starter, a main course, and a dessert. The dessert alone was the size of the Sears Tower, with the added bonus of having a cherry atop it. Ricky tried to drench his carb-heavy meal with black coffee, but this only served to make his guts sound like they were attempting whale song.

He stood up, paid the check, and went to the bathroom. After ten minutes, he realized nothing was going to happen, tried to stand up and experienced shooting pains in his legs so severe that he nearly fell back down and wedged his ass into the seat. Ricky slowly got up again, but this time his legs had gone completely numb and he briefly felt like a flying torso before he was compelled to sit down and massage his thighs for a couple of minutes.

"Are you OK in there, sir?" a voice asked from outside the door. It was a thin male voice and Ricky guessed it was just a teenage employee rather than an angry redneck with a full load.

"Fine," Ricky called back. One of his legs had nearly returned to life, so he hitched himself onto his feet and began to pull his cargo pants up.

"You're not taking drugs in there, are you?" asked the teen detective.

"Sure I am," Ricky replied, opening the door and pushing past the boy on his way out. He was so relieved to be out of there that he farted loudly as he passed an old couple celebrating their diamond wedding anniversary.

"Don't have the veal," Ricky told them as he headed for the door.

Ricky was in a good mood, despite his dinner and recent events, and he supposed it was the relief of – if not knowing, then being close to knowing. There were plenty of reasons for feeling better: one, he wasn't alone. Whatever it was, real or imaginary, body part transference was a *thing*, and a *thing* is always better than a *no thing*. Two, the thing had a name. Ricky imagined himself at a specialist medical center, with pretty nurses looking at him and whispering to each other, "That's Mister Smart. He's a victim of body part transference." It sounded impressive, like Munchausen syndrome by proxy, or phantom limb syndrome. And three, if something has a name, it can be, if not cured, then at least addressed. *The first step to recovery*, Ricky thought, *is*— He couldn't actually remember what the first step to recovery was, but it was something to do with naming things.

So when he pulled up outside the anonymous office block on 18th Street, Ricky was as happy as a man who woke up with someone else's hand on the end of his arm can be. He locked the car and was about to go into the building when he saw his camera bag lying on the passenger seat. Wary of thieves, he unlocked the car again, put the bag over his shoulder, and pushed open the door.

The lobby was deserted, just an empty security desk and an elevator. Ricky looked at his phone, checked the address, and saw that whatever he was going to was located on the second floor. He got into the elevator and went up.

The elevator opened on a blankly anonymous corridor studded with equally anonymous doors. Ricky stepped out, uncertain where to go until he heard laughter coming from an open doorway on the left. That and the smell of coffee told him he was on the right track.

He stood outside the room and looked in. There was an assortment of long tables pushed against the wall and a small huddle of plastic chairs in the middle. A cheap coffee machine was plugged in near the wall and there was a whiteboard with half-scrubbed writing on it. One of the chairs was occupied, by a young guy who looked like he went to the gym a lot, while two women – one older, the other young and wearing a baseball cap – stood by the coffee machine, talking intently to an energetic-looking guy in his late fifties.

Ricky knocked on the doorframe.

"Hi," he said, "Is this the—"

He couldn't quite bring himself to say it.

"The BPT group?" said the energetic-looking guy. He stepped forward and extended a hand. "Welcome, my friend," he said, and Ricky nearly burst into tears.

Once he was seated with a terrible cup of coffee and had blown his nose, Ricky began to get nervous. What if this place was just a nest of crazies? Nobody else, so far as he could tell, had anything physically odd about themselves. Some of them were, now he looked more closely, pretty strange looking in other ways. The older woman was wearing long sweatpants which didn't gel with the rest of her fussy, old lady outfit. The gym bunny was wearing a do-rag like a gangbanger but he had it pulled down over one ear like a pirate. And there was something familiar about—

The energetic-looking guy stepped into the middle of the room and clapped his hands together three times. Then he did it one more time, and one more time again.

I bet that routine gets old pretty quick, Ricky thought, but he listened just like everyone else as the guy said:

"OK, everyone, we're running late and the Boy Scouts of America need the room."

Blank looks.

"I'm kidding, but we all have places to be, so be seated and let's get started."

Everyone sat down and pulled their chairs into a vague circle.

"Great," said the guy. "And hi!"

Everyone said, "Hi!" right back.

"Welcome to our little group," said the guy. "My name is Don. And I…"

Don paused, and rolled up his sleeve. Ricky wondered why for a second, and then he saw it. Where the rest of Don's physique was reasonably burly and his skin robustly tanned, his arm was spindly and white. At first Ricky thought the guy must have had some kind of wasting disease, but then he realized.

"…and I am a victim of body part transference," Don finished.

After that, everything was a lot more relaxed. A lot more weird, as well, but relaxed. The gym bunny lifted up his do-rag to reveal a boxer's cauliflower ear, and the old lady told them – but did not show because ladies do not show – that her right leg had turned into a meaty caber of flesh overnight.

Ricky was about to take his hand from out of his pocket when the girl in the baseball cap and no make-up spoke.

"My name is Scala," said Scala Jaq. "And I am – you know."

She reached down to take off her gloves. Ricky stared like everyone else as Scala peeled off first one then another. She held up her hands like she had just got engaged and wanted everyone to admire her ring.

Her left hand was elegant and dark-skinned, the hand of a star. Her right hand was pretty much the same, with different nail paint.

"Is this a joke?" said Gym Bunny.

He turned to the others.

"I seen her on TV, this is *MTV Pranks* or something."

"Easy," said Don, calmingly. He looked at Scala.

"I'm guessing this is not a joke," he said.

"No!" Scala said. "This is not my hand."

The others moved their chairs forward to get a better look.

"The nails are different," said the old lady.

"Anyone could fake that," Gym Bunny said.

Scala looked at them all, hurt and defiant.

"It cost me a lot to come here," she said. "And this is not my hand."

"Are you one of those people?" asked Gym Bunny. "The ones who want to have their leg cut off?"

"It's her hand," said someone else.

"I know that," Gym Bunny replied. "Same idea, though."

Scala got up.

"This is not my hand," she said.

"Please," said Don. "Sit down. We believe you."

Scala looked doubtful.

"I said *we believe you*," Don repeated, looking at the rest of the group. "Isn't that right, guys?"

"I believe her," Ricky said, surprising himself. He looked Scala in the eye. "I believe you," he said.

He waited for her to say thanks or something like that, but instead she turned away.

Well, fucks a million, Ricky thought to himself.

"OK," said Don. "Someone else. Your turn, Ricky. Let's hear about you."

Ricky was ready. He even had a one-liner – "You wanna see someone else's hand? This is someone else's hand" – when Scala said:

"There's only one thing you need to know about Ricky. He's a fucking pap."

Don got to his feet. So did gym bunny whose name, apparently, was Tony.

"Is this true?" asked Don.

"He's got a camera bag," said Tony.

"Lots of people have camera bags," Ricky said. "It's not illegal."

"I saw him this morning," said Scala. "He was trying to take my picture."

"Are you famous?" asked the old lady, whose name now escaped Ricky.

"I knew I saw her on TV," said Gym Bunny.

They surrounded Ricky as he sat there like he was too stupid to get up.

"I can't believe he came here," Scala said. "I mean, I literally told him to fuck off this morning."

"Oh my," repeated the old lady.

"I didn't come here to take your photo," said Ricky. "Or anyone's photo."

He looked around. He had one chance. He took it.

"Look," he said, and took his glove off.

"Oh my," said the old lady again, whose name, Ricky now remembered, was Theresa.

"Jesus," said Tony.

"Well," said Don. "This is interesting."

"Interesting?" said Scala. "The guy's faking it to get in here and take more pictures of me."

"You got a high opinion of yourself," said Tony.

"Nice theory," Don said, looking at Ricky's hand. "But this is old ink. He may be a creep, but he's entitled to be here."

They took Ricky's camera off him.

"Not having much luck today," Scala said.

"It's not what you think," said Ricky.

"Dude, you just quoted the motto of the World Pervs and Stalkers Association," Scala replied. "If I had a dollar for every time some guy said that who put my head on a naked porn star's body or got caught jacking off onto a life-size cardboard cutout of me…"

"People do that?" said Tony.

"Happens all the time," said Scala. "Which is how I know this guy's a fucking creep."

"I'm a professional photographer," Ricky said.

"Let's bust his face," said Tony.

"Fuck off, do-rag," Ricky replied.

Redbeard lunged at him. Don stepped in.

"OK, Tony," he said. "First off, nobody's getting their face busted. Secondly, we don't use language like that."

"Sorry," said Ricky. Tony, he noticed, said nothing.

"And thirdly," Don said, "in this room we don't care who people are or what they've done. We're all victims, people."

He looked around the room.

"We're all in the same mess here."

FIVE

Everyone had some terrible coffee and calmed down. Scala looked at her lap while Tony glowered at Ricky and flicked fingers from his eyes to Ricky's face. Ricky ignored him.

"OK," said Don. "We've established that body part transference is real, and that we have been affected by it."

Reluctant nods.

"The question is – what do we do about it?"

Tony laughed. It was a dry laugh.

"I could get a new ear," he said. "Plastic surgery."

"Lucky you," said Theresa. "I can't get a new leg."

"People," Don said, and at that moment Ricky knew he hated him, "people, this meeting is not about surgeries. It's not about short-term solutions."

"What is it about, then?" asked Tony.

And who made you boss? Ricky thought but did not say.

Don sighed.

"It's about coming to terms with what's happened to us,"

he said. "And why it's happened. This is kind of an unusual situation, right?"

"I'll say," Theresa agreed.

Tony sighed.

"If you ask me, we're screwed," he said. "There's no way whatever the fuck this is can be reversed. All I want is to find the people who did this and ask them why."

"You think someone *set out* to do this?" Scala spoke for the first time. She sounded angry.

"Hell yeah I do!" said Redbeard. "This isn't radiation or pollution or some fucking accident. This is deliberate."

"You missed out one more thing," said Ricky.

They all looked at him, like he was a turd who just learned to talk.

"What's that, Ricky?" asked Don.

Ricky looked at them all, one to the other.

"How do we know this is it?" he said.

"What does *that* mean?" asked Tony, but he sounded scared, like he knew the answer already.

"We all woke up with a new hand, or a new leg or whatever," Ricky said. "What's to stop whoever did this making us wake up tomorrow with another new leg or hand?"

There was silence in the room. Clearly this idea had occurred to some present but not all.

"Holy fuck," said Tony. "You mean—"

"This isn't over," Ricky said.

"Oh, that's just ridiculous," said Theresa.

"Enough," Don interrupted, forcefully. "In this room we are all victims."

"Even the creeps," said Scala, sardonically.

"Even me," Ricky finished. "Any of us. Any of us could look in the mirror tomorrow morning and—"

He looked round at all of them.

"—not even recognize ourselves," Ricky finished.

His meaning sank in.

"You mean like a new face?" asked Tony.

"More than that," said Ricky. "How about a new head?"

Theresa moaned. "Stop it," she said. "It doesn't bear thinking about."

"But that's why we're here," said Ricky. "Am I right, Don?"

For the first time, Don looked less than certain. *I just gunged his ho*, thought Ricky, and the thought made him feel good.

"Don?" asked Theresa, worriedly.

Don swallowed. Then:

"This is everyone's first time here," he said. "So I wasn't going to address this, ah…"

"Head on," said Theresa, and immediately looked like she wished she hadn't spoken.

"…but, yes, Ricky has a point. We don't know where we're going with this journey and we need to prepare ourselves for any future eventuality."

"Journey?" Tony spat out. "It's not a fucking journey if you wake up with a new fucking head!"

"We need to stop focusing on heads," Don said. "Who knows," he added, "maybe us guys will wake up with some new equipment downstairs?"

There was an awful silence in the room, broken by the sound of tears. Theresa was crying.

"What are we going to *do*?" she said.

They talked for another half hour. It seemed to Ricky that Don either didn't know any more than anyone else did, or he did know more but he wasn't letting on. Either way, he had nothing to offer beyond bland reassurances which had no hard facts to back them up.

"This is happening all across the USA," Ricky said. "Around the world, even. So there are others I can talk to, people in the same situation."

"That's just talk, though," Tony said.

Don fixed him with a serious look, and Ricky suddenly realized that maybe Don wasn't all grin and grip. Maybe there was a bad fucker in there, too.

"Tony," he said. "How long have you had that ear?"

Tony flinched. "About two weeks," he said.

"Theresa?"

"Ten days," she replied.

Don smiled, tightly. "Everyone here, no disrespect, is new to this. A rookie. But there are people who've lived with this for *months*. Maybe longer."

"How do you know?" asked Scala, sharply.

"Because I'm one of them," said Don. "This arm came onto me eight months ago. Eight months and nothing since. And I'm not alone. There's a woman in Paris, she got a new hand ten months back. A guy in Brazil said hello to a different foot twelve months ago. A *year*, people."

He looked at them all.

"So we have time. Time to talk to the others with BPT. Time to put out feelers, and find out more. OK?"

There was nodding. Ricky noticed Scala didn't join in. She jammed her baseball cap down over her face and stood up.

"OK, everyone," said Don. "Check your emails for the next meet. And Scala, I'd like to talk to you for a moment afterwards."

She frowned. Don smiled.

"Relax," he said, "it's not work-related."

In the general buzz of people leaving, Ricky managed to pick up his camera bag and slip out. But he didn't follow the others to the elevator. His sixth sense – what his ex-wife used to call his *dick sense* – was kicking in. Not only that, but there was a famous person in the next room. Not only that either, but he didn't trust Don farther than he could spit: the guy was almost certainly a monumental bullshitter. Ricky had met a lot of bullshitters – managers, publicists, guys who said they could get you on the guestlist but never did – and he knew the type. Firm handshake, shaky everything else.

So he ducked into an open doorway farther down the hall and waited.

Eavesdropping is surprisingly hard in an empty office building, where the silence is more of a collection of hums: faulty strip-lights, vacuum cleaners on other floors, the occasional quiet whoosh of an elevator are continual, while conversation is muffled by ceiling tiles and office carpeting. On the other hand, the muffling makes it easy to sneak around.

Having prepped his camera, Ricky made his way silently back to the room he'd just left. The door was half open: he lay down, placed his camera on the floor, and listened. At the other end of the room, Don and Scala were having a conversation.

They weren't whispering, but they weren't exactly talking loud and clear either. Ricky wished he'd been able to bring some recording equipment; to be precise, he wished he *owned* some recording equipment. He knew paps who were tech heads and had every kind of snooping gear, from sensitive audio mics to actual fucking drones.

He leaned closer, but couldn't hear anything. Vexed, he fired off a few shots in silent mode, and crawled back out of there like a serpent in reverse.

Nothing doing.

He quietly packed up his gear and made his way down the back stairs.

If Ricky had been able to hear the conversation that Don and Scala were having, he would have been very little the wiser. It began after the others had left the room.

Don got up to close the door, but Scala said:

"Nuh uh. I don't know you."

Don smiled and sat down on the table.

"Fair enough," he said. "Though in point of fact, you do know me."

"No I don't," said Scala.

"You sure?" said Don. "Weren't you supposed to meet someone here tonight?"

"Yeah, but they never turned up – oh shit. You're him?"

Don nodded.

"Your pen pal," he said. "Don't look so surprised. Were you expecting maybe Justin Bieber?"

"Old reference," she said, "but yeah, someone maybe more my own age."

"Sorry," Don said. "I may have been less than honest with my, ah, cultural references."

"You told me you were big into Megan Thee Stallion," said Scala. "Actually, that should have given it away. Nobody says 'big into'."

"You're not mad at me?" Don's eyes were almost twinkling. Scala sighed.

"Everything else is fucking weird right now," she said. "Why not you?"

Don looked concerned. "You don't think – maybe this older guy, he was grooming me?"

Scala laughed. "Grooming? You can't even groom your fucking mustache, Don. If that is your—"

"It is my real name," Don said, mock-hurt, or maybe even mock-mock-hurt. "And it's a great mustache. Jeez, two months of friendship burned up just like that."

"You're the one who emailed me," Scala said. "No name, just right on my private secured account, saying you knew what had happened to my hand and you could help."

"That was always what this was about," Don said. "And for the record, I am big into Megan Thee Stallion."

Scala looked like she was about to either laugh or hit Don. Both, perhaps.

"OK," she said. "Here I am. We met. Now what?"

Don told her.

"Shit the fuck," said Scala Jaq.

SIX

Ricky walked back to his car. He was just putting his seat belt on when his phone pinged. It was a voicemail message from Coke Boy, left about three hours ago. Ricky pinched the bridge of nose, sighed, and played the message.

"Yeah, hi, right. This is George calling for Ricky, um, the girl, you know who I mean, she's heading into town, just thought you'd like to know. Listen, you owe me—"

Ricky deleted the message. *Too late, pal*, he thought, then: *George? I had no idea.*

He drove home.

Scala took a cab back to the Regality. She would have called her limo service, but she didn't want Jonty knowing where she was. She was aware he could have her followed or some weird private-eye shit like that, but she had a feeling that he trusted her, at least up to a point.

Ricky opened his front door and turned on the light. Immediately something hard and heavy smashed his arm down into his chest.

"Fuck!" he shouted and stumbled forward.

The heavy thing thumped into his neck this time, causing Ricky to fall to the ground. Then a crushing weight descended onto his back. The weight smelled of sweat and vape smoke so Ricky knew it was a human being: a big one.

"I haven't got any money!" Ricky shouted into the rug.

A yank at his neck brought the camera bag off. Someone tipped its contents onto the floor and Ricky heard the whine of the camera as it was turned on.

"Look at these pics," said a voice. "Fucken paedo."

"I'm a professional photographer!" Ricky shouted. His face was slammed into the floor.

"Yeah?" said another voice. "Then go down the beach, take photos of the pretty model girls."

A hand grabbed a hank of Ricky's hair.

"We know what you are," said the voice. "Get up."

Ricky was hauled up by his hair – *I didn't know I had enough hair for that to be possible*, he thought through the pain – and a face appeared in front of his. Ricky recognized the face: it belonged to the guy Jonty, who managed Scala Jaq.

"You've been taking pictures of my girl," Jonty said. "In her swimwear, you fucking paedo."

Ricky felt like saying *actually she's twenty-one* but realized quibbling was not the best option right now.

"It's my job," he said.

Jonty took a knife from his pocket.

"Yeah? Well, I got a job too," he said. "Protecting my investment."

He drew the knife across Ricky's forehead, hard. Ricky

shrieked in pain and fear. The groove the knife had made began to bleed down into Ricky's eyes.

"Relax, it won't scar. Probably," Jonty said. "Now, do you have any flash drives, memory sticks, that kind of thing?"

"I can't see!" Ricky shouted. Jonty kicked him in the balls.

"There's a laptop over here," said a second voice.

"Take it," Jonty said. "Oh but wait, it's your private property," he said to Ricky.

"Yes it is," Ricky said.

"That's disappointing," Jonty said. "I always kind of hoped that a guy who'd been kicked in the nuts would talk in a squeaky voice like in a cartoon. Oh well."

He picked up the laptop and smacked Ricky in the face with it.

"Sturdy," he said, then frisbeed it across the room into a wall, where it fell in half before landing on the tiled floor.

"Jump on that for me, would you?" he said to the heavy, who dropped Ricky onto the floor and then pogoed up and down on the laptop like an excited cartoon gorilla.

Jonty bent down to where Ricky lay on the floor.

"Listen, Ricky," said Jonty. "This may seem unnecessary after what's just happened, but if I see you within a mile of my client, you're dead."

He placed a foot on Ricky's face and pressed down.

"I mean that literally, by the way. Literally you will be killed. Oh God," he said. "Do you have to do that?"

The heavy finished pissing on Ricky's floor, shrugged, and put his dick back in his pants.

"I'm sorry about that," said Jonty, and left.

Ricky lay on the floor for a few minutes because it was easier that way. Then he got up and went to find a mop.

At the exact moment that Ricky was wiping someone else's piss off his floor, Scala Jaq was sitting in her hotel room with Jonas on her lap, trying of think of something. She wasn't sure what that something was but she wasn't stupid, far from it, and she knew that if she kept thinking, she'd get there.

With one hand she was stroking Jonas, and with the other she was scrolling through her email archive.

Scala had first received a message from the man she now knew as Don about eight weeks before she met him. It had been a short email, sent to her private, encrypted account, and it said simply:

I'm not a stalker but this guy is. You need to tell your people about him NOW.

She was about to delete the email when she stopped herself. Her private email account really was private: she'd had it set up by a European tech firm and nobody to do with her career even knew about it, not even Jonty. Scala only used it to talk to a few people – her best friend from school and her sister, both of whom were beyond bribery and corruption – and didn't even give the email address to boyfriends (who, also being celebrities, were not to be trusted).

She made a note to contact the tech company to see if they could find the sender's address and then, with a slight frisson of fear, scrolled down to see a photograph of a young white man with the caption *ERIC GREENLEAF*. The name and the image meant nothing to her, but she archived the email anyway.

The very next morning, Scala was scrolling through *USA*

Today online when she saw a picture of a singer she knew slightly called Sylvee, next to a picture of an ambulance leaving a club. The caption below the images said that Sylvee had been attacked by a man claiming to be her greatest fan. There was no photograph, but the fan's name was given as Eric Greenleaf, and he was apparently on the run after attempting to chloroform Sylvee and abduct her from the club.

An hour later, Scala received a second email from the same address:

Greenleaf is here:

followed by co-ordinates from a location app.

This time Scala did act. She went downstairs, walked to a public telephone, and called 911.

That night, watching a bulletin about Greenleaf's arrest after an anonymous tip-off, Scala received a third email.

Sorry about the magic trick! But I had to convince you of my bona fides.

Then:

Please keep this conversation to yourself for now.

Ever since, Scala had received regular emails from the anonymous account. Most of them were chatty and inconsequential, and none of them were ever again as dramatic as the first. One day Scala realized she was even looking forward to them. This worried her and she decided that now would be a good time to tell someone about her mystery emailer.

But that morning was the one when she woke up with a different hand and, after she had almost – almost – recovered from the shock, she saw an email alert on her laptop. After a moment's debate with herself, she clicked on the email. It read:

Something happened, hasn't it? Something bad. Don't worry, I can help.

Three weeks later, Scala was in an anonymous room with a bunch of strangers, talking about her new hand. All because the person emailing her, who called himself Don, had directed her there.

Scala had been a celebrity for much of her short life so far. She'd seen other, younger stars – men and women, boys and girls – crash and burn, fall victim to drugs, egos, bad management, and worse, and in relation to all this she had picked up a wide vocabulary of negative ideas and words.

One of those words came to mind now.

Groomed.

• • •

Ricky climbed into bed, every inch of his body aching. As a pap, he was used to the odd shove or blow, but this was different. It was a professional beating, thorough and unpleasant. He thought briefly about taking a bath, but his bath was shallow and narrow, designed for standing in while taking a shower, not for someone of Ricky's uncontained figure lying down.

After thumping his pillow into a shape that didn't jab at his new facial bruises, Ricky began to drift into an unpleasant sleep, where he dreamt of disembodied limbs kicking and punching him. Then a high beeping sound woke him: his phone, which somehow the thugs in their enthusiasm had forgotten to smash or cram down his throat.

Groaning, Ricky leaned over and found his phone on the floor.

"Hello?" he said.

"It's me," said Scala Jaq. "We need to talk."

SEVEN

"OK," said Don. "Thank you everyone for coming to this meeting."

"Ain't got nothing more important to do," said Tony. He laughed, but nobody else did.

"I'm sorry to call another meeting at such short notice," Don went on, "but, as they say, life comes at you fast sometimes, and there have been a couple of new developments."

He looked around the room as if inviting questions, and Ricky instinctively covered the huge bruise on the side of his face, being unable to do anything about the knife cut on his forehead. He didn't like being the focus of attention at the best of times, and right now was far from being the best of times.

In fact, Ricky hadn't wanted to come at all tonight, but Scala had... *made* him wasn't the right word, but it was close.

"We need to talk," she'd said on the phone.

"No, we fucking do not," Ricky replied.

Scala must have heard the anger in his voice.

"What's wrong?" she said. "First of all you're following me

around and now you're avoiding me? No wonder you're Miami's worst pap."

"That's not true," said Ricky with bruised pride. "Also, don't play innocent with me. You know what happened."

"Let's pretend I don't," said Scala.

"Your fucking heavies came over and beat the shit out of me," Ricky said. "Smashed up my stuff and—" Ricky found he couldn't bring himself to say *pissed on my floor*, "—left again," he finished, weakly.

"Jonty?" said Scala.

"And some big apes," Ricky went on.

There was a pause, followed by a sigh.

"Well, you can't say you didn't deserve it," Scala said.

"I dispute that," Ricky said.

"Which is why you got beat up," said Scala.

"Are we done? Because I think one of the conditions of me not getting beaten up just for doing my job was I keep away from you."

"That's unfortunate," said Scala. "Because I need you to do some work for me."

Now there was a longer pause.

"Excuse me?" said Ricky.

"You're a journalist, aren't you?" Scala said. "I mean, that's what you tell people."

"I'm a photographer," Ricky replied. "There's a difference."

"Yeah, but we're not talking portraits and special occasions, are we?" said Scala. "We're talking snooping around and sticking lenses up people's skirts. You pretty much are a sex pervert."

"I really have to go," said Ricky. "I need a new camera and a new laptop on account of your friends."

"Boo the fuck hoo," said Scala. "That said, if you keep out of Jonty's way, I'll make sure you get paid for this."

"Paid for what?" asked Ricky.

There was a sound on the other end of the line, like someone knocking on a door.

"I have to go," said Scala. "See you at the meeting."

"What meeting?" said Ricky.

Ten seconds later, his phone buzzed.

HI ALL. SORRY FOR SHORT NOTICE, CAN WE MEET TOMORROW, SAME PLACE SAME TIME? DON.

There were a couple more people in the room tonight, but apart from that it was the usual crew: Theresa the old lady, Tony the gym guy (who tonight was sporting an ill-advised beret over his ear), Scala and Don. The newcomers were a small, pop-eyed man in his forties called Larry and a quiet woman called Helen who looked like she was a librarian or something like that. Neither of them said much, but then nor did anyone else. It was as if the relief of the first meeting – finding others like themselves, realizing that whatever else was going on, at least they weren't alone – had given way to the deeper reality of the situation: it didn't matter how many new pals they had, everyone in this room was in some incomprehensible and terrible way completely fucked.

Ricky, who was completely fucked in a variety of ways both new and traditional, sat opposite Scala and tried not to think about the fact that the very person most likely to get him killed was the reason for him being here tonight.

He had very little doubt that Scala's promise to square things with her manager would have zero effect, and was more than slightly concerned that he would be set upon by Jonty and his primate pals as soon as he left the building. But for now at least he felt safe in the eye, as it were, of the hurricane.

"First of all," Don said, "I'd like to welcome our two newest members, Larry and Helen."

"Hi," said Larry, almost cheerfully. He even did a little wave. *Poor fucker thinks he's going to get better*, thought Ricky, *like he's at AA or something.*

"Hello," Helen said, nervously. She smiled a little.

"I've told Larry and Helen a little about our last meeting, what we're here for and who we all… are," said Don. "Now perhaps they'd like to tell us about themselves."

Here comes the reveal, thought Ricky, surprised how routine a fucked-up weird situation had become so quickly. Sure enough, Larry took off his shoe and sock to show everyone a foot that wasn't his foot, and everyone nodded in an *I've been there* kind of way, and Larry put his shoe and sock back on, relieved that he wasn't the only one.

"Helen," said Don.

Helen didn't roll up her sleeve or take her shoe off. She just stood up and looked everyone in the face.

"Hi," she began. "My name's Helen and like everyone here, I have, what do you call it—"

"BPT," said Don. "That's the term we use."

"Funny, it sounds like a disease," said Helen, and she was smiling as she said it. "Or a crime, you know, like DUI."

"It's a fucking sentence if you ask me," said Tony.

"I suppose so," Helen replied. "I can see how you might be scared of it."

"I'm not scared," Tony said, looking scared.

"No, I'm sorry," said Helen. "I meant like how anything new is scary. But when I got out of bed a month ago with this—"

And now she did indicate, with a brush of her hand, an arm that seemed thicker than its counterpart, longer even.

"—I was scared," she went on. "Because I saw it as an invasion of my person. An attack on my physical and mental self."

"Isn't it?" asked Theresa.

"Maybe," said Helen. "And I don't mean to sound rude or inconsiderate, but I can see how you might feel that way. Not everyone welcomes change, especially when it's unasked for."

"I'll say it's unasked for," said Tony, fingering his ear. "It's completely unasked for."

"Let her finish," Don said quietly.

"Not everyone likes change," Helen said. "But I do."

There were a few seconds' silence.

"You like this?" said Tony. "You like looking down and wondering where your body's gone? Where it's going?"

Helen shrugged. "It's just a body," she said. "I never liked this one: maybe I'll like the next one more."

"I don't get it," said Tony.

Helen shook her head. "I don't need you to get it," she said. "I've always hated this body. I've never been happy the way I am."

"What way is that?" asked Scala.

"The way that's me," said Helen. "I don't like the way I am outside and I don't like the way I am inside. I hate my reflection and I hate my thoughts. I would have killed myself years ago but all I have is this life. And now..."

She smiled.

"...now I have a chance at something different."

Everyone was silent for a few seconds.

"If it's any consolation," said Larry, "I hate my new foot."

"Thanks, Larry," said Don. "And seriously, thank you Helen for your perspective."

"Is that why we're here?" asked Theresa. "Did you ask her along so she could tell us, 'Good news everyone! Let's all look on the bright side!'"

"I'm just speaking for myself," said Helen. "I can go if I'm distressing you."

"No, don't," said Scala.

"I asked Helen here because, like I said before, we're all in the same boat," said Don.

"I don't wanna be in any boat she's in," Tony said.

"You are, though," Don said. "All of us are. We may have different perspectives but we're all in this together. Which brings me to my news."

He reached into the bag at his feet and pulled out a piece of paper.

"I set up a couple of alerts for anything to do with our condition," he said – Ricky noted the word, *condition*, and wondered if that was really what he had, a condition – "and I found this article."

"That's it?" said Tony. "You found an article on the internet? Any one of us could have done that."

Don gave him a look. "Yes, but nobody did," he said. "And this article, I didn't find it on Google or AltaVista—"

"What the fuck is AltaVista—" Tony began.

"—I found it doing *research*," said Don, and now he sounded angry. "And by research I don't mean I just typed in some keywords, I mean I went deep. Really deep."

"He's been on the black web," said Theresa.

"The dark web," said Tony.

"Isn't that just for drugs?" asked Theresa.

"There are other corners of the web," Don said. "There are people who've worked for the government, who are no longer happy to work for the government, who have information to share…"

"Are you saying what's happening to us is something to do with the government?" asked Larry. He sounded doubtful, and Ricky guessed that Larry was a decent taxpayer.

"Honey, everything's something to do with the government," said Theresa.

"Deep state," agreed Tony.

"I'm not saying anything," said Don. "Just that what's happening to us isn't an accident."

"Maybe it's like Chernobyl," Tony said.

"That was an accident," said Ricky, and Tony shrugged.

"What does your piece of paper say?" asked Scala.

Don held the paper up and everyone leaned in. It was a printout of a badly scanned document, a third- or fourth-generation photocopy with the typed words almost illegible, and whole paragraphs covered in thick black lines.

"Looks official, alright," said Tony.

"Heavily redacted," Don said. "But the person I spoke to, he's kosher, says this is the real deal."

"What real deal?" asked Larry, who was clearly uneasy with the idea that governments could be bad.

"In layman's terms," Don said, "certain government departments have been conducting experiments, the nature of which isn't known."

A silence fell.

"What the fuck," asked Tony, "does *that* mean?"

Don frowned. "Look," he said, "I'm just struggling toward the truth, same as the rest of us. But, and I don't wish to be rude, I'm making an effort, do you know what I mean?"

"He's doing the legwork," Larry said approvingly. "He's putting in the hours."

"Thank you, Larry," Don said. "I am putting in the hours. I mean, if anyone else feels like rooting around in dubious corners of the internet or wants to give their hard-earned cash to strangers for information, feel free."

He sat back. Nobody said anything.

"I didn't think so," said Don.

"So what does it say?" Ricky asked. "This document of yours. In layman's terms."

"Real layman's terms," added Tony.

Don crossed his arms.

"You really want to know?" he asked.

"Yes!" Theresa almost shouted.

"OK then," said Don. "You ever heard of something called teleportation."

"*Star Trek?*" Tony said. "Like sending one thing from over here to over there."

"I read they've been working on that for years."

"Who? UPS?" said Larry, and laughed. Nobody else did.

"Teleportation," said Don, "is a scientific concept which looks into the idea that somehow we could transport, say, that chair from where it is now to some other place. Say, the other side of the room, but also say, France. Or the moon."

"The moon," repeated Larry.

"For example," said Don.

"There's no such thing, though, is there?" asked Tony.

"They've tried," Don said. "I read how they sent a few atoms across a room and it cost something like a trillion dollars."

"UPS won't be using it for a while then," said Tony, glowering at Larry. Larry looked down at his feet.

"But it exists in principle," said Don. "Maybe more than that."

"What's this got to do with us?" Helen asked.

"Oh fuck," said Tony. "No."

"What?" asked Scala.

Tony's face was ashen white. He said, "I just got it."

"Got *what*?" said Ricky.

Tony leaned over. He lifted Ricky's right hand, his old hand.

"Transporting one thing from one place," he said.

He lifted Ricky's new hand.

"To another," he said.

EIGHT

Ricky heard someone swear, which was Tony saying, "Shit shit shit shit." He heard something fall, which was Theresa fainting. He saw Larry stand up and say, "You people are crazy."

He heard Don say, "People! Stay calm."

He heard himself say, "This doesn't make sense."

That seemed to do it. The idea that none of this made sense made everyone calm down again, as if the idea was so crazy – crazier even than waking up with someone else's foot on the end of your leg – that it couldn't possibly be true.

"Maybe it isn't," said Don. "And I have no evidence – literally none – to back up such an idea. But this document…"

He held it up, and this time Tony grabbed it. Don sighed and grabbed it back.

"…this document," he went on, "says that teleportation is real. It works. And that it's been tried out on human beings."

Larry peered at the document before Don put it back in his pockets.

"It says that?"

Don nodded. "On State Department headed paper."

"It's still a leap," Scala said. "From experiments to what's happening to us."

"Is it?" said Don. "You ever hear that saying, when you have eliminated the impossible, what's left, however unlikely, is the truth?"

"Einstein," said Ricky. "I saw it in a gif once."

"Sherlock Holmes," Don corrected.

"He wasn't real," Theresa said, as if that might help.

"Real or not," Don said, "does anyone else have a better explanation?"

Half a dozen hands went up.

"Transplants," said Tony.

"What?" Scala replied.

"Someone is removing our body parts with surgery when we're asleep and replacing them with other people's," Tony went on.

"Wouldn't we notice?" asked Larry. "Wouldn't there be scars?"

"Wouldn't it hurt?" Theresa asked.

"And that's another thing," said Scala. "How come these things—" she raised her hand, "—don't hurt?"

"God," said Theresa.

She looked at the others. "What?" she said. "It's as good an explanation as any."

"*God* did this to us?" said Tony.

"He does move in a mysterious way," Theresa said.

"This is more than mysterious," Tony said, "it's fucking baffling."

"Why would God do this?" asked Helen.

76

"Why would he test Job?" said Theresa. "Why would he visit the Flood on the Earth? Or sacrifice his only son?"

"It's a possible explanation," said Don. "But it's kind of a get-out-of-jail-free card. Open ended, you know?"

"The problem is," said Ricky, "none of this makes sense. Why would anyone do this to us? And how? Teleporting, you know, an ant is maybe possible, but hands? And like she said," he went on, nodding at Theresa, "why doesn't it hurt?"

"Well, a lot to think about there," said Don. "OK, I suggest we all go home, get some sleep. I'll get back to my research and everyone just hope for good news."

He looked at Theresa.

"Pray for good news," Don said.

NINE

Ricky sat outside the building in his car, looking at his phone. A few minutes later, the passenger door opened and Scala got in.

"You're going to get me killed," he said.

"The smell of this thing's gonna kill you first," Scala said. "This is like where fast food wrappers come to die."

"I eat when I can," said Ricky, defensively.

"Which by the looks of things is all the time," Scala replied. "OK, so what did you think of all that?"

Ricky presumed she meant the meeting.

"It was weird," he said. "But then, you know, it's all weird."

Scala turned in her seat to look at him.

"The thing is," she said, "I know Don."

"Don?" said Ricky. "What, is he your number one fan or something?"

She shook her head.

"He got my email address somehow," she said. "He's been

emailing me weird stuff for weeks. Like information about the guy who attacked Sylvee, only before it happened."

"Did you tell the police?"

"No," Scala said. "I wanted to know more before I did anything. And then—" she raised her hand, "—when this happened, he seemed to know about it."

She frowned at Ricky.

"He knows about stuff before it happens," she said.

"Normally if someone knows about something before it happens," Ricky replied, "it means they made it happen. You don't have to be Sherlock Holmes to work that one out."

"Yeah, I get that," Scala said. "But the Sylvee thing? I mean, Greenleaf was Canadian."

"He was from Canada, that doesn't mean he was a space alien," Ricky pointed out. "Anyone can find out about Canadians, even weird stalker Canadians."

"No, like he came out of nowhere," Scala said. "There was nothing on Greenleaf. He was totally clean, had no previous, had never even left his hometown. Then one day he turns up at the club and launches himself at her."

Ricky shrugged. "People do strange things," he said.

"You're not listening," said Scala. "I don't care if he was crazy his whole life or one day he just lost it. My point is, he had no history of anything – so how could Don know what was going to happen?"

"Maybe he has a police radio," said Ricky.

"Is that all you have?" asked Scala. "Because if you don't do better, I'm going to call Jonty and say you're in my car."

"But you're in *my* car," said Ricky.

"I don't think Jonty would care," Scala replied.

Ricky sighed.

"OK," he said. "Don is suspect. Every way suspect. He knows stuff he shouldn't know."

"Like the document tonight," said Scala. "Did you buy that? All the stuff about the dark web and the scientist? And he didn't even let us look at it."

"Oh yes he did," said Ricky. He held up his phone.

"What's that?" Scala asked.

Ricky said, "As soon as I could see he was going to hold it up, I zoomed in and clicked."

"You took a photo?"

"It's my job."

Scala snatched the phone.

"Hey!" Ricky said.

She peered at the image.

"It's hard to read."

"Of course it's hard to read, I had the phone in my lap at the time. But there's enough detail."

"Enough detail for what?"

Ricky looked at her.

"To see that he's bullshitting us."

He pushed a finger on the screen and enlarged the image.

"Can't see the writing too well, but there's no State Department logo like he claimed," Ricky said. "Also the text is wrong."

"It's mostly blacked out."

"Redacted, yeah. But look."

Scala leaned in.

"What am I looking at?"

"There are little headings before each section. Like headlines. Hard to read, I know, but try."

Scala squinted at the screen.

"WITNESS something," she read. "Something CHARGES."

"Does that sound like a scientific document to you?"

"Not especially."

Ricky took his phone back.

"Don got this off some true crime website or some shit like that. It looks official, it's got spooky blanked-out bits and it's hard to read. Wave it around at people while you're talking, it does its job. Which is to back up his argument for an hour."

"So it's fake."

"The document's not fake," said Ricky. "It's Don who's the fake."

"Shit," said Scala, leaning back and exhaling. "I mean, I had a feeling. But—"

"It's never nice to have it confirmed," Ricky said.

She turned her head to him.

"That sounded heartfelt," she said.

"I wasn't always this happy-go-lucky," Ricky said. "I used to have a life, someone I trusted. But you know how it is. You have a couple of habits and she walks out."

"Habits?"

"Booze habit, drink habit, porn habit…" said Ricky. "I'm fine now, but it's too late."

"You don't know that," said Scala.

"Oh, I do," said Ricky. "I have a feeling. Also, I kind of lied about being fine now. Anyway," he went on, "you said something about paying me."

"Right," said Scala.

"What is it?" Ricky said.

He turned in his seat.

"I'm a cynical hack, you know that. I'm only doing this for the money."

"I know," said Scala. "And I'm glad. Because if you were doing it for any other reason… I'd be calling Jonty right now."

Ricky frowned.

"What kind of name is Jonty anyway?" he asked.

"It's English," Scala said. "Short for Jonathan."

"Is he English? Jonty?"

Scala shook her head no.

"At least, I don't think so. I mean, he doesn't drink tea or say 'fortnight' but…"

Suddenly, to Ricky's surprise, she laughed.

"What's so funny?" he asked.

"Nothing. Except, you know, here I am maybe about to have my ass teleported to the moon or something," said Scala, "and instead of totally freaking out, I'm in a yellow Pontiac Aztek that stinks of cheeseburgers talking about whether my fucking manager is a Brit or not."

Rocky thought about that for a minute.

"Yeah," he said, "objectively, that is funny."

Scala laughed so much she was nearly sick.

"I better go," she said when she'd calmed down.

"You need a ride?" asked Ricky.

"Nah," she said. "Better not risk it."

"What you going to do then? International celebrity can't be walking round here all alone."

"This is a business district, nobody's here at night," said Scala.

"I'll walk to a well-lit street corner, call my driver, and say I just went for air."

"In the business district?"

"Most of his clients he has to pick up from strip clubs at four in the morning," said Scala. "Believe me, he lives for the quiet jobs."

"OK then," Ricky said. He got out.

"What are you doing?"

"Opening the door for you."

"Oh," she said. "Well, gee."

Scala got out. She pulled a sheet of paper from her jacket.

"This is a record of all the emails Don sent me," she said. "There's some, like, IP addresses and stuff there."

"Alright," said Ricky. "There are people I need to talk to."

"Great," Scala replied. "See you soon."

Ricky watched as she walked off.

He was suddenly struck by a powerful certainty that one of them was going to get killed.

As long as it isn't me, he thought, and was surprised to feel ashamed about it.

• • •

Ricky walked along the beach toward his destination, which was a beach bar called Beaner's that looked like an old fisherman's shack and smelled like one too. The spring-breakers came here sometimes because it was funky and weird, but the drunks came all the time because it was cheap. Ricky had spent a few nights here himself, until one night he'd found a bug in his drink so large that its wings splashed his face with rum when it took off.

But this sort of thing didn't seem to worry most of the lushes who spent their days at Beaner's, staring out at the ocean like it was the biggest martini in the world; and it certainly didn't worry Isinglass, who was the journalist contact Ricky had mentioned to Scala. Despite a pint-of-whiskey-a-day habit, Isinglass had somehow managed to keep hold of the shreds of his career as a freelance hack, probably because he had once been very good at his job. He still knew people, and this was why Ricky had called him (landline only, third attempt successful) and arranged to meet.

Ricky finally made it to Beaner's, and saw Isinglass sitting on the steps, trying to unkink a very dry-looking Lucky Strike. Ricky offered him a Marlboro Lite.

"Not for me," said Isinglass, in a voice like nails, "you need a cigarette holder to smoke those fucking things."

Ricky sat next to him.

"You want to go inside, have a drink?" he asked.

Isinglass coughed for about a minute without interruption.

"Barred," he finally managed to say.

Ricky was impressed. Getting barred from Beaner's was almost impossible.

"What did you do, kill someone?" he said.

"Tried to," said Isinglass. "Fucker moved my glass, so I put a sword in his eye."

"A sword?" asked Ricky.

"One of those little plastic ones that come in cocktails," said Isinglass. "It was red."

"His eye or the sword?"

"Both," Isinglass said, and let loose a machine-gun burst of coughing.

84

"Let me go in and bring us out something," Ricky suggested. Isinglass shrugged, which was the nearest, Ricky knew, he'd get to expressing gratitude.

"Rum," said Isinglass.

"Rum and what?"

"Rum and a pint glass," Isinglass replied. "Full to the top, no ice."

"You want Coke in that?"

"You want my balls on your chin?"

Ricky was about to reply to that when he realized it was probably a rhetorical question.

Inside the bar, he noticed that one of the staff had a red and swollen eye, so he waited until the other bartender was free.

"Isinglass, huh?" she said. "Asshole."

But she served Ricky the drinks.

Isinglass swallowed most of his in one go.

"Did someone piss in this?" he said by way of thanks.

"I need to talk to you," said Ricky, setting his Coke with no rum down.

"You are talking to me," Isinglass replied. He finished his drink and wiped his mouth with his hand. "Your round," he said.

"I just—"

"Time was," said Isinglass, "I would be offered thousands of dollars and turn it down. To keep my mouth shut, you understand. Now you want to pick my brains and you won't even buy me a fucking drink?"

"OK," Ricky said.

"This time get a pitcher. That way you won't have to keep

coming in and out," said Isinglass as Ricky stood up. "And get yourself a real drink, I hate drinking alone."

Ten minutes later, Isinglass was throwing pebbles at seagulls and Ricky was beginning to feel quite dizzy.

"Nearly got the fucker that time," said Isinglass as a gull squawked at him and flew off.

"I'm sure that's illegal," said Ricky.

"Bullshit, they're vermin," Isinglass replied. "I'm doing the city a favor."

He launched another stone and it hit a seagull. The bird immediately fell over in the sand.

"Shit," said Isinglass.

"We should go," Ricky said.

"Fuck off, we haven't finished the pitcher yet. Besides," said Isinglass as the bird got up and staggered groggily away, "fucker got up."

Halfway through the second pitcher, Ricky was feeling extremely dizzy. Isinglass, by contrast, was in a very good mood.

"Give me a quarter," he said, "I want to play the jukebox."

"I don't have a quarter," said Ricky, who felt he would have thrown up if he'd even tried to put his hand in his pocket.

"I want that song about Margaritaville," Isinglass said, and sang a few bars, horribly.

"'Margaritaville'," said Ricky. "That's what it's called."

"I never knew that," Isinglass said. He leaned back on a wooden pillar and closed his eyes.

After a while, Ricky said, "Isinglass? Are you asleep?"

Ricky went to the bathroom to be sick and when he returned, Isinglass was gone.

"Shit," he said.

He tried to get up to look for him but standing up made him feel nauseous again.

A few minutes later, Isinglass returned with a paper bag.

"Catfish," he said. "Want some?"

Ricky shook his head.

"OK," said Isinglass, taking a piece of fried fish from the bag and biting into it. "What is it you want?"

A white piece of catfish flew from Isinglass's mouth as he spoke.

Ricky leaned over and hurled into the sand.

Sometime later, when Isinglass had finished his meal and Ricky's stomach had settled down, Ricky said:

"I need you to find out about someone."

"Do you have a name?" said Isinglass.

"Don," Ricky replied.

"Well," Isinglass said after a moment, "that narrows it down."

"I don't have his second name," Ricky said. "But I do have some online stuff."

He looked at Isinglass, his dirty shirt, his stubble.

"It's OK," Isinglass said. "I'm fully computer trained. I have one of those, you know, Dells. The kind you can carry around."

"A laptop?" asked Ricky.

"Of course it's a fucking laptop," Isinglass said. "I'm kidding, you asshole. You think I brought down the Santanas with a quill pen?"

Ricky, who thought the Santanas might be a group, shook his head.

"Give me that piece of paper burning a hole in your shirt pocket," Isinglass said, and Ricky handed it over. Isinglass looked at it.

"Your boy sounds nice," he said. "I'm guessing this is some little girl he's been cozying up to?"

"Yes, but not like that," said Ricky, and as he said it, he wondered if it was actually true.

"Doesn't matter if it's sex or money or whatever," Isinglass said, "this Don guy wants something that she has and he's worked out the best way to get it is to grease his way in there."

"She thinks he's a fake," said Ricky.

"Fake?" Isinglass replied. "He's a fucking liar is what he is. This whole thing—" he waved the sheet of paper under Ricky's nose, "—nothing he says is true."

"You can tell?" asked Ricky.

"Hell yeah," Isinglass said. "He's a snake oil salesman. It's all farts and no figures, as my wife used to say."

He peered at the paper again.

"There's some real information between the lines here and there," he said. "Most of that will turn out to be misdirection, but that's fine. The fun part is working out what's behind the misdirection."

"You think you can find him?" Ricky asked.

"Yeah," said Isinglass, and he sounded almost sad at the prospect. "Anyone who sits down at a keyboard can be found."

Isinglass took a last swig of rum.

"The only question is," he said, "are you sure you want to find him?"

TEN

Scala sat in her room feeding Jonas fortune cookies, taking care to first remove the paper ribbon inside. She had ordered a Chinese meal from her favorite Miami Beach restaurant and the owners had with excessive generosity thrown in an entire box of fortune cookies. As Jonas crunched the hard shells, Scala unrolled the fortunes one by one.

"Looks like I got a whole range of possible futures going on," she told the dog.

She picked up a strip of paper.

"'Have regard for tomorrow, because it will be here soon,'" she read. "Well, duh. 'Do not let a liar force you into anything.' Hey, that one actually works."

Scala picked up a third.

"'Be yourself, because who else can you be?'" she read out. She crumpled the fortune up and tossed it into the air. Jonas leapt after it and, having sniffed it, looked at Scala judgmentally.

"Sorry," she said, "that one was too close to home."

There was a knock at the door.

"It's me," said a voice.

Scala got up.

"Has it ever occurred to you," she said through the door, "that 'it's me' is not great self ID?"

"Jonty," said the voice. "It's me, Jonty."

Scala opened the door. Jonty entered, with a very large man in tow.

"This is Tom," said Jonty. "Tom, go and sit on the bed."

The very large man was about to sit on the bed when Scala said, "Hey Tom? I don't like strangers sitting on my sheets."

Tom shrugged.

"I'll wait outside," he said, "if that's OK."

"Go," said Jonty.

"I've been meaning to ask you," Scala said to Jonty. "Are you English? Like half or part or anything?"

Jonty shook his head. "California," he said. "Encino, like George Lucas."

"Oh," said Scala. "Only the name."

"What's wrong with the name?"

"Nothing," said Scala. "So what's with Tim?"

"Tom. He's for you."

"I'm fine."

"If you're sure," Jonty said. "There's a lot of crazy people about right now."

"Anybody in particular?" Scala asked.

"No," Jonty replied. "Just better safe than sorry."

"Alright," said Scala. "But if there is any one guy, I'd like to know. A name can make a difference."

"Sure," said Jonty, absently. "Listen, are you packed?"

"No," Scala said. "Why would I be packed? We're here for a week, aren't we?"

Jonty shook his head.

"I wish you'd read your itinerary," he said.

"I did."

He looked at her like a tired principal.

"Your *revised* itinerary."

"Precis it for me."

"We've been offered *Midnight with McGovern*," said Jonty.

"Who dropped out?"

"Nobody," said Jonty.

"Seriously?"

"OK," Jonty said. "It was the K-Pop girl. Lily."

Scala shook her head.

"Wow," she said.

"You're doing the new drop and some comedy song with their band," Jonty went on. "Maybe a skit, too."

"Nobody says *skit*," said Scala.

"Noted," Jonty replied. "Anyway, we're leaving tomorrow morning, coming back next week for *MTV Flo-Raps*."

"Wait," said Scala. "I'm doing what with the band?"

• • •

"So you're going to New York," Ricky said. "Good."

He was thinking of Jonty's apes and how they wouldn't be breathing down his neck, or breaking it.

"It's not good," said Scala. She was in the bathroom talking to Ricky on her cell. "I won't be able to keep an eye on Don."

"You're paying me to keep an eye on Don," Ricky pointed out.

"OK, but I'll be missing the meetings," she said. "I mean, what if something happens?"

Ricky thought about this for a moment.

"Didn't Don say what happened to us was happening all over America?"

"All over the world," Scala replied.

"And didn't he also say there were groups like ours in most cities?"

"Yeah, but—"

Scala stopped.

"Oh my God. There's got to be a group in New York."

"Exactly. And New York is – it's New York."

"It's not Miami Beach."

"Right. It's not some torn-out piece of paper with fake names and dates."

"Jeez," Scala said. (*Jeez? Who says that?* Ricky thought.) "There might be somebody there who knows what's going on."

"They didn't call it the Manhattan Project for nothing."

There was a pause.

"Sorry," said Ricky. "I have no idea why I said that."

Scala called Don.

"Hi!" he said, sounding yet again like a (*cult leader*) counsellor for troubled teens.

"Listen," Scala said. "I have to go to New York for a couple of nights."

"Nice," said Don. "Give my regards to Broadway."

Scala wondered if he was drunk, or high, then remembered he was always like this.

"So I was wondering," she went on, "if you could tell me where the meetings are. In New York."

"Meetings?" said Don.

"Meetings," Scala repeated. She had the beginning of a sick feeling in her stomach, like she used to get when a boy said, "There's something we need to talk about."

"OK," said Don.

Several seconds passed. Scala was sure she could hear the black ether waiting in the phone system to hear what Don was going to say.

"There's something we need to talk about," said Don.

• • •

They met in, had they but known it, Ricky's favorite Denny's. Don had a decaf coffee and Scala had tap water.

"What's going on, Don?" Scala asked.

"I feel I owe you an explanation," Don replied.

"An explanation of what?" asked Scala. "I mean, at this point, I'll take anything."

"I appreciate it's a tough time for you," Don said. "It's a tough time for all of us."

"Same boat, I know, thanks for reminding me," said Scala. *Although I don't think anyone else is getting personal emails from you,* she thought.

"OK, this is the thing," Don said, and he actually looked around like he thought the waitresses might be eavesdropping. "I haven't exactly told everyone the truth."

He sat back in his seat, humble and defiant at the same time.

"I'm going to need more than that," Scala said.

"I know, I was getting to it," Don replied. "Look, this group –

these are vulnerable people. They're frightened, they're confused... they're not adaptable the way we are."

Scala noted the way he put himself and her together, and said:

"OK, so some people can't take it and apparently we can. Still doesn't explain why you are apparently not telling me something."

"I was going to," Don said. "I was waiting for the right moment."

He's three seconds away from "it's not you, it's me," Scala thought to herself.

"The fact is," Don said, "not everything I told the group is true."

"I got that," Scala said, fighting the urge to stab Don in the eye with the sugar dispenser. "So why don't you remedy that now? Just for me."

"Wow, you're tough for a teenager," said Don.

"I'm twenty-one," Scala replied. "Which I'm sure you already know."

The chill in her voice must have got to Don because this time he said:

"I know everything."

"About what?"

He leaned forward.

"About *this*," he said, grabbing Scala's new hand so hard it hurt. "Sorry," he said, letting go, but not before Scala wondered if she had just seen a flash of the real Don. "Just stressed out."

"Same boat," said Scala. "Also, please don't do that again. I have krav maga to level four."

"I don't play video games," Don said. "Joke," he added, without humor. Then:

"What I'm about to tell you," he said, "goes no farther than you, me, and the salt cellar. I think you can maybe just about cope with it, but the others…"

Don mimed a head exploding silently.

"Alright," said Scala. "Whatever nutty shit you're about to tell me, I'm telling no one."

Except Ricky? she wondered. It was an interesting point.

"There is no New York group," said Don.

"O-kay," Scala said. "That's weird, but not that big of a deal."

Don sighed.

"Nor is there a Chicago group, or a Los Angeles group, or a Pittsburgh, Philadelphia group," he went on. "New York, London, Paris, Munich, no groups there either."

"I don't get it," Scala said, but slowly she did. "Oh," she said.

"Ours is the only group," Don said, nodding. "And that means—"

Scala shook her head. "No, it can't be," she said. "You said this was happening everywhere. America, Europe—"

"I did, didn't I?" Don replied. Then, mystifyingly, "Do you believe everything the zoo tells you?"

"What zoo?"

"Figure of speech. It's like I said," Don went on, "these are vulnerable people. Theresa's old, Tony's… dumb, Helen is depressed or something—"

"Very empathetic," said Scala.

"The point is, they have enough to deal with already, they don't need to be told the truth."

"Which is what?"

"Which is that *it's just us*," Don said. "When I said there were others, I was giving them hope. Tell them there's only six of us or whatever, and hope is out the window. Flushed down the toilet."

"It doesn't make sense," said Scala.

"All of it or just that part?" asked Don.

"Why would we be the only ones? This is Miami Beach, not…"

"Area 51? Chernobyl?" said Don. "Like they say, everything's got to happen somewhere. Why not Miami Beach?"

"OK," said Scala, although she wasn't. "Why us? We're hardly a cross-section of humanity."

"I don't know," Don said. "You got your jock, your nice old lady, your pop singer…"

"It's not funny," said Scala. "And I don't believe it."

"You don't believe we're the only ones? Tony and you and me and Helen and Theresa and Ricky and the other guy?"

"Larry," said Scala. "And no, I don't believe it. No government experiment or whatever the fuck this is would take place like this. It's ridiculous."

"Ridiculous?" Don repeated. "I'll tell you what's ridiculous." He looked around one more time.

"I'm a time cop," said Don.

"A what?" said Scala.

"A time cop," said Don.

"You mean, like a cop who's been a cop for a long time? Or a cop who's done time?" asked Scala.

"No," said Don, "I mean a cop who travels in time. That kind of time cop."

"That kind," said Scala. "Fuck off."

"I said you wouldn't like it."

"Seriously, fuck the fuck off."

Scala got up. Don did too.

"This is why I couldn't tell you," he said. "Because I knew you'd overreact."

"I'm not overreacting," said Scala. "I'm *reacting*. There's a difference. Jesus, you meet me in a Denny's and tell me that."

"Does it matter that it's a Denny's?" asked Don, smiling.

"Fuck off," Scala said again. Don stood in front of her.

"It's the truth," he said, no longer smiling.

"It's bullshit," said Scala. "You must think I'm fucking twelve years old."

"You're twenty-one, and you're the most intelligent woman I know."

"Woman?" Scala repeated.

"Alright," said Don, "person."

He put his hand on her arm. Scala knocked it off.

"Ow," said Don. "Level four, alright."

"Is this man bothering you?" said a voice. It belonged to a big woman sitting at the next table with a young, equally big man who looked to be her son.

"I don't know yet," said Scala.

"Well, my son will fuck him up for you if needs be," said the woman.

"Good to know," Scala said.

She sat down again. Don did, too.

"A time cop," said Scala again. "Like in—"

"Like in that movie," Don finished for her. "*Timecop*."

"Are you saying we're in a movie?"

"No, I'm saying if you've seen the movie, it might help to explain the concept."

"There's no concept," Scala said. "Unless 'you are nuts' is a concept."

"This is what happens when people tell the truth," Don said. "If I'd said, oh, we've all got a new disease caused by cell phones or something, you'd have believed me."

"Because it's almost possible," said Scala. "Unlike you being a time cop."

"Why?" asked Don, pushing his seat back from the table and putting his arms behind his head like he was testing his favorite pupil.

"For a start, you'd need a time machine or something," said Scala, "and there's no such thing as time machines."

"That's true," Don said.

"Excuse me?"

"Time machines don't exist," said Don. "They can't exist because if you build a machine to go somewhere, there has to be a place for it to go. And time isn't a place."

"OK," said Scala. "So time travel isn't possible but you're a time cop. That's like being a mall cop without a mall."

"That's good," said Don. "I'll tell that one to the other time cops. If," he added, "I ever see them again."

He picked up the salt and pepper cellars.

"You going to explain how time travel works?" asked Scala.

"No," said Don, "I was just making some room for this."

He put the condiment set to one side and took out a book.

"*An Experiment in Time,*" said Scala. "Is that Stephen Hawking?"

"Now that's a great book," Don said. "This one, less so. Turgid.

Over-argued. Illogical. But," he added, slapping the cover of the book for emphasis, "it's also right."

"Right about what? That you're crazy."

"Listen!" Don said, loudly. He slammed his hand down on the table.

"You OK, honey?" asked the large woman.

"I think so," said Scala.

"Apologies, folks," said Don. He turned to Scala again.

"Sorry," he said. "I just don't get how you can accept having someone else's fucking hand on your arm but time travel's a crazy idea."

"Good point, well made," said Scala. "I guess because I actually *have* someone else's fucking hand on the end of my arm, but I don't see any actual time travel. Just a weird guy with an old book who says he's Doctor fucking Who."

She was as angry as Don now. *Take a breath*, Scala told herself.

"OK," she said. "We're here. I do have someone else's hand and that is weird and fucked-up. So go ahead. Tell me how you're a time cop."

Don looked down at the table.

"Thank you," he said. "I know this all sounds slightly insane, and I guess it is on some level, but it's real."

He let out a breath so deep it sounded like it had been inside him for years, and said:

"Let's leave aside the mechanics of the thing for now. All I'm going to say is that traveling in time, it's not like taking a cab, it's more like…"

He waved his hands around, as though trying to pull his thoughts from the air.

"It's like you threw a die, and it came up the number you were thinking of, except you weren't thinking of the number until the die showed it to you," he said. "It's like finding a door in a wall that wasn't there before, and nor was the wall, until you needed it to be. It's like—"

"It's like bullshit is what's it like," said Scala.

Don smiled.

"OK," he said, "I guess I'll leave the chat about remote viewing and precognition for another day. Like I said, it's best we leave the mechanics aside," he concluded. "What you need to know is the whole time-cop thing."

"Oh boy," said Scala. "Do I."

"A long time from now there will still be a world," said Don. "And it'll work. It'll be messy like now and right won't always beat wrong, just like now, but it'll work."

"Good to know," Scala said.

"And one day, the world won't work anymore," Don went on.

"Don't tell me, we collide with Mars," Scala said. "No, plague. Wait, nuclear war."

"We call it the Pulse," said Don. "It stopped everything. The air turned black, the animals died, everything crashed. I mean literally, planes fell to the earth."

"When does this happen?" Scala asked. "I feel I should tell people."

"We tried," Don said. "Some of us. It didn't work."

"Is that why you're here?" said Scala. "Noble Don, flying back in time to warn the people of old."

"I'm getting to that," Don said, shaking his head. "See, the world recovered. Kind of. It was bad for a long time, but it began to get better. But the Pulse changed things."

"And that's why you're a time cop," Scala replied.

"You got it," said Don.

He took a swig of coffee.

"People aren't so different in the future," he said. "They're happy and sad and worried and cruel. But mostly…"

He seemed to be searching for the right word.

"…they're resentful," he said.

The restaurant was emptying. With a nod to Scala, the large woman and her son were leaving, too. She was alone with Don and the waitresses.

"Resentful?" she said, reluctant to go along with Don's story but not really having a choice.

"People had had their lives ruined," Don said. "I mean, most of it was top-down shit, government and military doing what they do best. But there was this lobby, this huge mass of people, saying, we lost husbands, mothers, providers while others went unpunished. And the authorities said, sorry, can't help you, the bad guys are all dead. Which is true, by the way."

"I'm lost," said Scala.

"Short version," Don said. "You can't bring back Uncle Joe when he's dead, and you can't punish the guy who killed him, because there was a war, and he's dead too. Sad but true, right?"

"I guess," Scala said.

"Wrong," said Don.

"I didn't say, 'right'," Scala replied. "I said, 'I guess'. I'm not actually agreeing with you. But yeah, I would tend to agree that when people are dead, they're dead."

"And that was the issue," Don agreed. "You can make people's descendants pay for shit, reparations and all that, but you can't make the actual bad guys suffer. Because that would involve—"

"Time travel," Scala said. "Shit."

"You got it."

Don ordered two coffees.

"I don't drink coffee," Scala said.

"They're for me," said Don. "I love caffeine."

"What, is it illegal in your time or something?" asked Scala.

"No, but it's hard to get the beans," said Don. "Anyway, back to time travel. You see, there had been experiments. Not so much travelling in time as what you might call remote viewing."

"I would never call anything remote viewing," Scala said.

"Remote viewing is like you can't be in the past, but you can see it," Don said. "Fly-on-the-wall kind of thing. Then someone worked out if you can see something, you must in some way be in the place where that something is. Like there's no fly on the wall, that's impossible, but what if there's a picture of a fly in the room?"

"That makes no sense," Scala said.

"And yet here I am," Don said.

"Here you are," Scala agreed. "Making no sense."

The coffees arrived.

"Anyway," said Don, using the word as a blanket to throw over everything she'd just said and suffocate it, "years passed, work went on, and they figured it out."

"Time travel?"

"Kind of."

Don took a sip from one of his coffee cups.

"I told you about putting the picture on the wall, right?" he said. "There has to be a picture there already for that to work. It can be the same picture only older, it can be a different picture, but there has to be a picture."

"I'm confused *and* bored," Scala said.

"It's a metaphor," Don said.

"I got that."

"It doesn't have to be a picture."

"I got that too."

"It just has to be something in the past occupying the same space in the future. A statue, or a chair. Or an animal."

Scala looked at him.

"An animal?"

Don smiled at her.

"Or a person."

"What?" Scala said.

"You heard me."

"A person?"

"Yeah. Not the same person, like it's not the same picture. But you replace a person in the past with a person in the—"

"That's impossible," she said.

"It's not impossible at all. It's just very difficult," said Don. "Which is why we do it one piece at a time."

"No," said Scala. She looked at her hand in horror.

"Yes," said Don. "We call it the Victim Replacement Program."

Scala looked at him.

"OK," said Don. "Shall we do this from the top?"

ELEVEN

"The world I live in," said Don, "the world I'm from, it's not so different from this one. Everyone talks about the future, or used to talk about the future, like it was this shining city of tech, where everything's kind of white, or translucent blue, and clean. Kind of like the future is a giant clinic."

"And is it?" Scala asked.

"Like a giant clinic?" said Don. "No."

The future (Don said) was not what it was cracked up to be. There were no flying cars, no droids serving tea – no droids at all – and no giant computers telling everybody what to do. The Pulse kind of fucked all that up. It made the human race take three steps back – maybe five – before it figured out how to take one step forward again.

But neither (Don went on) was the future like one of those movie apocalypses. The landscape wasn't bleak and barren, not all of it anyway, with nothing going on but burning heaps of rubble and cities of rats and plague and upside-down shopping carts.

The future was just *shitty*.

After the Pulse, all kinds of shenanigans went down. There were little wars that tired themselves out after a while, because nobody really had the energy apart from a few people who liked uniforms and torture. Then there was some business with a train that Don didn't quite remember, and things kind of settled down.

Life was never going to be that different when human beings were involved. People went about their business like they always did, building stuff and growing stuff and having kids and generally just getting on with it, like people do. They worked, they played, they tried to get on, and if they couldn't get on, well, there were options. Like crime.

Crime in the future was like crime now. There were no new future crime categories: crooks just carried on doing various kinds of bad stuff, on a spectrum of a bit naughty to just horrible, the way crooks always had. But there was one difference: not in crime, but punishment.

"The Pulse changed everything and nothing," said Don. "It remade the world, rebooted it kind of in a grim way, and the people just got on with it. And in the end, it wasn't so different to how it had always been. The sun started shining again, people found love and happiness and all that whimwham, and life went on. You know? Like it does."

But (he went on) the world was not quite as it had been. The Pulse had done something to the world. Nobody was quite sure what it was, but the world felt different. Like sometimes there was a different taste to reality. You'd wake up in the morning, and the air felt different. It was hard to put your finger on, but it felt somehow like things were possible now that weren't possible before.

And then one day somebody worked out what those possibilities were.

"It was a psychiatrist, some French lady," Don said. "She was doing some research into regression therapy, seeing if you really could go back to the pre-memory stage, and she decided to experiment on herself."

The French lady was named Marie Fevrier and she was thorough. She went back to her childhood home – it was still in the family – and sat down on the floor of the room she had slept in as a baby. She had her favorite childhood toy, a battered cloth puppy, and she placed it in front of her and just *stared* at it. For minutes. For hours.

Nothing happened. Not for the longest time.

And then Marie Fevrier heard a noise. It was a child crying in a cot. She shook herself awake – not that she'd been asleep, but she realized she'd gone into a kind of trance – and looked up. She was in the same place, but instead of everything in it being kind of faded and neglected, the room was freshly decorated. There was the wallpaper she remembered being there her whole childhood, the little chair and the table she used to play at. And in the playpen next to her was – she couldn't quite believe it but it had to be true because everything else was true – a toddler, a girl who she knew, quite definitely, was her.

The girl looked up and smiled in her direction.

Marie fainted.

"She didn't give up," said Don. "She kept going back. Because what she'd discovered wasn't a way to revisit your past memories, it was a way to *revisit the past*."

"Time travel," said Scala.

"Not really, because she was just looking," Don said.

The Fevrier Method, as it was known, didn't work for everyone. Most people just couldn't do it, and those who could were soon recruited by various government agencies, because this was a fucking useful skill by anyone's standards. But not that useful. Certainly, the Fevrier Method was great if you wanted to just look at stuff. Historians and that kind of person loved it: that was pretty much it, though.

The Pulse had loosened reality enough for human beings to look, but they couldn't touch. That came later.

"People started trying to send things back," Don said. "It didn't work. There was just a lot of fools getting nosebleeds from staring at mice."

"Mice?" asked Scala.

"Like guinea pigs," Don said. "They were the cute ones, right?"

One day, someone did it. He was a guy from Oregon called Frank Allen and he took a ten-dollar bill from just before the Pulse happened, put it in a metal box about the same age, and concentrated on it for a whole morning. That didn't work, so Frank took the box to an old church that had been there for about a hundred years and put it on a shelf in the crypt.

Frank sat down in front of the box and cleared his mind. Time passed. He found he was in a kind of trance, just like Marie Fevrier. And when he came out of it, he was still in the present day, and so was the box.

He was disappointed, but kind of expecting it. Frank went over to the shelf – and noticed that the box was covered in a thick, filthy layer of dust, like it had been there for a long, long time. He opened the box, with some difficulty, because the lock was rusted, and took out the bill. It hadn't changed: at least, not any more than something that's been kept in a box for decades in a damp crypt would change.

A few days later, Frank got a job offer from a government agency and vanished from public view forever.

"After that," said Don, "people got really interested in the past. Lost inheritances, that kind of thing. And reparations."

"Reparations?"

"Yeah. Not just from the time of the Pulse, but before," said Don. "Think about it. People have been crapping on each other for centuries. Occupation, slavery, genocide. Imagine someone took your land. Your house. Your father's house. Your grandfather's *life*. You can't stop that happening, but you can get payback. Or try to, anyway."

Which is where the Victim Replacement Program came in. Civil rights lawyers were inundated with requests – demands, really – to open up old cases where someone suspected injustice toward a forebear.

"People used to just want a pardon for Great-Aunt Mary," said Don. "Now they want to go back and punish the person who framed her. Or the person who killed her."

Such procedures were impossible at first. Then it was discovered that the government had been experimenting with body part transference. It was crude, and most of the prisoner volunteers who weren't actually volunteers died in transit, but eventually they got it right. If you wanted a historic wrong righted, and you didn't mind never coming back, you could be transported into someone else's body, bit by bit.

"Why?" Scala asked.

"Because if you do a whole person in one go, they die."

"No, why would you want to go back in time, live someone else's life?"

"My time isn't that great," Don said. "A lot of people would like to go back to happier times. I mean literally. So why not go back in time, kill the person who ruined your family, and take their life? Also literally. Literally take their life, and live their life, with all that entails."

"It seems kind of complicated," said Scala.

"Oh, it is," Don agreed. "And it needs policing. Which is where I come in."

Don was a regular cop, he said, when he was approached by someone high up in the Victim Replacement Program.

"There had been mistakes," he said. "Records from the past are scanty at the best of times, and people were abusing the system. They were faking their case, just to get back to the past. So the VRP asked me if I would help out."

"And you generously agreed to give up your entire life and go back in time and never return," said Scala.

"I was a cop," Don said. "My life was pretty crappy. No family, no savings, and nothing to look forward to but death. You think it wasn't better to live the rest of my days in the twenty-first century?"

He looked at her. "You people," he said. "You had no fucking idea. You were living in paradise and you didn't even know it."

TWELVE

"Nothing," Isinglass said. He pushed a sheet of paper across the bar at Ricky.

"What do you mean, nothing?" asked Ricky. The paper was covered in a jagged scrawl that was more like the death throes of a very thin snake than someone's handwriting. "And what's this?"

"Nothing means nothing," Isinglass replied. "The IPs you gave me led nowhere. They don't exist. And that's my expenses."

"I can't read it," said Ricky.

"Four hundred dollars," Isinglass said.

"For what?" Ricky asked, incredulous.

"For talking to the IT guy at the paper," said Isinglass.

"But he didn't know anything," said Ricky.

Isinglass said, "It's still information."

Ricky sighed, and took a lump of twenties from his wallet.

"This is all I have," he said. "You'll get the rest when… when I've got it."

Isinglass unfolded the money with distaste like it was a tiny, filthy diaper.

"OK," he said, and waved one of the crumpled notes at the bartender.

"I need more information," said Ricky.

"So do I," Isinglass said. "I mean, from you. So far all I have is the guy's called Don and he sends emails."

Ricky thought for a minute. "So, the lady told me her account was private and secured," he said. "Which means Don broke into her emails. Also there's the fake IPs. That means he's got hacker skills."

"'Hacker skills'," said Isinglass contemptuously. "You sound like the nineties."

He sighed.

"I'll ask my guy again," he said. "In the meantime, get me something to go on."

"Like what?" asked Ricky.

Isinglass gestured hopelessly at the air.

"Anything. I feel like I'm at a séance."

"OK," said Ricky, then: "Wait a minute."

"What?"

"I just realized something."

"Shit, I thought you were going to buy me a drink for a moment there."

Ricky took the hint and ordered a pint of rum. He waited until Isinglass had swallowed some of it before saying, "He rents a room for the meetings."

"Who? What fucking meetings?"

"Don, of course. He holds these meetings, like AA sessions."

Isinglass looked at him over the top of his rum glass.

"And this was something you didn't feel I needed to know until now?"

Ricky grimaced.

"I didn't want to tell you about the meetings," he said. "They're… weird."

"Like your fucking hand is weird," said Isinglass. "OK, give me the name of the place and I'll look into it."

Ricky wrote down the address of the building. "He has to give a name to rent the room, right?" he asked.

"Look at you, Sherlock Holmes," said Isinglass. "I'm going for a piss," he added and left Ricky at the bar.

When Isinglass hadn't come back ten minutes later, Ricky went to the bathroom to see if he was OK. He found Isinglass standing at a urinal, head leaning against the tiled wall, completely unconscious.

"Isinglass!" he shouted. "Wake up!"

Isinglass grunted but remained comatose.

"Pull his dick, that'll wake him up," said the man at the next urinal, who was barely awake himself.

With difficulty, Ricky opened one of Isinglass's eyelids, saw the veined eyeball move, and decided it was OK to leave.

Once he was home, he checked his messages and emails to see if Scala had been in touch, but there was nothing.

Probably dancing the night away, he thought, turned on the TV and fell asleep during *Saturday Night Live*.

• • •

Scala wasn't dancing the night away. She was still sitting in Denny's, trying to ignore the staff as they humped chairs onto tables, lifted cups to wipe under them, and all the other little signs that they wanted to close up – and Don was still talking.

"It works," he said insistently.

"It can't," said Scala. "It doesn't make sense."

Don held up his own arm, the arm that looked thinner and paler than its partner.

"And this does?" he said. "Technologies change, you know that. We can replace organs, why not limbs?"

"Because—" Scala began, and stopped, realizing she didn't know. She took a deep breath. "Because what you're saying is insane."

"It's not insane, it's just new to you. You feel threatened."

Don's face took on a sympathetic look.

"It must be hard for you. This is an information overload. But it's real."

"Real?" Scala said. "You're saying that in the future, people will be able to trade bodies with people in the past."

"That's a crude way of putting it, but yes," said Don. "The transference method enables a form of punitive justice to occur."

"Punitive…"

"Justice," said Don. "An eye for an eye. Literally."

Scala looked at her hand again.

"This can't be true."

"And I can't keep saying, *look at yourself*," Don said. "Look at your own body."

"OK," Scala said. "Let's say you're not crazy. Let's say that this—" she held up her hand, "—is someone else's hand, someone who was the victim of a crime in the future—"

"I see where you're going with this."

"Are they *my* victim?"

"That's—"

Scala grabbed Don's arm.

"Because that's where this falls down." She laughed. "I mean, apart from the fucking time travel shit. Apart from the body part transference and the future war and all that."

There were tears in her eyes now.

"All that I can apparently swallow," said Scala. "But on top of that, I'm supposed to believe that I'm being punished for some sort of *crime*?"

Don nodded.

"It's wrong," he said. "It's wrong, and you're right. And that's why I'm here."

"Here for what?" Scala asked, and now she really was crying.

"Here to fix it," Don said, smiling. "I'm the time cop, remember?"

• • •

Don called a cab and had it drop Scala back at her hotel. He walked her to the lobby.

"Goodnight," he said.

She said nothing. She was drained and exhausted.

"I know this is a lot to take in," said Don. "If it helps, you're the only one I could tell. Which makes me feel better, at least."

Scala took a step toward him. Her eyes flared with rage.

"Wrong thing to say, OK," Don said. "Sorry. But two things to remember. One, the others can't know this. They won't be able to take it. And two, I'm here to fix this. And I will fix it."

He put his hand on Scala's arm. She stepped back and he removed it.

"I just have one question," Scala said.

"Go ahead," said Don.

"How did *you* get here?" Scala asked.

"Let's save that for next time, assuming you want to see me again and there is a next time," said Don.

He smiled at her. It was a worldly-wise, weary smile.

"Try and enjoy New York," he said. "We'll talk more when you get back."

. . .

Ricky still couldn't get hold of Scala, so he went outside for a cigarette. He didn't smoke much now, but he'd never given up anything in his entire life and he couldn't get the hang of vaping so he still smoked the occasional cigarette.

He stood outside his apartment, and he was so engrossed in trying to get his mom's old Zippo to work that he didn't notice when the rain began to come down, lightly at first and then harder and harder until both Ricky and the cigarette were drenched and he was forced to go inside again.

When he got inside, he saw his phone was vibrating. He picked it up.

"Scala," he said.

He could hear nothing at the other end.

"Hello?" he said.

Now he could hear her. Great heavy gouts of misery erupting from inside. She was *sobbing*, that was the right word.

"Sorry," Scala eventually said.

Ricky said something to her he'd never knowingly said before.

"Are you OK?" he asked.

"Not really," Scala said. "I need to see you."

"Now?" said Ricky. "But it's raining. I think the weather's changing."

"Fuck the weather," said Scala.

They met at a cutesy retro diner on the corner. The TV was on in the corner, a big map of Florida filling the screen. A weather girl droned on about storms coming in as the waitress came over to their table.

Ricky ordered a millionaire shortbread and Scala had a glass of tap water.

"Nighthawks," said Ricky.

Scala looked at him.

"It's a painting," he explained.

"I know," said Scala. "I was just thinking, are you all that stands between me and whatever the fuck."

"I could go," said Ricky. "I mean, people want to hurt me because of you, it's no big deal."

"I know that," Scala said.

"Also, right back at you. It's not ideal for me that my only—" Ricky hesitated; he didn't like to use the word *friend*, "—ally is the Britney Spears of the twenty-first century."

"Jesus, how old are you?" said Scala. She almost smiled. "And it's the Lisa Left Eye Lopes of the twenty-first century. She was cool."

"Are we cool?" Ricky asked.

"You?" Scala said. "Never."

Now she did smile, briefly, before beginning to cry. Ricky, inexpert with tears, gave her a handkerchief.

"What the fuck is this?" Scala said, pushing it back to him. "Your beating-off rag?"

"I'm really glad you made me come out tonight," Ricky replied.

"Sorry," said Scala.

"Why did you make me come out?" asked Ricky.

Scala told him everything.

Ricky was silent for quite some time. Occasionally he opened his mouth, about to speak, and then closed it again, as though whatever he had to say wasn't ready yet. He looked at his own hand a few times, clenched it, rubbed his eyes, and shook his head.

After a while, Scala said:

"You need to say something now. Even if it's just, 'you're nuts'."

"That's a given," Ricky said. "Or Don is. Shit."

He touched the back of his new hand, a gesture that Scala had seen him make a few times lately. She wondered if he knew he was doing it.

Then he said:

"Why?"

"I don't know," Scala said. "I guess it's like revenge. You kill me, I get your body. I get your body, I get your life."

"How does it work? I mean, it can't work, so how does it?"

"It's the future, they can do it. That's what the future is, right? It's the place where they can do stuff we can't."

"Why don't they just, I don't know, stop the crime from happening in the first place? If they can travel in time and all?"

"I guess they only know the crime has happened after it's happened," Scala said. "And even then, I imagine they have to prove it, you know."

"Prove it?"

"Yeah. Hire a lawyer and, I don't know, a historian, and say, 'Hey, this happened to my mom, or my wife,' and then, you know – prove it."

Ricky looked both blank and angry.

"OK," he said. "Let's say all of this is true – the time travel, the victim thing, the cop bit – but why us? I haven't done anything."

"Me neither," Scala said. "I mean, I think. No. Nothing so bad that someone would do…"

She touched her own hand.

"Maybe," she said, "he's here to fix things."

"Yeah, right," Ricky said. "Because he's done such a great job so far."

"It's not Don's fault we're like this. He's the same as us, remember."

"Doesn't mean anything," said Ricky, but he sounded unsure.

"Jesus," Scala said. "I'm not happy either, you know."

"Sorry," Ricky said. "It's just this is so fucked up."

"You know what?" Scala said. "I just realized what we are. With these… new parts. Coming from nowhere, piece by piece."

"What?"

Scala looked at him.

"We're downloads," she said. "Like an album dropping one track at a time, song by song, until one day – bang, the whole thing is there. And we're gone."

"Thanks," said Ricky. "I feel so much better."

Scala looked at her phone. It was nearly three a.m.

"I have to be up in four hours," she said. "Any news from your sleuth guy?"

"He's not a sleuth," said Ricky. "Even though he does drink a lot. Hey, do you have my money?"

"Oh, your money," Scala replied, but she took out a small roll of dollars and passed it to him.

"Careful," said Ricky. "Someone might pap you and think I'm your dealer."

"You worried about my reputation?"

"No," Ricky said. "I'm worried about someone else getting the scoop."

"But—"

"I know. Listen, as soon as my guy has something, I'll call."

Scala shook her head.

"You can't," she said. "Jonty's going to be with me the whole time. I know he peeks when I use my cell."

"Then how—"

Scala slid a piece of card across the table.

"These are all my details," she said.

"Including the email address Don hacked?" asked Ricky.

"Good point," said Scala. "So use it only in an emergency."

Ricky waited a few minutes, then paid for his shortbread before putting on his coat and leaving.

Outside in the rain, Tom, the man who'd beaten Ricky up a few hours before, watched as Ricky got into his car and drove home.

THIRTEEN

Scala braced herself for the inevitable shuddering and bumps as the plane touched down at JFK.

"We should have hired a private jet," said Jonty, who had talked nervously throughout the entire flight, turbulence and all.

"Save the planet," Scala said. "Besides, I hate private jets. You just know some oligarch's been fucking in them."

Jonty collected their few items of luggage from the locker as Scala smiled at people she didn't know.

"You don't have to smile at all of them," Jonty said. "Just the ones who might be influencers."

"Social media," said Scala, beaming at a thin grumpy kid with an Aquaman beard. "They're all fucking influencers these days."

Midnight with McGovern was transmitted from an old TV theater near Times Square and was billed as live, which it mostly was, apart from the occasional backup recording of rehearsals if a sketch went really wrong or a guest act turned out to be unusually offensive.

"We know that won't happen with you," said the smiling PA who met Scala at reception. "I'm such a fan," she went on, not offering any evidence of said fandom. "Here we are," she said a few minutes later when they reached the dressing room where Scala would be spending most of her week.

"Anything you need, you know where I am," said the PA before vanishing into the network of corridors again.

Scala looked around the room. It was comfortably furnished and entirely windowless.

"I got my own bunker," she said to no one in particular.

The first day was unexceptional. Scala met the writers, who were all huge fans, and the head of the network, whose kids were huge fans, and was assured that she would meet the host, Kendra McGovern, at some point, except she didn't like to meet guests before she interviewed them, so maybe she wouldn't meet her until after the show. Scala was shown the skits, which were fine, and Jonty vetoed one of them for language and another for content, and the song she'd be performing with the house band turned out to be not a comedy song, but an old blues standard that they knew she would be able to sing because she had such a great voice.

The second day was pretty similar, except all the sketches were dropped for a topical routine about the President, which Jonty wasn't sure was right for Scala's audience and Scala wasn't sure was actually funny.

The third day was completely different, because on the morning of the third day Scala woke up, raised her arm to look at her watch to see what time it was, and screamed.

This time it wasn't just her hand that had changed. It was

her entire arm, from the top of her shoulder to her fingertips. The skin was the same pale color as her hand – her old new hand, she thought wildly for a moment – and there were some freckles, but apart from that it wasn't a bad match. With make-up or gloves nobody would notice.

Nobody but me, Scala thought.

She sat on the end of the hotel bed with her eyes shut for as long as possible. When nothing happened, which of course she had known would be the case, she opened her eyes again and looked for her phone. It was shocking, really, how easily she adapted to her situation. Her new fingers worked as well as her old ones, and even the slight change in hand size made no difference to her balance or ability to grip things. Only the constant visual reminder that *this isn't my fucking body* made her aware that something was wrong.

Scala picked up her phone and was about to dial Ricky when she stopped herself. She thought of Jonty and his security concerns. She thought of Don and his hacking skills. And then, absurdly, she thought of her audience, the *demographic* as Jonty called them. Huge swathes of people on every continent on the planet, most of whom she would never meet, and most of them neither rabid stalkers nor dewy-eyed teens who worshipped her.

At twenty-one, despite a brief but near-seismic wobble at the end of her teens, Scala had no intention of biting the hand that fed her. She was a realist, and knew that if she fucked up, she would be at best playing theme parks until she died, and at worst might end up singing her own songs at kids' parties. So she paid attention when Jonty talked about career paths and unexpected changes of direction, she avoided (these days) drug abuse and excessive alcohol, and she took care not to piss off the fans. She wouldn't lie or engage in fake relationships, but at the same time she wouldn't do anything that might mark her out as nuts or too weird.

And now here she was, about to text someone she barely knew, whose job was to publicize in the most negative manner possible the activities of people like her, and she was about to do it on a phone that might conceivably be hacked into by someone she knew even less well, and could equally conceivably have already been hacked by her manager.

I'm turning into a monster, thought Scala, *and all I'm worried about is social media.*

She put the phone down again. Immediately it buzzed. Jonty.

Hi. Do you need anything?

Scala thought of texting:

Sure, my old body back.

Instead she sent:

Can you get me some gloves? To wear on the show.

Immediately he texted back:

Are you sure?

Yes, she replied. *It's the look right now. Trust me.*

OK, Jonty replied. *Boxing or driving?*

Ha the fuck ha, she replied, and went into the bathroom to see if anything else was different about her.

• • •

Ricky woke up early that morning. He winced when he saw just how early: Ricky wasn't someone who liked to enjoy the

123

morning. He preferred to skip the morning, and found the nocturnal life of the pap suited his mental clock. Now here he was, awake before dawn, and he knew he wouldn't be able to get back to sleep again.

Ricky thought about masturbating, but decided it was too much effort, so he got up and went into the bathroom to piss. He stood there, listening to the sound of his own urine hitting the pan, and looked at his reflection in the bathroom mirror.

Oh fuck, he thought.

Something was different.

Ricky stopped pissing and took a step nearer to the mirror. What was it? His face seemed the same as it had last night but there was something different. He turned his head from side to side.

And then he saw it.

That's not my ear, he thought.

Ricky's new ear looked nothing like his other ear. He had always had small, round, delicate ears – "like a Japanese girl," someone had said once. Now he had one small delicate ear and one large, ragged, dirty-looking ear with, he was horrified to realize, a chunk torn out of its lobe.

Hurriedly he brushed his hair over his ears, but the new one was too large and it stuck out again like an ogre trying to hide behind a curtain.

I guess I could say I caught a bad ear infection, Ricky thought to himself.

"A really fucking bad one," he said out loud.

He thought about telling Scala, but decided there was no point. Either she would freak out, which was bad, or she wouldn't give a shit, which was worse. So he found some old hair gel and tried to matt his hair over his ear, watched it bounced back, gave up and went and made some coffee.

It was still only five-forty in the morning.

. . .

Ricky was woken at eleven by his phone ringing. He sat up, immediately covering himself in lukewarm coffee from the mug he'd made earlier and fallen asleep holding. His groin dripping, Ricky looked for his phone and eventually found it on the toilet lid.

"Hi," he said, moving his leg slightly to separate his drenched scrotum from his thigh.

He was answered by a deafening fit of coughing.

"You took your fucking time," a voice said after the coughing had finally subsided.

"Isinglass," said Ricky. "How are you?"

"Fucked like your mother," Isinglass answered cheerfully. "Is this a bad time?"

"No," said Ricky, looking at his stained crotch.

"Great. Get a pen and paper."

Ricky found a pencil and a scrap of paper and sat down.

"OK," he said.

"OK what?"

"OK, I'm ready," said Ricky.

"Right," Isinglass replied. "Sorry, I had a bad night."

He coughed again, as if producing evidence.

"You still there?" he asked.

"Still here," said Ricky.

"Got a pen?"

"Yes," said Ricky, trying to sound patient.

"Good, because you need to write this down."

"Hence the pen and paper."

"Nobody says 'hence'," Isinglass said, "except a fucking asshole."

"Are you going to tell me anything?" asked Ricky.

"Don't rush me," Isinglass said.

Ricky heard an odd scraping sound and realized Isinglass was unscrewing the lid from a bottle.

"Isinglass, are you drinking?"

"It's nearly dinner time," Isinglass said. "Cheers."

Ricky moved the phone to his other ear, which felt weird for some reason until he realized he was holding it against his new ear. Hastily he moved it back again.

"Alright," Isinglass said. "Listen to me, and listen carefully."

Ricky listened. Then he started writing on the Post-it note. A few seconds later, he ripped the note off the pad and began writing on the next note. Then he went in search of a writing pad and began writing in earnest.

"You don't sound very surprised," Isinglass said when he'd told Ricky everything he'd found out.

"I guess it's a lot to take in," Ricky said. *Plus you have no idea what I've already taken in*, he thought to himself.

"I guess," Isinglass said. "Anyway, if you want me to continue, I'm gonna need a lot more money."

"Why?" said Ricky. "I mean, this is just research, right? Library visits and internet searches."

"Yeah, but I like money," said Isinglass. "Also, no offense, but if you want to do it, be my fucking guest, fat boy."

Ricky rang off. He needed to write up what Isinglass had told him properly before it all got confused in his head. He opened a note in his phone and after some thought named it INFORMATION. That was vague enough to deter snoops, he decided.

DON, he typed, remembering what Isinglass had told him.

"First of all," Isinglass said. "There is nothing on this guy. I mean, shit all."

"What about when he hired the room?" asked Ricky.

"Paid cash," said Isinglass.

"How? Nobody takes cash."

"Went to the ATM and took out three hundred dollars."

"That's a lot of money for two hours in a meeting room."

"Which is why they took cash," Isinglass said. "If you ask me, the office manager charged him a hundred and took the rest for himself."

"Did he sign anything?"

"Did he balls," said Isinglass. "Just winked at the guy and said he trusted him to take care of the paperwork."

"And I suppose he didn't have to produce any ID or anything like that?" Ricky said.

"No," said Isinglass. "The manager's corrupt but he's not stupid. He told me he was a little bit worried that your guy might be using the room for, what did he say… nefarious purposes."

"Nefarious purposes? He said that?"

"Like someone's going to rent a meeting room for sex trafficking or cutting up a body, right? Anyway, the manager didn't want to be left holding the baby, his words not mine, so he asked Don for some kind of ID. Which Don gave him."

"What? Just like that?"

"Yeah. Just like that."

"Was it valid ID?"

"No, it was a drawing of a dick. With your name underneath it."

"Isinglass, are you drunk?"

"I fucking hope so, I've had about a quart of rum."

"Maybe we should speak later."

"Maybe you should listen now. The ID your friend gave the manager – it was right but it was also wrong."

"Definitely call me back when you're sober."

"*No.* Listen to me. The ID was a driver's license. A completely legit driver's license, the guy's real name, everything, except one detail didn't make sense."

"You going to tell me the detail?"

Isinglass belched at the end of the line and Ricky recoiled.

"Sorry," said Isinglass. "The detail that didn't make sense was your guy's DOB."

"How so?"

"The manager told me your guy—"

"Don."

"Sure. He said *Don* looked to him to be forty-five, fifty years old."

"Yeah," Ricky said. "That's about right."

"The DOB on the driver's license begs to differ," said Isinglass. "It makes him out to be seventeen years old."

"It's a fake," Ricky said.

"The manager checked it out," Isinglass said. "It's real."

"The manager made a mistake."

"He scanned it," Isinglass replied. "Put it on the photocopier when Don was on his phone and scanned it."

"He has a photocopier?"

"He's an office manager, what else would he have?"

There was a clink of ice at the end of the line as Isinglass took a swallow of rum.

"The license is real," he said. "I got a printout of the scan and it checks out."

"So there's someone out there with the same name as my guy," Ricky said.

"Was," Isinglass replied.

"What does that mean?"

"I looked him up. The seventeen-year-old," said Isinglass. "He was killed in a home invasion about six years ago. The killer was never caught."

"Is Don the killer?" asked Ricky. "Did he assume the kid's identity?"

"I don't know," replied Isinglass. "You're the one who's met him. Did he strike you as the kind of person who'd go to Alaska to kill someone just for their driving license?"

"Alaska?"

"Yeah."

"This makes no sense."

"You're wrong," Isinglass said. "This is the part that does make sense. Keep listening, there's more."

Having typed DRIVER'S LICENSE and ALASKA into his document, Ricky squinted at his notes again. This time he typed SCALA.

"I figured out who your girl is," Isinglass said.

"That's not what I asked you to do," said Ricky.

"I don't like to be kept in the dark," said Isinglass. "When I'm working, I kind of like to have the full picture."

"I understand that, but it didn't seem necessary was all."

"You wanted to keep her to yourself is all," Isinglass replied. "You're not exactly a savory character, Rick boy."

Ricky said nothing.

"It's OK," Isinglass went on after deciding that Ricky wasn't going to speak. "Everyone likes to hold something back, doesn't matter if they're a marathon runner or a pervert. But look, you can't tell me half the story."

"Of course, I get that now," said Ricky, who had no intention of telling him any more than he needed to. The whole thing was fucked up enough already without freaking out a man who'd probably won the Pulitzer Prize for drinking.

"Good," said Isinglass. "Because when I found out who she was, I naturally figured what anyone else would. Namely that the guy was a stalker, a what do they call them now?"

"A stan," said Ricky.

"Right, that. But again, there's nothing. I mean, your girl, she attracts the crazies like moths to a fart. Which explains the booze habit."

"What booze habit?"

"Jesus, and you call yourself a journalist. Never mind. Anyway, this Don character, seventeen or seventy-seven, he's not on any police sheet, he doesn't pop up in any chat rooms, there are no fan sites warning people about him… So if he is planning to abduct her or anything like that, there's no evidence to suggest he will.

"In fact," Isinglass went on as Ricky tore another sheet off the notepad, "there's no evidence of him anywhere."

"Tell me his name at least," said Ricky, pen in mouth.

"Don Marx," Isinglass said. "Like the brothers and the communist. Listen, I have one lead."

"Oh yeah?" Ricky replied.

"The murder in Alaska," said Isinglass. "There was one interview the police did, with some old geezer who says he was nearby when it happened."

"That's it?" Ricky asked.

"That's it or that's shit," Isinglass replied. "Old geezer's still alive, so I think I'll go see him."

"In Alaska?"

"Of course not," Isinglass said. "The fuck would I go there. Nah, he's an old geezer, he did what all old geezers do when they retire."

It took Ricky a moment to work out what Isinglass meant.

"No way," he said.

"Yep," said Isinglass. "He retired to Florida."

Ricky wrote OLD GEEZER in the document and added MARX to Don's name. It wasn't much, but it was a start: and, while he'd never have said anything to Isinglass, he reckoned he was getting more than his money's worth.

He saved the document, poured the rest of the cold coffee down the sink, and decided he wasn't too tired to masturbate after all.

• • •

Scala experimented with make-up on her hands before deciding it would be easier to go with the gloves. She rejected a lacy pair as too porn, a studded leather pair as too weird, and a single white glove as too eighties, and eventually settled on a nice black pair that didn't draw too much attention to her hands.

Jonty sat in his office with his laptop, looking at a clone of Scala's cell phone display. There was nothing new, and even though she had no idea about the clone account, she hadn't put the email account she used for private stuff on the home screen. But she sometimes got impatient and texted people she shouldn't. He could wait.

• • •

Tom sat outside Ricky's in his hired car. It was gray and of a make so dull that people's eyes just slid off it. He knew Scala was in New York so she wouldn't be meeting with Ricky, but that didn't matter. All he needed was to be told by Jonty that one of them had emailed or texted the other and he would go to work.

• • •

Isinglass drained the last of his rum and went to bed. On the way he stood in the cat's litter tray, cursed, and threw the contents of the tray at the cat. Then he found his bedroom and collapsed onto the threadbare counterpane in a close approximation of a coma.

• • •

The various members of Don's group were all going about their daily business, trying not to think about what was or wasn't happening to them. Only Tony, the gym bunny, was feeling different from usual.

He had this pain behind his eyes.

FOURTEEN

The hotel was the pinkest thing Isinglass had ever seen, and he'd lived in Miami Beach for thirty years. It looked like it was made entirely from marshmallow. It didn't smell like marshmallow; it smelled of old people. There was a strong odor of cleaning fluid, and decay, and meals that had died years ago. No piss smell, Isinglass noted: these old geezers were kept clean, which meant they had money. *Money can't buy you happiness,* he thought, *but it can keep you from smelling of piss.*

He was standing at the main desk and waiting for the clerk to call off the search for whatever was hiding inside his nostrils. At last the clerk removed his finger, wiped it in his hair, and said, "Yes?"

"Oh hi," Isinglass said. "I've come to visit my uncle."

"Name?" said the clerk.

"His or mine?"

The clerk sighed. Isinglass made a mental note to come back and slit his throat in the night.

"Both," he said.

"I'm sure you get this all the time," said Isinglass, putting a cheerfulness into his voice that would have shocked Ricky. "The fact is, we have the same name. Close family, I guess. You see, Dad—"

"Name," said the clerk again, and Isinglass amended his plan to cutting the man's nuts off and shoving them down his throat before slitting it.

"Mackie," Isinglass said. "Doug Mackie."

"He's in the lounge," the clerk said.

"Fuck you," Isinglass muttered and walked away.

"Excuse me?" said the clerk as Isinglass headed into the lounge.

"Thank you!" Isinglass shouted back.

The clerk frowned and went back to reaming out his nose.

The lounge was mostly empty. There was a widescreen TV showing a music channel, some tall armchairs with people sleeping in them, and a table where a game of dominoes was taking place. One of the players was asleep so Isinglass guessed they weren't playing for high stakes.

"Can you turn that off?" someone said. It was a skinny old guy in a red plaid shirt, seated in a wheelchair in front of the TV which was showing an old Kiss video.

"My pleasure," said Isinglass and picked up the remote. It didn't work.

"Needs a new battery," said the skinny old guy. "You have to turn off the set."

Isinglass found the off button and the racket disappeared.

"Thank fuck for that," said the old guy.

"My pleasure," Isinglass replied. "Hey, I'm looking for Doug Mackie."

"That's me."

"Mister Mackie, I'm Isinglass, this is my card. I'm a journalist and—"

"Son, I don't care if you're Jack the fucking Ripper. Wheel me the fuck out of here and buy me a drink."

"Right away, sir."

"This here's an OK place," said Doug as they approached a sport bar on the main drag. Isinglass opened the door and pushed Doug's chair inside.

When they both had beers with chasers, Mackie said:

"You're that writer."

"I prefer hack."

"You busted those guys."

"Long time ago."

"You look retired."

"Yeah."

"So what do you want?"

Isinglass handed Doug a piece of paper. It was a copy of a newspaper cutting.

"Shit," said Doug. "This again."

"Again?" Isinglass asked.

Doug slid the paper back to him.

"Every five years someone calls me up, says they want to talk about the murder," he said. "Sometimes it's some freakshow TV program, sometimes it's for a book."

"I'm sorry," Isinglass said. "But this is important."

"Yeah, they say that too."

Mackie gave Isinglass a look.

"You don't strike me as the sensationalist type," he said.

"I hate sensation," Isinglass said.

"I thought as much," Mackie replied.

"Besides, it's not the murder I'm interested in," Isinglass said. "It's the kid."

Mackie took a sip of his beer.

"The kid," he said. "Don."

"Don," Isinglass agreed.

"I don't remember as much as I used to," Mackie said.

"I can pay," said Isinglass.

"No, I don't want money," Mackie replied, irritably. "I mean my memory is shot. You know when people say they can't remember what they had for breakfast but they do remember what they were doing forty years ago?"

"I've heard people say that."

"Well, not me. I can't remember shit about anything."

"Alright then."

"That said—" Mackie reached for his chaser, "—I do remember Don. He wasn't the kind of kid you took to. Kind of pushy. Like a salesman or a Jehovah's Witness. You could see him going door to door with a big fake smile."

"Insincere," Isinglass said.

"Enthusiastic, too," Mackie said. "It was tiring, especially if you lived next door. 'How you doing, Mister Mackie?' 'Sure is a beautiful day, Mister Mackie.' Like that movie."

"Which movie?"

"The one with the pod people. You know, they're always smiling and raising their fucking hats."

"*The Bodysnatchers*. Great movie."

"Book's good too. Anyway, that was Don. His mom and dad were pretty quiet but he was always in your face. Belonged to every committee and club in town, always collecting for something. He was fucking annoying."

"And then he got murdered," said Isinglass.

"Yeah," Mackie said thoughtfully. "He did."

Mackie finished his beer. Isinglass fetched two more.

"It was weird about the body, though," said Mackie.

"Weird how?" asked Isinglass. There was nothing in the paper about a body.

"Well, there were the usual signs of struggle at the house alright," Mackie said. "Blood and broken glass and valuables were taken. But there was no body. The police thought maybe the kid had done it."

"Robbed his own parents?" asked Isinglass. "Smashed the place up and vanished?"

"Yeah, didn't make sense," Mackie said. "And then they found a body. Five months later, up in the woods when the thaw came. Came down the river. Animals had been at it, wasn't much left. But there was a high school ring and a watch that his parents identified. So that was it."

Isinglass frowned. There was something in Mackie's expression that made him ask:

"Was it?"

Mackie hesitated.

"No, it wasn't."

He looked at Isinglass and said:

"Because I saw him again."

"Don? You saw Don after he was murdered?"

"Yeah. Only it wasn't him."

"What do you mean, it wasn't him?"

"I have to go. Take me back."

"Mister Mackie, please. How could it be Don and not be Don?"

"I'm not crazy, you know. I forget things but I don't have dementia."

"I know that. My mother has dementia."

Mackie fixed Isinglass with a glare.

"Is that true?"

"OK. Had dementia. She's gone now."

Mackie sighed.

"Alright. A week after the murder happened, I was in my bedroom. It was late and I'd fallen asleep on the bed."

"Had a drink?"

"Could be. Anyway, I woke up because the dog was barking. It was my wife's dog and the fucker lived to bark. I went to the window to see if it was something I needed to worry about, like a bear, and I saw him. Don, outside his parents' house. Only it…"

"It wasn't him?"

Mackie seemed to be struggling.

"It was. And it wasn't. He moved the same, for sure. But then the security light came on and I saw his face and – and it was older."

"Older?"

"Yeah. A lot older."

"Could it have been his father? A relation?"

Mackie shook his head.

"Don looked like his mother. And there were no relations to speak of. It was him. And it wasn't him."

Mackie put down his beer.

"Can I go back now?" he asked.

Isinglass took Doug Mackie back to the hotel.

"Did you have a nice time with your nephew?" asked the clerk, in a voice that mixed boredom with a complete lack of interest.

"I've had worse," Doug replied. He looked up at Isinglass.

"Can you take me to my room?" he asked.

Doug was silent in the elevator and said nothing until Isinglass had wheeled his chair into his room. Then, the door closed, he got out of his chair and went over to a cabinet that was too large for the room.

"I can walk OK when I need to," he told Isinglass, holding on to the side of the cabinet.

He opened a drawer and pulled out a large tan envelope.

"I never told the TV people or anyone else about this," he said. "You can have it. You seem on the level, maybe."

"Maybe is OK by me," said Isinglass, taking the envelope.

"Open it later," said Doug. "Now get out, I need to sit in that damn chair over there and I don't want you to see me go over on my ass."

"Sure thing," Isinglass said, and left.

Isinglass walked home. It wasn't far and that way he still had money for wine. Once inside his own apartment, he drew the blinds, turned on the light, and opened the tan envelope.

Inside were some documents and a couple of photographs.

"Son of a bitch," said Isinglass.

There was a birth certificate for Don and, as if to bookend, a death certificate, which confirmed not only date, time and place, but also that he had been seventeen years of age at the time of the murder. An identical version of the newspaper cutting that Isinglass had. A photograph of the teenage Don. And a series of five photographs – real photographs, from a real camera. Three of them were too dark and blurred for anything to be clearly visible in them, but the remaining pair had been taken, presumably, when the light went on. The figure in them was some distance from the camera but was obviously an older version of the teenager in the other pictures.

Don, thought Isinglass. *And Don.*

There was a click behind him. Isinglass turned to see his front door opening.

FIFTEEN

S cala couldn't stop looking at her reflection.

"You look amazing," said the make-up woman, whose name was Midori. "I feel like I hardly need to be here."

Scala made herself smile.

"I bet you say that to everyone who sits in this chair," she replied.

"Honey, you haven't seen who's sat in that chair," said Midori. "Some of them don't need me, they need *surgery*."

She beamed at her own joke, then frowned.

"None of my business, but it's awfully hot under those lights," she said. "You might want to think again about those."

She inclined her head toward Scala's gloved hands.

"I'm fine, but thanks for thinking about me," said Scala. "Listen, can you do something about my eyes? They look kind of—"

"Tired?" said Midori, a little too eagerly. "I didn't like to say anything."

She set to work finding brushes and tubs.

Scala looked at her own reflection again.

At least it's just the hands, she thought.

. . .

Several hundred miles to the south, Ricky was also looking at his reflection. He was trying on a green plaid hunting cap with the side flaps untied and wondering if he could get away with it.

The salesclerk said something. Ricky lifted up one of his flaps.

"Excuse me?" he said.

"I said," replied the salesclerk, "do you actually do any hunting?"

"No," said Ricky. "It's just..."

He stopped, having failed to come up with anything.

"It's your ear, isn't it?" the clerk said. He sounded sympathetic. "My cousin had this terrible infection, totally messed her ears up. She looked like she'd gone ten rounds with – I'm sorry, that was tactless," he finished.

Ricky took off the cap.

"Do you have any berets?" he asked.

. . .

There was very little furniture to smash in Isinglass's apartment, and bottles were the only glass, but it was clear to the cops when they finally arrived that there had been one hell of a struggle.

Books were scattered everywhere, the wall was dented in two or three places, and the only table was in splinters: but mostly there was a lot of blood. The cops, who were used to that kind of thing in the neighborhood, were surprised only by one thing: there was no body.

. . .

Scala was taken down to the studio. There was the familiar interviewer's desk and couch, with the band's gear to one side. She stood by the backdrop which, like every talk show she'd ever seen, featured the city skyline, and watched the house band murder her new single.

"I thought we were using my band," she said to Jonty when her manager finally appeared.

"That's not going to happen," said Jonty, helpfully. "Even Springsteen used the house band."

"He's a rock singer," said Scala. "He's used to singing with bar bands. I'm going back to my dressing room."

"I'll come with you."

"That's not going to happen," said Scala.

She walked off, and Jonty followed.

"Is everything OK?" he asked. "I mean, you've worked with house bands before so—"

"It's not the house band," Scala said.

"Then what is it?"

Well, the main thing is I'm turning into someone else, Scala thought.

"I'm just not comfortable with this whole thing," she said.

"That narrows it down," Jonty replied.

Scala turned to him.

"You know what? Fuck this, I'm not doing it."

"The rehearsal? They won't like that."

"The show."

Jonty walked briskly behind Scala as she tried to find the main entrance.

"At least let's discuss this," he said.

"There's nothing to discuss," replied Scala. "The band sucks, the show sucks – everything sucks."

She stopped when she reached the lobby. There was a large crowd of fans outside.

"OK," Jonty said. "We get your band from wherever the fuck four corners of the earth they are right now. We don't do the blues song. And if you really want we skip the interview. Tell them you're ill."

"Ill and I can sing?"

"You're a trouper. You're fucking Judy Garland."

"Judy Garland wasn't a trouper."

"She was born in a trunk."

"How is that even possible?"

Scala found herself smiling.

"That's better."

"Fuck you."

"Whatever you say."

"Alright," Scala said. "I'll do my song, with their band. And I'll do the interview. But no personal stuff."

"Got it."

They walked back to the studio floor where the house band were still trying to kill Scala's song.

"What was the cover going to be?" asked Scala.

"'Cocktails For Two'," Jonty replied.

"You're kidding me."

Jonty shook his head.

"I told them you were old school," he said. "I guess they took me literally."

• • •

Ricky pulled his new hat – green wool, with a red pompom on the top – down over his ears and walked back to his car. He looked at his phone: no calls. Ricky dialed Isinglass.

"Hello?" said a voice he didn't recognize. "Who is this?"

"Who's *this*?" Ricky answered back.

"Police. Now tell me your name."

"Why are you answering this phone?" said Ricky, who found the police annoying.

"We have your number," said the cop on Isinglass's phone.

"No you don't," said Ricky, "I have an app to make sure that doesn't happen. Is Isinglass dead?"

"He's—" the cop began, and then there was a rustle, and a new voice said:

"This is Detective Rourke. Mister Isinglass is missing. Any information you have will be gratefully received."

"To hell with you," said Ricky, and rang off.

He started the Aztek and headed into the evening traffic.

• • •

Scala got through the song somehow and, after scattered applause from the studio crew, said to Jonty:

"Maybe someone could show them the actual chords?"

"I'll give them all a CD," Jonty said.

"You sure they know what those are?" asked Scala. "Some of them look like they just found out about vinyl."

"Let me speak to the MD," said Jonty. "In the meantime, your costume is ready."

"Costume?"

"For the sketch," Jonty said. "It's like a skit on the new *Star Wars* movie and you're playing—"

"What sketch?" asked Scala.

"We can't drop it," said the producer.

She was sitting on the guests' couch on the set as carpenters worked around them and she looked unhappy.

"Well, you can do it," Jonty said, "but Scala won't be in it."

"There's always a sketch with a guest star," said the producer. Her name was Fleur and she had red asymmetric glasses on a chain round her neck. "Even Radiohead did the sketch."

"Scala Jaq isn't Radiohead," Jonty said. "She's uncomfortable with acting."

"Really?" said Fleur. "I thought she was in a teen drama for like seven years."

"Which is why she's done acting," Jonty said.

Fleur sighed and put her glasses on.

"It'll reflect in our metrics," she said. "And hers."

"I know," Jonty said. He sat on the couch next to Fleur. "Believe me," he said, "I'm as unhappy about this as you are. If she won't do this, what's next? SNL? Not that there's any comparison," he added.

"OK," Fleur said. "She can do her song and fuck off, if that's what she wants."

"Thanks," said Jonty. "You won't regret it."

"Why not?" asked Fleur, then: "OK, now you're off the hook, but you need to tell me the real reason for the shitfit."

"Oh, it's real prima donna stuff," said Jonty.

"Not enough kittens in the dressing room?" asked Fleur.

"Worse than that," Jonty said. "She doesn't want anyone seeing her *hands*."

• • •

Ricky sat on his own couch, drumming his grubby nails on his mom's old coffee table. He was nervous, not just because of the news about Isinglass but because of what he was about to do, which was something he really didn't want to do.

Ricky was going to call his sister.

Ricky did not get on with his sister Katie. Maybe it was because Katie had devoted her entire childhood to making Ricky's life miserable. From the age of four, when she'd tried to bury her toddler brother in hot sand on the beach, to the age of sixteen, when she'd falsely reported him to the police for selling dope, Katie had waged an unremitting war against him. If asked why – and Ricky, tear-stricken and bruised, had often asked her why – she would just smile and say, "I guess 'cos it's fun."

But her hoax call to the police had had one positive side effect: taken down to the station in a cop car for questioning, Katie had suddenly found a focus for all the hate and resentment that broiled inside her. She became a cop, found happiness, and never tortured her brother again (but then, she had no need to, because all Miami was now her bitch).

Now that their parents were dead, Ricky and Katie found it easy to avoid each other. Ricky's frequent encounters with the police – mostly for obstruction – didn't involve his sister, who was now doing well in Homicide. Which was why Ricky needed to call her now.

"Fuck off," Katie greeted him.

"You don't know why I'm calling," said Ricky.

"Well, it's not to say you're dead," Katie said. "And even a desperate whore wouldn't marry you, so it must be 'cos you want something from me. So fuck off."

"No," said Ricky.

"Aw, I miss you saying no," Katie said. "You'd look at me with your little red eyes, all wet from crying, and you'd say, 'No, Katie, stop it, Katie.'"

"You never did," Ricky said.

"I know," Katie sighed. "My, but those were great times. Anyway, nice talking to you, good to know you're still a fucking beaker of living snot, see you in hell."

"I need to talk about a case," said Ricky.

"A what?" Katie sounded like she might be coughing and Ricky realized she was laughing. It was a horrible sound, like a dog being strangled.

"A case."

"Rick, you're a fucking paparazzi. You take pictures up girls' skirts. Did you kill someone? Oh God, if you did, can I bring you in?" Katie's voice was a hot whisper. "I'm serious, Rick, have you killed someone?"

"No," said Ricky. "Come on! If I killed someone, don't you think it would be you?"

"Right," said his sister. "OK, I'm almost interested. What case? Wait, I'm going to take a dump."

"What?"

"It's OK, I'm kidding, I just took one. *What case?*"

"It's the reporter, Isinglass."

"Oh, him. 'Reporter' is pushing it. Guy practically keeps Jim Beam going single-handed."

"He's missing. There was a big bust-up at his apartment."

"You want me to find him for you?" asked Katie. "Once again, fuck off."

"No," said Ricky. "He was doing some work for me, I need to know what he found out."

"That's more like the sniveling little shit I know," said Katie. "What do you need?"

"You're gonna help me?"

"You know what, Isinglass was OK," said Katie. "Little too heavy on people's fucking rights, but I like him. So I'd be doing this for him, not you."

"Alright," said Ricky. "Anything you can find that looks like he was working on something new, I need. And, obviously, anything about where he is. Poor guy," he added, and pretty much meant it.

"Sure thing," said Katie. "If I find anything, I'll let you know."

"Thanks," Ricky said, with virtually no difficulty.

"No problem, shitboy," said his sister. "Hey, if I do find what you need…"

"Yes?" replied Ricky.

"Can I taser you?"

Ricky rang off.

• • •

The car didn't exactly speed through the night, because traffic in Miami Beach is bad, but it went as fast as it could, and fairly soon it was outside the city. The driver parked as near to the house as he could and loaded Isinglass's unconscious body into an old shopping cart, which he then wheeled into the yard. Opening the rusty garage door with a remote control, he pushed the cart inside and closed the door again.

• • •

Scala sat in her dressing room, ready for the run-through. She was wearing her normal clothes with the gloves she planned to wear on the night. They were, as gloves tend to be, pretty warm, but there was nothing else she could do about her hands. So gloves it was.

McGovern's stand-in was coming to the end of her autocued introduction. Scala stood up just as Jonty appeared.

"Break a leg," he said as he stood back to let her pass.

"Balls," said Scala.

• • •

Ricky's phone rang.

"Asshole."

"Hi Katie."

"I got the stuff," his sister said. "Fuckin' weirdo."

"Isinglass?"

"You. It's just some newspaper clippings and a couple of photos. One's a teenage boy, and the other must be his dad."

"Must be?"

"They look pretty much identical. Oh, there's a birth certificate and a death certificate."

"Can you bring them over?"

"No, I'm gonna burn them."

"What?"

"Joke. Meet me at the Denny's near the station."

She rang off.

Ricky felt sick, and didn't know why.

• • •

The run-through was fine, even though the keyboard player, who'd done a tour with Adele and thought he was fucking Rachmaninov, kept adding fills that weren't on the song. A death stare from Scala fixed that, though.

"Good work," Jonty said.

"Is that it?" asked Scala.

"Yep," replied Jonty. "We just do it again for the cameras tomorrow night."

"We?" Scala said, raising an eyebrow.

"And there's the interview too."

Jonty frowned.

"You going to wear those gloves on the night?"

• • •

Ricky parked outside the Denny's, which was smaller than the one he frequented, and full of cops. He could see his sister inside, eating a knickerbocker glory. A pink folder lay on the table in front of her. Ricky thought it might as well have TOP SECRET COP BUSINESS written on it. He took a deep breath and went inside.

The moment the door opened, his sister gave him the finger with both hands.

• • •

Isinglass woke up. He was tied to a chair, and it was dark wherever he was.

A light flicked on, and Isinglass looked up.

"What the hell, Mehitabel," he said.

SIXTEEN

"Here it is," said Katie. She pushed the folder toward Ricky. He was about to open it when she slapped his hand, hard.

"Don't open it here, you fucking idiot," she said. "Do you want to get us both in trouble?"

"Sorry," said Ricky. "Thanks," he added.

"Don't ever thank me," Katie said. "Just the idea of your gratitude makes me want to throw up."

Katie's cop radio crackled and she spoke into it.

"Fuck," she said.

"What is it?" Ricky asked.

Katie smiled.

"That guy of yours – they found him."

"Is he OK?"

"No, of course not. He's dead."

Ricky said nothing. Katie stood up and, as if feeling generous, said:

"Hey, you wanna come see him?"

Ricky looked at her.

Katie nodded at the folder.

"You've read the book," she said. "Now see the movie."

Ricky had been in a cop car before, but never one with all the lights and sirens on that was going way too fast in traffic.

"Can you slow down a little?" he asked.

"Let's see," said Katie. She thought for a moment. "Nope," she said, and accelerated.

They arrived at the house a few minutes later. It was a rundown one-story building in what used to be a pleasant part of town, and it still had a garage and something that had once been a yard. The garage was lit up and a few people in crime scene suits were milling about. One of them approached Katie.

"Who's this?" they asked.

"My brother," said Katie. "Is that a problem?"

"No," said the crime suit. "Just don't let him touch anything."

"Are you sure," Katie said, "because I was going to let him finger the corpse."

The crime suit shook their head and walked away.

"Asshole," said Katie, and went into the garage. Ricky followed.

There was a body on the floor.

"Is he dead?" asked Ricky.

"What do you think?" Katie replied.

She crouched down. Ricky did the same.

"Oh my fuck," said Katie.

When Ricky saw what she was looking at, he nearly vomited. Someone had put a shovel right through the back of Isinglass's neck, almost severing his head.

"Well, that's new," Katie said.

Ricky went outside, and this time he did throw up.

"Mind my fucking crime scene," said a cop.

Ricky was about to reply when he saw something shining on the asphalt. It was a coin. Without really knowing why, he leaned over and picked it up. It was a perfectly normal nickel but there was something odd about it, something different. Ricky put it in his pocket for later.

"Stealing change now?" said Katie. She was stood over him, holding the pink folder. "You forgot this, dickballs."

"Thanks," said Ricky, and Katie hit him in the face with the folder. He took it from her.

"Next time I see you it better be when your coffin's going into the fucking fire," said Katie and walked back to her car.

Ricky didn't ask for a ride home.

When he'd finally found a cab prepared to come out there and had got back to his own apartment, Ricky put the folder on the table and lifted out its contents. They were just as Katie had described them: birth certificate, death certificate, cuttings, and photographs of a teenager and an older guy. Both of whom, Ricky realized at once, were Don.

"Well, that makes no sense," he said out loud.

Something had fallen out of his pocket when he sat down. He picked it up: it was the nickel. Ricky examined it more closely. It seemed to be made of a different metal to whatever nickels were normally made of: it was both shinier and cheaper looking. He flipped it over and then he caught his breath.

The date next to Jefferson's head was over fifty years in the future.

Ricky spent a few minutes looking up "nickel dates" on the internet, learned a lot of useless stuff about coins, then gave up. The thing was clearly a fake.

Then he looked at the picture of teenage Don in the newspaper from six years ago, and the photo of Don now, taken – he looked at the date stamp on the back – also six years ago.

"No fucking way," Ricky said to himself.

He looked at his phone for a minute or two before finally calling Scala. The phone went to voicemail, so he just said, "Call me," and hoped he didn't sound too freaked.

• • •

Scala's phone was in her dressing room, because Scala was live on stage with the house band, performing her new single on *Midnight with McGovern* in front of a studio audience and several million viewers, none of whom were Ricky, because he'd decided to have a bath.

She got through the single fine, even though the keyboard player had now discovered a similarity between the main riff of her song and some old fucking Herman's Hermits song and was playing both at the same time like he'd just heard the King of Assholes had died and he was hoping to be crowned the New King of Assholes, and managed to smile and do the "no, you were great, why would I want my own band when I could have Old Father Time and his orchestra" gesture at the end. Then she crossed from the band area to the couch, as rehearsed, and sat down beside Kendra McGovern's desk.

"Scala Jaq, everyone!" Kendra all but hooted. "Scala Jaq!"

"Thanks!" Scala half-gasped, half-gulped, like she was so psyched from performing she couldn't come down to earth just then.

McGovern held up the new album, which came in a nice box like it was Korean or something, made a couple of generic gags about downloads and what even are they, like she was fifty-three instead of thirty-five, and then turned the full beam of her attention on Scala.

"So," said Kendra McGovern, "are we debuting a new look tonight?"

The fucking gloves, thought Scala, and made a note to kill the producer if there was time. "Why? Are you looking for tips?" she said, and laughed like she would never dare suggest such a thing.

"Me? I buy my clothes bulk like pet food," Kendra replied, and the audience laughed. "But seriously, the gloves. I mean, did Stevie Nicks die and leave them to you?"

"Stevie's a mentor and a guiding light to me," Scala replied. "I wish she'd give me some of her stuff. And never die," she added, piously.

"Of course. I don't think the Mac can ever die," Kendra went on. "Like cocaine is the secret of eternal life or something."

"If it was," said Scala, "I'd be the first to know." She gave herself a point in interview bingo: *mention your weakest point first*.

"Amen to that," said Kendra, who as far as Scala knew had never taken any drug without a prescription in her life. "But I feel we've strayed from the look."

"You're not going to let this go," Scala said, baring her teeth a little. That way, Kendra could claim she'd dug something from the interviewee but still back off with dignity.

"It's just such a statement look from you," said Kendra.

"If you like 'em so much, I can get you a pair," Scala said.

"With these hams?" Kendra replied, holding up the hands of a large doll. "OK, OK, I talked about the gloves too much. I'm sorry."

"That's OK," Scala said, smiling like she had been given the best compliment of all time.

"But they are *great* gloves," Kendra said.

This is about me not doing the fucking sketch, Scala thought but did not say. She waved her gloves at the camera benignly and waited for Kendra to say something else.

Then a man in the studio audience shouted:

"Take 'em off!"

There was some laughter. Kendra frowned.

"OK," she said. "We don't—"

"The gloves!" the man shouted. "Take 'em off!"

He began to chant.

"Take 'em off! Take 'em off!"

A couple of other men and a woman joined in.

"Take 'em off! Take 'em off!"

"Oh what," Kendra said. "Scala, I'm sorry – we're going to wind this up now. Scala Jaq, everyone."

Scala forced herself to shake McGovern's hand and wave to the audience. As soon as she saw the credits roll on the monitor, she got up and walked off the set.

Jonty knocked on the dressing room door.

"Scala? I'm here with the producer."

No response.

"She's here to apologize personally."

Nothing.

"Scala?"

Jonty opened the door. The dressing room was empty.

"Shit," he said.

The fire door closed behind Scala and she made her way down the alleyway in the rain and hailed a cab.

"Leon's," she told the driver, and gave him an address.

Jonty looked at his phone.

"Double shit," he said.

Leon's was surely the grimmest bar in New York. It had survived every kind of rent hike and gentrification, possibly because it was so grim, and remained a haven for people whose sole interest was being really drunk inside a fairly warm room.

Scala had come here when she was first recording in New York with her then boyfriend, a fourth-rate producer who had somehow stumbled across a first-rate star. She liked it for the same reasons as all the other drunks in the room, all of whom were either too old or too drunk to know or care who she was. In those days, Scala was experimenting with alcohol. Now she had discontinued her experiments and was two years sober.

But here she was.

She ordered a beer, changed her mind, asked for an alcohol-free beer, received a disdainful look from the barman, who probably didn't even have alcohol-free water, ordered a Jim Beam, and sat down by the ladies' toilets, which were probably the most undisturbed part of the bar.

She looked at the bourbon and tried to remember what it tasted like. She raised it to her nose, sniffed it, and put it back down again. Then her phone vibrated, and vibrated again, and again. Soon it was vibrating so much it felt like she had a hyperactive hummingbird in her pocket. She took her phone out. Her social media was going nuts: notification after notification was popping up on every platform like bubbles.

Scala took a deep breath, and clicked. Every single post contained three words. There were gifs, memes, jpegs and videos, all captioned with the same three words: *TAKE 'EM OFF*. Some of the posts were cheerful, some were sweet, but most of them were nasty and a lot of them – unsurprisingly, given the words – were aggressively sexual.

"Thanks, the world," said Scala. She put her phone down and picked up the shot glass again. "Care to join me?" she asked the glass.

She was about to drink it down in one go when this time her phone actually rang.

"Fuck you, Jonty," said Scala.

RICKY, the caller ID corrected her.

Scala shrugged. She raised the glass to her lips. Then:

"Ah, Jesus," she said.

She put down the glass and picked up the phone.

"I've been trying to get you for hours," said Ricky. "Where the fuck have you been?"

"I guess you don't watch TV," said Scala.

"Why?" said Ricky. "What happened?"

Three minutes later, Ricky said, "New hand, eh."

"That's all you have to say?" asked Scala.

"Sorry, I'll watch online later," said Ricky. "Also, you know, I have a new fucking ear."

Scala was silent for a moment.

"I'm sorry," she said, then: "Hand trumps ear."

"This isn't rock paper scissors," said Ricky, but she could tell he was actually amused.

"No, fine, OK," she said. "Now tell me your news. I can't see how it could be worse than mine."

"Oh," said Ricky, "it's much, much worse than yours."

"Tell me," she replied.

"First I have a question," Ricky said. "Where do you stand on time travel?"

"You're kidding me," said Scala.

Jonty watched *Midnight with McGovern* for the third time on his laptop. Then he brought up the cloned phone screen.

RICKY.

He was about to call Tom when he saw the time and realized Tom would either be asleep or at some weird club.

We can always waste him tomorrow, Jonty thought, and texted Scala instead.

Scala read Jonty's text.

Really hope u r alright. Car to airport six a.m., it said.

She got up and left the bar, placing the shot glass in front of a shaky-looking man in a baseball cap.

"On me," she said.

The man focused for a moment, then leered.

"Take 'em off," he slurred.

Scala pulled her hood up and went outside to call a cab.

• • •

Ricky found a gas station map of the USA, some tacks, and a ball of string. He stuck the map to the wall, put the photos of young Don and old Don on either side, and linked them to Alaska and Florida with lengths of string. Then he stood back and looked at his handiwork.

"Well, that helps," he said. "Not."

SEVENTEEN

"Time travel," said Scala.

"I know," Ricky said, "it sounds incredible, right?"

"You have no idea," said Scala.

They were sitting in the darkest and quietest corner of Beaner's. Scala's face, who was pretty recognizable most of the time, was everywhere this week, and she was taking no chances. It felt like everyone was either shouting or whispering *Take 'em off* at her all the time.

"By the way, I saw the show," Ricky went on.

"Oh great," said Scala. "Love the hat, by the way."

Ricky glowered.

"Anyway," Scala said, "you were saying."

"It's the only explanation," said Ricky.

He spread the pictures out again.

"I get it," Scala said.

"It's the same guy," said Ricky. "Same time, same guy. How can that be?"

"Well—" Scala began. Ricky interrupted.

"Time travel. It's the only explanation. For this, too."

Ricky showed Scala the coin. She didn't speak.

He looked at her.

"Why aren't you saying I'm crazy?" he asked.

"Maybe because you keep interrupting me," Scala replied. "Or maybe it's because I've heard it before."

"From who?"

"From Don," said Scala. "You asshole," she added.

"That's bullshit," Ricky said, a few minutes later.

"Says Mister Time Travel."

"OK, but he's a cop?"

"A time cop. How is that more nuts than time travel?"

'I guess because being a space cop—"

"Time cop."

"—it's like one step too far."

"Yeah, you're right," Scala said. "It's fine one minute he's seventeen and the next he's fifty something. It's fine he's a time traveler. Oh, and it's totally fine that you and me and half of Florida are switching fucking body parts every ten minutes. But a time cop? That's way unfeasible."

"Alright," Ricky said. "So if he's a cop, and he's like you say, back in time investigating who's guilty and who isn't – and don't they have search engines in the future by the way?"

"Ricky," said Scala. "There was an apocalypse. A big one."

"Convenient," Ricky said. "But anyway, all that on one side – how come he's visiting himself?"

"Maybe he wanted to see the old homestead one last time."

"The night he was murdered?"

Scala nodded. "Why not? Isn't that exactly what a cop would

do? Visit the scene of a murder? I mean, if I was a cop and somebody murdered me, I'd be keenly interested."

"That's another thing," said Ricky.

"Oh good, another thing," Scala echoed.

"If he was murdered when he was seventeen, how can he be still alive now? Like if you go back in time and kill your grandfather, you can't be born."

"But he didn't kill his grandfather," Scala said.

"Clearly I'm not explaining myself very well," said Ricky.

"Never mind," Scala said. "Look, neither of us has a clue what's going on. But we know it's weird, and we know Isinglass got killed over it. So we need to be careful."

"You got a plan?" asked Ricky. "Because I don't."

Scala pulled her hood up tighter.

"I do," she said.

Ricky ordered two more Cokes, and when the barman had stopped laughing and served him, he took them back to the corner.

"The first part of the plan is we just keep on doing what we would be doing," Scala said. "Go to Don's meetings, act like we don't know anything."

"That's easy," said Ricky. "We don't know anything."

"And we listen," Scala said. "For anything that doesn't sound right. Anything that might be a clue."

"What's the other part of the plan?" asked Ricky.

"That's a little more intricate," said Scala.

• • •

Don had texted to say there was a meeting tomorrow night if that was OK with everyone. *Like we've got something more pressing to do,* thought Scala as she texted yes back to him.

"Where are you going now?" said Jonty as she tried to pass him in the lobby of the Regality.

"Out," she said, like a teenager with a dumb dad.

"We need to talk about the show," Jonty said.

"Later," she said. "This is important."

"Walk with me," said Jonty.

"Nobody actually says that in real life," Scala said, but she walked with him anyway.

It was raining outside.

"Florida weather, eh?" Jonty said, then: "So where *are* you going?"

Scala looked at the ground.

"You can tell me," said Jonty.

"I don't want to," Scala replied. She exhaled. "OK," she said. "But this goes no further."

"No worries."

"I mean it. If I see anything online or anywhere, you are fucking fired."

"I said no worries."

Jonty tried to look hurt, and nearly succeeded.

Scala took a deep breath.

"You know I used to drink," she said.

"And the rest," Jonty replied. "You're not back there, are you?"

"I came close a few times recently."

"How recently?"

"The last few weeks I've been doing that thing. Walking past bars and wondering what it would be like to go in and maybe

165

think about having a drink. In fact, last night," said Scala, "I came really close to having a drink. Which is why…"

She stopped.

"Why what?" asked Jonty.

"…which is why I've been going to meetings," Scala finished.

Jonty looked at her. It was meant to be a piercing gaze.

"You didn't tell me," he said.

"I know."

"I need to know these things."

"Well, now you do. And I'm going to be late."

"OK," Jonty said, still processing. "I'm glad you're walking the line. But we still need to talk."

"My car's here," said Scala.

Jonty watched as the car drove off. This time he did make a call.

By the time Scala got to the meeting, Ricky was already there. He nodded to her from across the room and she nodded back.

"People!" Don called, clapping his hands together. "Peo-ple! Let's get to it!"

Everyone sat down, and everyone was there, even Larry the scared man. Helen took her seat, looking unruffled as ever. Theresa, chatty like she was visiting her family. Ricky, head down and saying nothing. And Tony, looking – *different*, Scala thought. *Different and scared.*

"OK," said Don. "Now everyone's here, I have a brief announcement. I think we're a little closer to getting some real information on what's happening out there."

Scala edited Don's words in her head like they were a

press statement. They were completely devoid of content, she realized.

"Has something new happened?" Theresa asked, trying to sound hopeful.

"Not as such," Don replied. "But my research has revealed the names of some government initiatives that I'm pretty sure are related to what's going on here."

He started unfolding a sheaf of paper which Scala was certain contained a list of random conspiracy rumors from the internet. But she wasn't here to upset the apple cart – not yet – so she kept silent and let the others speak.

"Fucking government," Tony growled. "They got a finger in everything. It's the deep state."

"We don't know it's the government," said Larry nervously. "It could be foreign powers."

Tony said nothing, but Scala noticed he was clenching and unclenching his fists.

Helen said, "I know it matters who did this to us, but isn't it more important to find out why? I want to know what I'm becoming."

Theresa shivered. "I'm not sure I do. I just want it to stop."

"We're working on all these questions," Don said. "And I'm sure—"

"Stop?" Tony interrupted. "It's never going to stop."

"Well, we don't know that," said Don.

"My ear changed," said Ricky.

"My hand," Scala said.

Theresa pointed at her tiny foot, less tiny now. Helen stroked her arm like it was a cat.

"Like I say," Don repeated. "We're all in this together."

"Right," Tony said. "An ear. A hand. A foot. Yeah."

He lifted his head up and now Scala saw what was different about him.

"My eyes," he said. "Two days ago they were blue. Now they're brown."

Tony started crying.

"I have someone else's *eyes*," he said. "How the fuck does that happen?"

After that, the meeting fragmented a little. Theresa moved away from Tony, and Larry just kept saying he didn't believe it. Only Helen seemed unperturbed.

"How does it feel?" she asked Tony, and her voice seemed to calm him.

"The same, I guess," he said. "I mean, I can see fine. And I can cry, so I guess they're working, right?"

"They look great, if that helps," said Ricky, immediately sensing that it didn't help.

"Alrighty," said Don, making Scala want to jump on his back and ride him through a window. "I'm going to call this one. We need to regroup."

"What does that mean?" Larry asked, but nobody was listening.

• • •

The meeting broke up and people began to drift home. Helen walked out with Tony, still talking.

Scala nodded almost imperceptibly at Ricky, who headed out, leaving Scala with Don.

"Hey," she said.

"Right back at you," said Don.

"I guess you saw the show," she said.

"I was out," he replied.

"Jesus, does nobody have catch-up?" Scala said. "Joke," she added.

"I heard about it," Don said. "She had no right to ask you that."

"It'll blow over," Scala said, although she wasn't sure if anything ever did blow over nowadays. "Listen, about what you said…"

"Yes?"

"I believe you."

She looked around to make sure nobody had come back in for their hat or their umbrella.

"About the time cop stuff."

"That's great," Don said. "Wow!" he added. "I feel so much less isolated. Thank you."

"The only thing I don't get…" said Scala.

"What's that?"

"How do you do it?"

"Now that," said Don, "is a tale which requires coffee and donuts."

"Donuts?" said Scala. "Gee, you really are a cop."

The donut shop was quiet, perhaps because three broken strip lights are one broken strip light too many. Don brought over two colorful donuts and two drab coffees, neither of which were large.

"Wow, tiny," Scala said.

"Maybe we're getting bigger," Don said.

"Great," replied Scala. "That's all I need, turning into a fucking giant."

"Or ogre."

Scala drank some coffee. It tasted worse than it looked.

"So how do you do it?" she said again.

"Well," Don said, "you know how in the movies you get into something – like a hot tub or a DeLorean?"

"Yeah."

"It's nothing like that."

"Oh."

"It's kind of a Zen thing."

"Great, you've totally explained it. Thank you!"

Don smiled.

"You could do it now," he said.

"What?"

"All you'd have to do is clear your mind, like you were meditating. Think of… not where you want to be, or even when, but – and this is the hard bit – the state of being in the past."

"Right."

"Map it out in your head. What the room in the past you want to be in looks like. Ideally, the room you're in already should be kind of decked out like it is the past. Same for what you're wearing. You should have on clothes from the era. You should also be using soap from the period."

"Soap?"

"Soap, toothpaste, shampoo, that kind of thing. And you should have eaten food and drink available at that time. No donuts for Ancient Greece."

"Has someone gone back to Ancient Greece?"

Don smiled.

"Maybe. How would we know?"

"OK."

"Then you just stop thinking."

"For how long?"

"For as long as it takes."

Scala stared at him.

"That's it?"

"Yeah," said Don. "But you have to keep doing it until something happens. Which can take... months. Years, even."

"How long did it take you?" Scala said.

"About eighteen months," Don said.

And did you kill your teenage self when you did it? Scala wanted to ask.

"Wow," she said. "So what's to prevent me just going back in time right now?"

"Nothing," Don said. "If you're prepared to spend an indefinite time trying, and you're prepared to live out your life in a different time."

"Like you?" asked Scala.

Don said nothing.

"OK," said Scala. "I'll buy that."

"For a dollar," Don said.

"But this doesn't sound like how the Victim..."

"Victim Replacement Program."

"...works. I mean, how can a foot decide to go back in time?"

Don was silent for a while. Then he said, "The time travel guys have a saying. 'There has to be a space to occupy.'"

"Like a room to land in?"

"Kind of," said Don. "It doesn't have to be a room."

Scala frowned.

"A park?" she asked. "A field?"

"It's like you said," Don replied. "How can a foot go back in time? The simple answer is it can't, because if it does, it's just a foot. So—"

"There has to be a space for it to occupy," Scala repeated.

"And generally," Don said, touching his own too-thin arm, "that space is already occupied."

"That's horrible," said Scala.

"No different to a cuckoo," Don answered. "Big fat fucker pushing the other chicks out of the nest. Or those wasps that hatch their young inside other bugs."

"Because that's a delightful example," Scala said.

"Welcome to the horrific world of time travel," Don replied.

• • •

Ricky sat at home, listening to Scala and Don's conversation on headphones through his phone. It was hard to hear, because there was a menu on Scala's phone, but he could hear most of what Don was saying. He wasn't great at taking notes, though, and missed a few words here and there as he tried to get it all down on paper.

"They're called scorpion wasps," he muttered as he wrote.

"OK," said Scala. "Enough explaining for now."

"Thanks for listening," Don said. "Hey, you're not planning on leaving town anytime soon are you?"

"Not after the TV show," Scala replied, shaking her head. "Why?"

"No reason," Don said. "Just I might have some news for you soon. Real news," he added, seeing her look change.

"You just going to keep stringing everyone along in the meantime?"

"I don't really have any choice," Don said. "Unless you want to tell Tony his new eyes belonged to a murder victim."

"No thank you," said Scala.

She got up.

"Just let me know when something happens, OK?"

"I will," Don said.

It seemed to Scala that he smiled when he said it.

• • •

Ricky video-called Scala from an internet cafe full of Danish teenagers.

"Why are they all Danish?" Scala asked.

"I have no idea," Ricky said. "Maybe Denmark is a terrible place for a spring break."

"Did you get it all down?" Scala asked. She was wearing a hooded top and huge pink sunglasses, and she was sitting in the same internet cafe as Ricky. She figured nobody would be expecting that.

"Pretty much," Ricky said. "You think he's telling the truth?"

"No way of knowing unless you try it," Scala replied.

"Wait. Me try it?" Ricky said.

"I can't do it," said Scala. "People will miss me."

"Oh, thanks."

"I don't mean it that way," Scala said. "Like I have a schedule and everyone will notice if I'm not at the places I'm supposed to be at. Also, I kind of do mean it that way. Nobody cares if you live or die. No offense."

"None taken," said Ricky.

He sighed.

"One thing I don't get," he said. "Why do you want me to go into the past? Is it to find out more about Don's life or stop him being killed or what?"

Scala lowered her shades.

"I don't want you to go into the past," she said. "I want you to go into the future."

Ricky stared at her image. Around them, there was a lot of boisterous behavior in Danish.

"Excuse me?" he said.

"We need to see if Don's telling the truth," Scala explained.

"I thought you said he was telling the truth."

"About some things, maybe," she conceded. "But in the way people do when they give you a small bit of truth so you believe the big lie they're also telling you."

"Good psychology," Ricky said. "But Jesus, the future."

"It'll be fine," said Scala. "You just look around and come right back."

"Yeah, just transport myself limb by fucking limb into some future guy and then what? Reverse the polarity? I don't think so."

"No," Scala said. "You don't have to physically go into the future."

"But you said—"

"An expression Don used," Scala replied. "The first time he told me about all this. He said something about remote viewing."

"Isn't that drones?"

"No," Scala said. "It is not drones. I looked it up. It's like you can see things in your mind. Also precognition, which is seeing things that haven't happened yet. Except," Scala frowned, "they have happened, because time isn't linear."

"Oh boy."

"It's a theory," Scala said. "But it might work."

"It might not."

"We need to try it."

Ricky looked at his hand. He thought about all the things that had happened to him lately.

"No," he said.

"Why the fuck not?" Scala asked, exasperated. "Nobody else can do this."

"That's not true. You could do this."

"I can't."

"Why not?"

"I told you," Scala said. "If I disappear, people will miss me."

"Because you're a revenue stream, not because they love you," said Ricky. "Anyway, if you turn into another fucking person, they'll miss you more."

Scala said something that Ricky missed.

"What?" he asked.

"I said I'm scared," Scala repeated. "I'm terrified as it is, without going fuck knows where and maybe not coming back."

"Because you're young," Ricky said.

"Oh, now I'm a child," said Scala, huffily.

"That's not what I meant," Ricky replied. "I mean you're young so you're full of life."

"I know what you're full of."

"You think you're mature because you're still racing ahead

on the whole, I don't know, sheer fucking *momentum* of being alive," Ricky said. "Like there's fireworks inside you and they're still going off. Then one day they stop and you're just alive."

"Wow, this is poetry," said Scala, but she wasn't in a huff anymore.

Ricky sighed.

"Like me," he said, "I'm just alive. Every day is the same, inside at least. And the only thing I have in common with other people is that they hate me, and I hate me too. So you win."

"I do?"

"Yeah," said Ricky. "I'll do it. I'll go and look into the future."

Scala's idea was simple. They would break into the house where Isinglass had died and take it from there.

"That is kind of basic as plans go," said Ricky.

"Basic is good with plans," Scala replied.

"Why that house, though?" Ricky asked, even though he could guess the answer.

"You found a coin from the future," said Scala.

"Alright," Ricky said.

It was easy to get into the house. The garage was the crime scene, so the cops hadn't bothered to secure anywhere else. Scala and Ricky entered through the back door. They found an upstairs room that was clearly being used as an office: there was a kitchen table with a computer on it.

"Password protected," said Scala.

"Can we hack in?" Ricky asked.

"Of course we fucking can't," Scala replied. "You got the coin?"

Ricky produced the nickel.

"Good," said Scala, taking it from him.

"How do you know this is going to work?"

"Gotta be honest, I don't. I'm literally guessing here."

"What?"

Scala frowned.

"Don't act pissed," she told Ricky. "It's a good guess."

"How is it a good guess?"

"OK," Scala said. "It's like this. When Don told me all about the time travel stuff, he said the first time someone did it they didn't actually go back in time, they just… could see into the past."

"That's nice," said Ricky. "But we don't want to see into the past. We want—"

"To see into the future. I know, dummy. Which is what the nickel is for."

"Please explain some more, because I'm not confused enough yet."

Scala exhaled loudly.

"The woman who saw into the past, Don said she did it by focusing on some old stuff from when she was a kid," she explained. "So it must stand to reason that if you want to look into the future—"

"Then you need to focus on something from the future."

"Which for most people would be an issue. But not for us."

"Because we have something from the future."

Scala nodded.

"Finally," she said, and pushed Ricky onto a couch.

She placed the nickel in his hand, and turned on an old anglepoise lamp so that it shone right down on the coin.

"What are you doing, interrogating me?" asked Ricky.

"Helping you focus," she said. "Just concentrate on the coin."

"I feel stupid."

"That's because you are stupid. Listen, just look at the coin, and instead of thinking, *wow, a coin from the future*, think of it as an ordinary coin. It's not from the future at all. It's just a regular coin that you see every day."

"Like I just got it in my change."

"That's it."

"My change in the future."

"Your change *now*. Ricky, this is the whole point. There is no future, there is no then. There's just now."

"There's just now," Ricky said. He stared at the coin.

Time passed. It seemed to Ricky that he had never been so bored. He kept on looking at the coin, and nothing happened.

"I've been staring at this nickel for an hour now," he said.

"Ten minutes," Scala replied.

Ricky kept on looking at the nickel. It blurred in and out of focus, and sometimes he found his eyelids closing, but he kept looking.

"How long have I been looking at it now?" he asked.

"Just keep looking," Scala said.

After a while, Ricky heard Scala's breathing soften. He wondered if she was asleep. There seemed to be nothing but him and the nickel in the room. In the world.

Ricky was no longer sure where he was. Everything was just a gray cloud. If there were any sounds, he didn't hear them.

It was just him and the nickel.

After what could have been an hour or ten seconds, he gave up. He put down the coin and said to Scala:

"It's not working. I'm sorry."

But Scala wasn't there.

EIGHTEEN

Ricky was in a room. It was clearly the room he had just been in, but different. There was a fireplace, for example, full of burning logs – it looked hot enough but Ricky couldn't feel it. There were chairs, and a table. And that was pretty much it. The clutter of the room he had just been in – *the other room, the same room* – was gone.

This is the future, he thought, and wondered how he knew that. If it was the future, there were few signs of it. No giant silver wings flying past the window outside, no robots walking about, nothing.

In the future, he saw – because he could look even if, as he now discovered, he couldn't move – there were still plug sockets, which mean people still plugged things in. There were still pictures, if the drab still-lifes on the wall were anything to go by. And there were – he struggled for the word – picture rails. Ricky found the idea that humanity still had picture rails in the future weirdly reassuring.

He was in the future and not in the future. He was back

in his own time, in the room that was the same and not the same, and he was in the room that wasn't the same and was the same, and he was in the future.

Ricky was just wondering if maybe he should be taking notes or even pictures with his phone – was his phone even here? – when the door opened and six people came in. Instinctively he tried to hide, then realized, as the small group sat down, talking among themselves, that while he could see them, they couldn't see him.

Ricky, who had nothing else to do, listened.

There were five men and one woman. They looked just like normal people, but then, Ricky thought, they would, unless mankind in the future was breeding with aliens or splicing dinosaur DNA into its genes. They also looked – to someone who was judgmental, which Ricky very much was – like bad guys. Some of them had bad tattoos. A couple of them were scowling. One or two had the combination of workout bodies and pasty skin common to men who had spent a lot of time in jail.

Two of the men were big guys, two were kind of average, and one was small, with muscles. The woman was beautiful. She looked like a model, and she looked cruel (*also like a model*, Ricky thought). Even without hearing her speak, Ricky could tell she was the boss.

One of the big guys was saying something. He had a strong New Jersey accent and Ricky wondered if New Jersey was still a thing in the future or if the accent had survived on its own, like a chicken without a head. Then he decided to stop wondering about stuff and start listening.

"No, Mig," the woman was saying. "We can't stop now."

The big guy called Mig shook his head. "I think we got to stop, Jane. We've lost too many people." He had a shaved head and there was something weird about his ears. *Been there*, thought Ricky.

"We lost two," said the small guy. He was wearing a T-shirt with a picture of a dog on the front. It struck Ricky that fashions in the future hadn't changed much: either that, or these guys were really into retro.

"Lima got through, Andy," the woman called Jane said.

"Lima?" Andy replied. "How do you know?"

Jane took something out of an envelope. It was a yellowed piece of newspaper.

"He put an ad in the paper, Andy, that's how," she said.

"How old is this?" said Shaved Head Guy.

Jane smiled.

"Old enough," she said. "It's him alright."

"Imagine," said the small guy. "That ad waiting for us. Where did you find it?" he asked.

"Public library," Jane said. "And I also have people scanning internet archives, any hard drives the museum has – anywhere, really, where Lima might be able to leave a message."

"All that time," said one of the average guys.

"It's all about time, Gary," Jane replied.

Shaved Head took the clipping.

"'Lima,'" he read. "That's it?"

"It's enough, Will," the woman said. "The point is, it's possible. He did it, so we can do it."

"Well, great," said the other big guy. He had long blond hair and a matching mustache. "Let's do it."

He reached out a hand to look at the clipping.

And then Ricky did shout, so suddenly that he couldn't believe they hadn't heard.

It wasn't the clipping. It was the blond guy's hand: it was dark and scarred and there was something written on the knuckles. Just one word, with an exclamation mark after it.

YOU!

Ricky just stared in horror. He closed his eyes, hoping maybe to be transported somehow. But when he opened them again, he was still in the room.

He looked down at his hands. One of them was the hand he'd known all his life, but the other – the replacement hand, the new hand – was dark and scarred, like the blond guy's hand. And the tattoo on the knuckles:

FUCK

perfectly matched the tattoo on the blond guy's knuckles.

Ricky felt dizzy. He grabbed at a chair for support, but the chair wasn't there (*because I'm not here*, Ricky remembered). He breathed deeply and felt calmer; not a lot calmer, though.

I'm looking at myself, he thought, then corrected himself. *I'm looking at my future.*

The blond guy whose hand Ricky had was talking, for some reason, about cats.

"Not this again, Joe," said the man with the shaved head who was called Will.

"I like cats," Joe said. "It's a shame is all."

"I felt worse about the nickels," Will replied.

"Shut up," Jane said, and everyone did.

"We have a limited window for this," she said. "I know the

cops are on our asses, so we better pray that Lima is shifting his ass."

"I need to shift more than my ass," said Joe, and laughed. All he got for his trouble was a death stare from Jane.

"Lima went through hell for us," she said.

"What he did," said Will. He shook his head.

"Gotta be honest," he said, "gives me the creeps."

Jane raised her head.

"He's worth ten of you," she said. "And what he did, he did it for all of us. Remember that."

She stood.

"OK," she called out, "I'm ready."

The door opened and something with a sack on its head was thrown into the room. Joe pulled the sack off.

The newcomer was a young man who was sniffling and crying. Both his eyes were swollen and his face was bruised and beaten.

"Let me go," he said, looking at Jane, "I didn't do anything."

"That's not what I heard," she replied. "Joe, put his face in the fire."

"Excuse me?" said Joe.

"You heard me," Jane said.

Joe the blond guy said, "Can't we just shoot him?"

"No point wasting bullets," she replied. "Put his face in the fire."

Joe was about to say something else when he thought better of it.

"Take his arms," he said to the others.

The man began to scream and beg as he was pulled forward.

As soon as he had been placed in front of the fireplace, Joe closed his eyes and pushed his face down into the flames like he was baptizing him.

Ricky couldn't look but he didn't have to. The man screamed the whole time he was able, until finally he was silent.

Joe pulled the faceless body out of the fire and onto the floor.

"Jesus, the smell," said Will.

"Get him out of here," Jane said to the men who'd brought him in.

"What do you want us to do with it?" one of them asked.

"Leave him outside the police station," Jane said. "As a warning."

They dragged the body out again.

Ricky felt sick. The whole thing was like watching a nightmare happen in front of him. But, just like a nightmare, there was nothing he could do. He thought of Isinglass and wondered if that was what had happened again; then thought of the blistered and charred mess he had just seen and decided not.

Then Joe held his hand up.

"What now?" asked Jane.

"I been wondering," he said.

"Bad move," said Will.

"Seriously," Joe said, ignoring him. "I just want to know, when we get there, when we get our own bodies again..."

"Yes?" Jane said.

"What happens to *them*?" asked Joe. "The bodies we go into?"

"Interesting question," said Jane. "The government certainly doesn't want us to answer it. All they want us to know is that it works. We can go there, we can take their bodies, and take their lives."

"Yeah," said Joe, pressing his point. "But do they trade places with us, or do they just die?"

Jane looked at him. She grinned. It was far from being a nice grin.

"Three words," she said. "Nobody. Fucking. Cares."

He felt dizzy. The room was going in and out of focus, like a faulty projector. Voices were indistinct.

Ricky closed his eyes. When he opened them again, he was lying on the floor and Scala was standing over him.

"Did it work?" she asked.

Ricky threw up all over the floor.

"I guess that's a yes," said Scala.

She got him back onto the couch and gave him something in a glass.

"What's this?" he asked.

"Tap water," she said.

He handed it back to her.

"Jeez, picky," said Scala, but she took it and came back a moment later.

"Vodka," she said.

Ricky drank it down in one.

"Fuck you," he said. It was tap water.

"You needed water," Scala said. "I have no idea what happened to you just then, I'm not giving you alcohol."

"I saw my hand," Ricky said. "I saw a guy with my hand."

"Shit," Scala said.

When Ricky had told her everything and she had asked enough questions, Scala found some vodka. She gave Ricky the bottle, and when he'd had enough, took a slug herself.

"I guess that explains this," she said, taking a jar down from the shelf.

She opened it and spilled the contents onto the floor. It was all nickels.

Scala picked one up.

"Future coins," she said. "They must have been sending them through as test subjects."

"How do you send coins through time?" asked Ricky.

"Like Don said," Scala replied. "There just has to be a space to occupy. If you know there's a nickel in our time then you can send a nickel from your time. Oh, and talking of Don—"

She turned and opened a drawer. It contained a passport. Ricky picked it up and opened it. There was a photo of Don inside.

"Figures," he said. Then he remembered something.

"Cats," he said.

They were out for a few minutes at the back of the house when Scala said, "Look."

She shone her flashlight down at a pile of something. It was tangled and looked like hair and blood.

"Jesus," said Ricky, and threw up again.

"Guess we found the cats," Scala said.

• • •

"Lima," said Scala. They were in Ricky's Aztek again, driving back into town. "Do you think that's a name or just a codeword?"

"Could be both," Ricky said. He had stopped throwing up

now but didn't feel entirely great. *Which is hardly the fuck surprising*, he thought to himself.

It was raining hard, and Ricky found it difficult to see. The wipers were on maximum but all they were doing was making his eyes flicker, and that was tiring.

"Stop here," said Scala. They were three blocks from the Regality.

"It's really throwing it down," Ricky said.

"Then I'll get wet," said Scala. She looked at him. "Are you actually *concerned* about me?" she asked.

"If you get pneumonia, I'm going to be doing this on my own," said Ricky.

"That's my creepy stalker," Scala said. She patted him on the shoulder, pulled her hood up, and got out.

Ricky watched her run down the street in the lashing rain. He watched until she had vanished from his sight.

"Cute kid," said a voice from the passenger seat.

Ricky turned in surprise to see Tom the ape.

"What—" he began.

Tom punched him in the face.

• • •

Ricky, who lately was spending a lot of time unconscious, woke up in a brightly lit room with no windows. He was tied to a large swivel chair with his legs, rather worryingly, spread open.

"Hey, paedo," said Tom. His voice echoed in the room, which Ricky now realized was made of metal.

"Am I in a shipping container?" he asked. By way of reply, Tom punched him in the balls.

"Fucking paedo," Tom repeated.

"I'm not a paedo," Ricky managed to say when the agony had subsided. "I'm a professional photographer."

"Paedo," said Tom again. He moved toward Ricky.

"Please don't hit me in the balls again," Ricky said.

"OK," said Tom, and punched him in the face.

After that, Tom seemed to lose interest in doing any more things to Ricky – *or maybe he just needs to rest his fists*, thought Ricky – and the time passed in silence. Ricky, who was unable to move, decided he might as well rest, while Tom stared at him, presumably just repeating the same word in his head over and over.

Sometime later, when Ricky had, to his great surprise, managed to drift into an uncomfortable sleep, there was a hellish racket of grinding metal and the door to the container opened.

"Is he still alive?" asked Jonty as he closed the door behind him.

"Yeah," Tom sighed.

"Good, because I need a little chat," said Jonty.

"Wake up," Tom said to Ricky, slapping his face.

"I am awake, you dick," Ricky replied. "Stop fucking hitting me."

"Don't tell Tom what to do," said Jonty. "Tom, you can hit him."

"Thanks," Tom grunted, and punched Ricky in the stomach so hard that the swivel chair wheeled backward into the wall of the container.

"Pull him back over here," Jonty sighed.

Tom obliged, and Jonty stood in front of Ricky.

"You've lost a tooth," he said.

Ricky probed his mouth with his tongue. He found the tooth and spat it out. It landed on Jonty's shirt.

"Sorry," he said.

Jonty flicked the tooth onto the floor.

"No worries," he said. "I've got plenty of shirts, whereas you have a finite supply of teeth."

"Can I pull his balls off?" asked Tom.

"No," said Jonty. "Jesus, that's just weird. No, we're just going to kill the cunt."

"OK," Tom said. He sounded happy with that, thought Ricky.

"You can't kill me," he said.

"Don't see why not," Jonty replied. "You've got no friends, no family, and you're a fucking pap. We'd be doing the world a favor."

"Paedo," Tom added.

"Wait," Ricky said. "You're going to kill me? Because you think I'm stalking your client?"

"That's right," said Jonty.

"Can't you just get a restraining order?"

"Used to do that," Jonty said. "And it works. But this is different. I know she's been going to meetings again. No idea if it's AA, NA, CA or fucking A, but it's bad for business. Social media gets a sniff that she's fucked again, she's down."

"What's that got to do with me?" asked Ricky.

"She's going to meetings with her fucking stalker?" said Jonty. "Might as well be screwing you. No, we need you out of the way. Delete, put you in the trash, reboot."

"What about Scala?"

Jonty made a face.

"She'll be fine. I can see to it she gets into something legal. Prescription drugs, that kind of thing. It's a lot easier when a client is on heavy meds. Anyway," he smiled, "less talk, more action."

"Wait," said Ricky. "Do I get a last request?"

Jonty laughed.

"No, of course you fucking don't," he said. "I mean, unless it's 'kill me'."

He looked quizzically at Ricky.

"Is it 'kill me'?" he asked.

"Nah," said Ricky. "Actually, it's 'please don't turn around'."

The door opened behind Jonty.

"Who—" Jonty began.

And then his chest exploded.

Tom stared in disbelief, spattered in bits of Jonty.

"What the fuck?" he said.

"Let him go," someone said. "Before you go the same way."

Tom brushed a bit of bone from his jacket and took a knife out. He cut the cords holding Ricky and stood back.

Don stepped forward and pointed the gun he'd just killed Jonty with at Tom's head.

"Thanks," he said. "I presume you won't be taking this any further."

Tom shook his head vigorously.

"I didn't see a thing," he said.

Don smiled.

"Good to know," he said. Then he nodded at Ricky.

"Can you help me get this poor guy out of here?" he asked Tom.

Tom helped Don get Ricky to Don's car.

"Thank you," said Don.

Tom waited, looking uncertain.

"You can go," Don said. "It's fine."

Ricky watched Tom walk away.

"You're going to let him go?" he asked.

"Yeah," said Don. "He's dead in six weeks anyway. Mob hit."

Ricky stared at him. "How can you know that?"

Don smiled. "Way to go with the innocent expression," he said.

"I don't know what you're talking about," Ricky replied.

"We need to talk," Don said.

Don's car was new, and extremely comfortable. Something jazzy played on the stereo as Don drove through rain-speckled streets and Ricky began to feel less like a living punchbag. The painkillers Don told him were in the glovebox helped, too.

"I really do not know what's happening," said Ricky.

Don laughed.

"Sure you don't," he said. "Like you really don't know what this is."

He took out his cell phone. Ricky looked at it and saw an image on the screen.

It was Scala and him breaking into Don's house. The quality was excellent, and Ricky guessed that Don's surveillance cameras were as classy as his car.

Don took the phone back and beamed at Ricky.

"Do you think they'll let us into the Regality dressed like this?" he asked.

• • •

Scala was trying to coax Jonas out from under the couch when the door opened.

"I thought I locked that," she said as Don and Ricky came in.

"You did," Don replied, "but I'm from the future, remember?"

"What, and in the future people can just open doors with their minds?"

"No, but we're good at stealing room keys from managers who probably shouldn't have them."

"Jonty had a key to my room? I need to speak to him."

"That might be tricky," Don said.

Scala picked Jonas up.

"Nice dog," said Don. "I've been meaning to ask, why is he called Jonas?"

"His second name is Brothers," Scala said.

Don looked blank.

"Jonas Brothers?" said Scala.

"I got it," Ricky said.

"Oh, right," Don said. "I'm more a Skynyrd guy."

Now it was their turn to look blank.

"I feel we've strayed," said Don. "Can I get a drink? Drinks in the past are so much better than they're going to be."

Don had a whiskey from the mini-bar – which, since Scala was in the Penthouse Suite, was an actual bar, only lacking a bartender – and Ricky had a beer. Scala had a mint tea and a look of surprise and horror on her face.

"You killed Jonty?" she said.

"You can get another manager," Don replied. "Also, he was trying to kill your boyfriend here. Had it all worked out, secure location and everything."

"He's not my boyfriend," Scala said.

"That's your reaction?" said Ricky. "Not, 'fuck, my manager tried to kill someone,' or 'fuck, Ricky nearly got murdered.' Just I'm not your boyfriend."

"Well, you're not."

"Yeah, Ricky, deal with it," said Don, stone-faced.

"Shit," said Scala. She sat there in silence for a moment. "Jonty's been my manager since I was seventeen."

"Time for a change, I'd say," Don remarked. "Besides, he was clingy."

"Also, he tried to murder me," Ricky pointed out.

"Let it go, Ricky," Don said. "I saved your life, didn't I?"

"About that," said Ricky. "He shot Jonty. Right in the chest."

"I don't want to know any more," Scala said.

"But you killed Isinglass with a shovel," Ricky went on.

"Who's Isinglass?" Don said.

"The guy found dead in your house," Ricky said.

Don spread his hands.

"Wasn't me," he said. "I swear. I didn't even know until I came back to the house and saw the police cars."

"You didn't think to maybe stop by and say hello?" Ricky asked.

"Dude," said Don, "I'm from the future. My ID says I'm twenty-one years old. And there was a crime scene in my house."

He stood up.

"We have other things to talk about," he said.

"Like what?" Scala asked.

Don frowned.

"Like what the fuck you guys think you're doing," he said.

He turned to Scala.

"I need to talk to you," he said. "On your own."

"Nice," said Ricky.

Scala took Don into the bathroom, leaving Ricky in the lounge with instructions not to touch anything.

"What?" she said.

"I need you to stop playing Starsky and Hutch," Don said.

"What?"

"Never mind," said Don. "I'm not good on cultural references. I mean, stop snooping. I get that it's hard to trust me, but you know I'm telling the truth."

Scala thought of the jar of nickels, what Ricky had told her.

Right now all I know is you're lying through your teeth, she thought. *I just need to know what you're lying about.*

"OK," she said.

"You sure?"

"Yes," Scala said. "Sorry. But you know – everything lately, it's so messed up."

"I get that," Don replied. "Listen, I'm so close now, I just need to get us to the tape."

"Who's *us*, exactly?"

"Everyone," Don said.

"That's kind of general."

"It's also kind of true. But please believe me, this is all going to come to a head in the next few days."

"I get it. So what do you want me to do?"

Don smiled.

"Support me. Back me up. Don't question my words or my deeds. And don't sneak around behind my back."

"A few days?" Scala said.

"Yep," said Don. "So, are you going to help me? You and lover boy out there."

"OK," Scala replied.

"Scout's honor?"

"Fuck off."

"Got it," Don said, and actually saluted.

When they came back into the lounge, Ricky was sitting with Jonas on his lap watching *VH1*.

"What do you know," Don said. He pointed at the TV, where some big men in Stetsons were performing loudly. "Skynyrd."

After Don left, Scala took Jonas from Ricky.

"It's not that I don't trust you with him," she said. "Just that you look so much like a big lump of meat right now he might try and eat you."

"I didn't think I could get any less sympathy," Ricky said.

"Looks like you were wrong," Scala replied.

She looked round the room.

"Did you touch anything?" she said.

"Like what?"

Scala picked up the TV remote and clicked on "last station." Two naked people immediately appeared on screen.

"Like yourself," she said.

"Damn, you're good," Ricky replied.

Scala's phone beeped.

"Shit," she said. "The police found Jonty. They're coming here to talk to me."

"I'm out of here," Ricky said.

"You fucking bet you are."

"I'll see you at the meeting."

Scala looked at him.

"There's a meeting?"

Ricky smiled. His face really was a mess.

"There's always a meeting," he said.

NINETEEN

When Ricky woke up the next day, he ached all over. His face, his chest, his – *my arm doesn't hurt*, he realized. Ricky got up and went into the bathroom. He took off his T-shirt.

He had a new arm, right above his replacement hand.

"I'm a lot more Joe than I used to be," he told his reflection.

His reflection didn't think it was funny.

Ricky tried to call Scala but got voicemail. He supposed she was talking to the police, and wondered if they thought she'd done it. Then he wondered if Tom had kept his mouth shut. Ricky decided Tom was the type to keep his mouth shut – after all, he'd barely said one word to Ricky (*paedo*) – and felt about as good as a man who had nearly been murdered then woke up with someone else's arm could feel, which was not very good at all. If he was honest with himself, which increasingly he was being forced to be, the past twenty-four hours had been the worst time of his entire life.

The only good part, he decided, was that Scala had left her

laptop open while she and Don went into the bathroom. And even that was only good if what Ricky had done worked.

Guess I'll find out soon enough, Ricky thought.

• • •

"Can I go now?" Scala asked the detective. They were not at the police station – one of the privileges of celebrity – but in a conference room at the Regality.

One of the detectives – a too-thin man with the last combover in America – looked at his partner, a bird-like woman in a mismatched blouse and jacket. She shrugged.

"I don't see why not," said the combover cop. "But don't leave town. OK?"

Scala was about to thank them and get out of there when her phone beeped.

"Excuse me," she said.

It was a message from Don.

"Important text?" said the bird woman.

"Meeting," Scala replied. "AA, you know."

"Been there," said the combover cop, then looked embarrassed.

• • •

Ricky, who had been fine with Joe's hand – not fine, exactly, but able to cope – found it hard to manage his new arm. For a start, it was about two inches longer than his old arm, and was muscular in a kind of ropey way. This meant that he was a little too vigorous with the clutch when driving, and almost wrenched the door off when he got into the Aztek (which had remained intact where it had been left, presumably because there was nothing of value in it, except possibly the fold-out tent).

He parked outside the office building and went inside. Don wasn't there, but everyone else was (including Scala, who by common agreement wasn't talking to him), drinking terrible coffee and chatting, just like they were drunks or cokeheads or other normal kinds of people.

To his surprise, Helen came over to speak to him.

"You're Ricky," she said, more as a statement than a question. "Helen."

"I know," Ricky said, which sounded rude so he said. "Sorry, I meant I remember you."

"That's OK," Helen said. "I'm just glad I made an impression."

"Yeah," Ricky agreed. "Most people here, they're pretty scared. But you…"

"I'm scared, too," said Helen. "But I suppose I'm different because I know I'm not happy as I am."

"Kind of drastic, though," Ricky said. "There's other ways of changing than this. More… voluntary."

Helen shook her head. "I never even thought about change before," she said. "I know people do that, but I've never felt that was the answer. Not so much happy in myself as unhappy in myself, if you know what I mean."

"Not really," said Ricky. "Actually, yeah, I do know what you mean. I'm not happy. I never have been."

Ricky was surprised to hear himself say it, but he *was* saying it, so he supposed it must be true.

"But I don't want to change this way," he said. "If I did change, I guess I'd want to control it."

"Does anybody get to do that?" asked Helen. "Change, I mean. Most people who want to change, they want to become who they really are. I don't: I literally want to be someone else."

"Well, good luck to you," said Ricky, sounding cross even to himself. "I just hope this stops," he said, unrolling his sleeve to show his new arm.

"Snap," said Helen. She pulled up the sleeve of her jumper. Underneath, the skin was lighter, thicker. Then she did the same with the other sleeve.

"Double snap," she said, and laughed.

When the meeting began, it turned out that Helen and Ricky weren't the only ones who'd changed some more. Tony, who was getting used to his new eyes, also had new arms, and Theresa's legs were different.

"I have to wear my baggiest pants," she sighed.

"Hey, Larry," said Tony, "you're awfully quiet. What's happening with you?"

"I don't want to talk about it," Larry said, looking at his shoes.

"What is it, new feet?" asked Tony. "New neck? New—"

He stopped.

"Oh my God, Lar," he said.

"I said I don't want to talk about it," Larry repeated.

"No way," Tony said.

"What is it?" Theresa asked.

"Shut up," said Larry. He stood up, his fists balled. "I don't make comments about your eyes."

"OK, man," said Tony. "I'm sorry."

Then he turned to the others with a stupid grin.

"It's his cock," he said. "Larry got a new—"

Larry flew at Tony and punched him in the face.

"Shut up!" he shouted as Tony yelped in pain.

At that moment Don walked in.

"I see we're all feeling a little fraught," Don said.

"Fuck you," Tony replied. "I think I got a black eye."

"Gee," Larry said, a new tone in his voice. "Last week you had blue eyes, then you got brown eyes, and now—"

"Leave it, Larry," Don said. He sounded wearier, Ricky thought, than perhaps he'd intended to. Clearly the stress of whatever the fuck he was up to was getting to Don.

"This isn't helping," Scala said. "We're here to help each other."

"Says the rich lady pop star," Tony replied.

"What's that got to do with it?" Ricky heard himself saying. "She's up the same creek as the rest of us."

"Is she?" Tony said. "Because I don't see any new fucking legs or arms."

Scala took her gloves off and held her hands up.

"Could be make-up," Tony sniffed.

"Wow," Ricky said. "I see you're a hundred percent asshole now."

"That's enough," Don said. "Like the lady said, we're here to help each other. Unless you all want to go home? I don't have to do this. None of us do."

"Sorry," said Tony. "My bad."

"I'm sorry too," Scala said.

"Alright," said Don. "Now I can see that there have been a lot of changes in people, and I know it's scary, but we just have to accept that we knew this was going to happen and carry on."

Helen put her hand up.

"Yes?" said Don.

"How long have we got?" she asked.

There were groans.

"Don't fucking *say* that," said Tony.

"Sorry," Helen said. "But I need to know. I have to put my affairs in order."

"Ooh-la-la!" Theresa sang, and Ricky wondered if maybe she had lost her mind. "Affairs!"

"We're not at that point just yet," Don answered. "With luck we may never be."

"So what now?" said Larry.

Don looked grave.

"I have news," he said.

"Good news?" asked Theresa hopefully.

"I think so," Don replied. "There are some people who can help us."

Everyone started talking at once.

"What people?" asked Larry.

"I can't say at this stage," said Don.

"I bet it's the fucking CIA," Tony said.

"It's not the CIA," Don replied. "It's not the FBI or the KGB either."

"Angels!" Theresa exclaimed. "Is it angels?"

"No," said Don, "it's not angels."

He stood up, got himself a coffee, and sat down again.

"I've been trying to get in touch with other people like us," said Don, looking Scala in the eye as if daring her to contradict him. "And I've had precious little luck. I'd get a fix on another group of people somewhere, and I'd try and call them, but they wouldn't reply."

"Suspicious." Tony nodded. "Can't blame them."

"Maybe they were being watched," Theresa said.

"Maybe we're being watched," said Larry, sounding worried.

"And then," Don said, "I got a call."

"Who from?" asked Helen.

"The angels," Theresa replied.

Don frowned. He was definitely looking a lot more tired these days.

"If you like," he said. "Listen, I can't say too much at this stage, but what I can say is this. These people know what we're going through. They've been through it themselves and…"

He looked at them all.

"…they think they can stop it."

Nobody was talking all at once now. They were all shouting.

After a few minutes, Don managed to calm everybody down.

"OK," he said. "Alright people, just chill."

"Are you sure this is on the level?" Tony said.

"Of course it is," Theresa replied. "Angels don't lie."

"I want everyone to go home and wait for my call," Don said.

"How long is that going to be?" asked Larry.

Don shrugged. "I honestly don't know," he said. "But hold this thought: there will be a call. That's all we need to know right now."

The meeting wound up. Scala and Ricky were waiting for the elevator when Don appeared.

"Hi, guys!" he said cheerfully. "Can I get a ride with you?"

• • •

"Where am I going?" asked Ricky.

"Doesn't matter," Don replied from the back seat. "Just drive."

"None of that was true, was it?" said Scala, twisting in her seat to speak to him.

Don spread his hands.

"It was and it wasn't," he said.

"That's helpful," Ricky said.

"Look," said Don, "I'm as much in the dark as you are at this point. I get my instructions and I carry them out."

"Who from?" asked Scala. "The other time cops?"

"Yes, the other time cops," said Don. "I don't know why that sounds so unlikely to you."

"Sorry. And what are the other time cops telling you? Specifically?"

Don sighed. "That some kind of breakthrough in our investigation has been reached."

"Your investigation? Have you actually been investigating anything?"

"At their end," said Don.

"But I thought you were the one doing all the spade work," Scala said.

"This is all new to me," Ricky said.

"I thought I told you Don was a time cop," said Scala.

"Stop the car," Don said.

They pulled over in the parking lot of a coffee shop.

"Listen to me," Don said. "I realize you're in the dark about what's going on, but so – to some extent – am I. And when I say there has been a breakthrough, that's all I fucking know."

"So are we meeting *your people* or not?" asked Scala.

Don was silent.

"I believe so," he said eventually. "Yes."

"They're coming here?"

"Yes again," said Don.

"How?" Scala said. Her voice was light but to Ricky she sounded concerned. "Don't they need to – what's the phrase – occupy the space?"

"I can't say any more than what I've said," Don replied.

"Mind if we go home?" asked Ricky. "I'm really fucking tired."

They dropped Don back at the office building.

"He's fucking lying through his teeth," Scala said as they watched Don walk away.

"You think?" said Ricky.

"What's going to happen?" Scala asked. "I mean, not just to us."

"Only one way to find out," Ricky replied. "Wait and fucking see."

Ricky left Scala a block away from the Regality.

"Sleep well," he told her.

"Ha the fuck ha," she replied.

As soon as Ricky got into his apartment, he noticed the light bleeping on his answering machine. Only one person used his landline.

"Hi, fruitloop," said his sister's voice.

TWENTY

Two days after the last meeting, Ricky went out and bought one copy of each of the day's newspapers. He skimmed through each one in turn until he found what he was looking for and then dropped the lot in a trashcan.

Scala had no more calls from the police and, on the advice of her record company, went into a complete media shutdown, citing in her online press release "deep personal distress at the loss and apparent murder of her manager."

Don walked on the beach a lot. Most of the time he just looked like a worried guy in the sand, but once he stopped, looked all around, and said, "This cannot be right."

Ricky went to see his sister.

"Sup, asshole," she said.

They were in the Denny's she liked.

"Nothing much," Ricky said.

"What's wrong with your arm?" said Katie.

"Infection," Ricky lied.

"My ass," Katie said. "You've been jerking off so much, it got muscular."

"I believe," said Ricky with all the dignity he could muster, "that you called me."

"Oh yeah. I just called to say I love you. And—" she held up a finger to silence him, "—to tell you, you dick, that the cops have some CCTV of a guy who looks like you at the scene of a murder."

"What?"

"Man, your innocent face is dumb," said Katie. "Fortunately for you, it was dark, and the footage is grainier than your dusty spunk, so you're in the clear for now."

"Oh wow, I feel so relieved."

Katie leaned over and grabbed Ricky's eyelid between finger and thumb.

"Listen," she said. "I don't think you have the actual balls to kill a person, but I know something's going on. I don't want to know, either, but I'm just saying…"

"What?"

Katie let go. She looked confused, as though feeling emotions rare to her.

"I don't care if you live or die, you know that," she said. "But if anyone's going to fuck up your life, I want it to be me."

"I'm touched," Ricky said, and he was.

"I gotta go," said Katie.

She looked at him.

"Keep in touch," she said.

• • •

Scala braced herself to look at social media. She logged on under a false name that she used solely for the purpose of reading what people were saying about her. She was the subject of several threads and topics, most of them veering between the kind ("pray for scala") and the sadistic ("she did it I know she did"). After a few minutes of reading this nonsense, she signed out and turned the TV on.

"And winds are in excess of twenty-five miles an hour," said the weather girl. "Hard to say if this means we'll be getting—"

She turned off the TV: it was time for bed.

"Tomorrow," she told Jonas, "is another day."

• • •

Don sat on a bench at the edge of the beach. He had a map in his hand, a real one, printed on paper, as well as his tablet, opened at a world map search site, and his phone, which was showing an almost identical app. He kept looking first at the paper map, then at the maps on the phone and the tablet, as if trying to convince himself that someone had made a mistake.

Finally he stopped looking. He folded up the map and gazed out at the beach.

"Fuck," he said. "This really is the place."

• • •

Police Officer Katie Smart of the Miami Beach Police Department sat down at a computer with a coffee and a donut.

"Really breaking the stereotypes there," said one of her colleagues.

"You ever see that movie?" Katie asked.

"Which movie?"

"*When Fuck Met You.*"

"Jesus, it was just a joke," the other officer said, but he left the room.

Katie licked the sprinkles off the donut and typed her password into the computer.

"Good movie," she said to nobody in particular.

. . .

Ricky went out and bought a new camera. He hadn't worked for days and the rent was nearly due. He caught a few tips from the internet and drove down to a big movie premiere in Miami.

After ten minutes of jostling outside the velvet rope, he shouldered his way out of the pack, almost knocking a young pap with curly hair to the ground.

"Hey, wasn't that Ricky Smart?" said the curly-haired guy to the paparazzo next to him, an older guy with gray hair in his beard.

"Yep," the older guy said. "Looks like he was in a fight."

"Looks like he lost it, too. What's his problem?"

The older man sighed and lifted his camera. The stars of the movie were going in now.

"There's only so long you can do this job," he said. "One day you just burn out."

"Not me, pal," said the younger man, and began firing off shots at celebs like they were ducks in a shooting gallery.

. . .

Scala dreamed she was an angel, flying through heaven. It was a weird kind of heaven, with puppies instead of people, but she didn't mind: all the puppies looked like Jonas and none of them were on social media. She flew higher and higher until suddenly the blue sky and white clouds of heaven turned into the black night of space.

There was no air in space (of course) and Scala found she was choking. She groped at her own neck as she fell and fell.

And when she woke up, she found she had her hands around her throat.

Not my hands, Scala remembered. *Someone else's hands.*

. . .

Don sat at home in a web of blue police tape and waited.

Finally a message came.

"OK," he said. "OK."

He began to breathe slowly in and out, as if he was trying to stop himself hyperventilating.

"This," he said out loud to himself, "is why you're here. This is it. This is actually it."

. . .

Katie Smart opened folders, clicked on security camera footage, and read reports. When she was done, she knew more about what her brother had been doing for the past few weeks than she had before, but was still completely in the dark.

She called across the room to another woman cop.

"Hey," Katie shouted, "is the armory still open?"

. . .

Don called Scala. She was still shaky after her dream.

"This is it," he said.

"This is what?" she asked. "Sorry, groggy."

"Not at all. This is… it's time," said Don. "It's happening."

He sounded excited, and nervous.

"OK," Scala said, sitting up in bed. "You mean the people are coming. The time cops or whatever."

"That's right," said Don. "I mean, that's the general idea."

"Did we establish how they were coming?" Scala asked.

Don said nothing. Scala remembered a story she'd read about a movie producer once. He got mixed up and said to someone, "Sorry, which lie did I tell?" Scala wondered if Don was trying to remember which lie he had told.

In the end Don said, "Can I just go with 'all will be revealed'?"

Scala shrugged, then remembered Don couldn't see her shrugging.

"Look," Don said. "These people, they're on our side. They can help us. I really can't tell you any more than that. Will that do?"

"I guess," she said.

"Great," said Don. "I'm texting you the location now."

"Location?"

"It's kind of a very specific place."

Scala's phone beeped. She looked at the text: it was a map reference.

"Wow," she said. "That is specific."

• • •

Ricky got a text. Immediately he called Scala.

They met in a beachwear store less than a mile from Don's location.

"Should I be wearing sunglasses?" asked Scala.

"It's raining," Ricky said.

"I meant because we're clearly being spies."

"This is serious," Ricky said.

"I know," Scala replied. "I just wish I knew what was happening."

"Weirdly," said Ricky, "I actually do know what's happening."

Scala looked at him.

"You never know what's happening," she said.

"On this occasion," said Ricky, "I do."

"Ricky," Scala replied, a warning tone in her voice. "What have you done?"

Ricky told her.

TWENTY-ONE

The day was fighting to be sunny, which made no real difference to the unpopular stretch of beach. There were no tourists making their way past the shops and restaurants, because there were no shops and restaurants. Just a woman in full bridal gear surrounded by bridesmaids who was smiling at a photographer while trying to walk on sand in white court shoes.

"Aw," said Ricky, "her big day."

"It's not a real wedding, you dork," Scala said. "It's a fashion shoot."

"Pretty convincing," said Ricky. "They got bridesmaids and those little guys and everything."

"They're called pageboys," Scala replied.

"Someone's on edge," Ricky remarked.

The bridal shoot wasn't the only thing happening on the beach. A group of people with tanned skin and red swimwear had also assembled on the beach.

"Are those models?" asked Ricky.

"Lifeguards," Scala said.

She gave him a look.

"Are you sure you're from Florida?"

Ricky all but pouted. "Way back," he said, "my grandpa owned an alligator farm on the edge of the Everglades. And my dad had a hardware store about half a mile from here."

"Wait," said Scala. "An alligator farm?"

"Yeah," Ricky said. "But the fuckers wouldn't breed. So he sold the land and moved to Miami Beach."

"Cool story," Scala replied. She didn't sound like she meant it.

Ricky noticed the tone of her voice and said:

"Are you still pissed at me?"

"Next time you do something as dumb as that, let me know," said Scala.

"So you can stop me doing it?"

"Pretty much, yeah. I mean, no offense, but thanks to you I already have a dead manager."

"He was trying to kill me."

Scala shrugged. It wasn't a good shrug.

"Look at that old van," Ricky said, more to fill the silence than anything else.

"What about it?"

"Just odd, that's all. Who leaves a van on a beach?"

Scala turned to Ricky.

"Maybe don't say anything unless it's useful?" she suggested.

"I guess someone dumped it there," said Ricky, and got a powerful death stare in return.

The fashion shoot ended, brought to a close by the clouds gathering overhead.

The lifeguards ended their pep talk, got into their cars, and went off somewhere more photogenic.

It was just Scala, Ricky, and the old van.

Scala saw figures in the distance.

"It's them," she said.

"Oh, so *you're* allowed to talk," Ricky said.

Don was leading the group – Tony, Helen, and the others – across the road, for all the world like a tour guide. He only needed a tiny umbrella and the look would have been complete.

"You'd think they'd never been outdoors before," said Ricky.

The little group certainly looked unsure of itself. Theresa jumped when a car pulled out in front of her, Larry kept looking from side to side like he half expected to be arrested at any minute, while Tony was squinting as though the sun hurt his eyes (*his new eyes*, Ricky remembered). Only Helen seemed happy, smiling like a person enjoying their big day out.

They seemed to take forever crossing the road, and made their way across the sand like they were walking on the surface of the moon.

"So this is it," Scala said to Don. "Whatever *it* is."

"Are you OK?" Ricky asked Don. "You look worried."

"I'm fine," Don replied. "It's just all this is happening kinda suddenly. I thought we'd have more time."

"More time for what?" asked Larry. He really did look unhappy to be here, like a mouse on a rollercoaster.

"To prepare," Don said. He clapped his hands.

"I'm not going to miss him doing that," said Ricky.

"This isn't funny," Scala said.

"OK, people!" Don called out. "I want you all to follow me."

"Follow you where?" asked Theresa. She was struggling to walk in the sand, so Helen took her arm.

"Just to that van over there," said Don.

"I fucking knew it," Ricky muttered, throwing Scala a look.

The van was an old Ford Econoline, brown with cream trim, and it looked like it had been halfway round the world before finally giving out in the middle of the beach. Despite its weathered appearance, Ricky noticed, the van had four brand-new tires and was fairly clean. He also noted that Don kept putting his hand in his pocket as though checking that something was there.

"This is it, people," Don shouted. "This is as far as we go."

The group huddled round the front of the van, for all the world like a weird bunch of rock fans at a music festival.

"Well," said Tony. "Here we are. On a beach."

He looked around. Ricky wanted to ask him if the world looked different when you saw it through somebody else's eyes.

"Ain't the kind of place I'd choose for a meeting," he said.

"Who says it's a meeting?" Larry asked. Larry and Tony were no longer agreeing on anything and their exchanges, while few, were always snipey.

"Is anyone else excited?" asked Helen.

"I'm terrified," said Theresa.

Larry said nothing. In the morning sun his face was white like bone.

"So what happens next?" asked Helen, and Ricky had to admit she did sound eager.

"We wait," said Don, but he didn't sound very certain.

"Wait for what?" Tony asked.

Don opened his mouth to speak, but nothing came out.

"Look at that," Ricky said to Scala. "He's lost for words."

Scala didn't reply.

After a while, people began to get bored. Tony took out a pack of cigarettes (he didn't offer them round). Helen continued to look around keenly, while Larry just stood there with a terrified expression on his face.

Then Don lifted his hand. It was trembling.

"What's up, Don?" asked Tony.

"They're coming through," Don said.

"What?" Tony said. "What do you—"

Tony's hands went to his stomach.

"Jesus!" he shouted.

"What is it?" said Theresa.

"My guts!" Tony roared. "My fucking guts!"

He cried out in pain, then clutched his chest.

"What's fucking happening to me?!" he shouted.

"God, man, what's wrong with you?" Larry said, but he stood up.

Now the group were standing around Tony, who was shouting and trying to grab his own chest and stomach at the same time.

"Does it hurt?" Don said. He sounded interested, rather than concerned.

"Of course it fucking hurts!" Tony shouted. "Jesus, make it stop!"

He fell backward – although to Ricky it looked more like he had been thrown backward – and started to jerk about in the sand, whipping grit into their faces as he convulsed on the ground.

"Somebody do something!" shouted Theresa, but nobody moved.

"Hold him down," Don said.

"You hold him down," Larry replied.

Don nodded at Ricky and they both bent down and tried to keep Tony still. Tony screamed and lashed out, punching Ricky in the side of the head. Ricky staggered to one side as Don stood up rapidly and said:

"Guess we'll just have to let it happen."

"Let what happen?" asked Larry.

"You'll see," said Don.

Tony continued to spasm on the floor, his cries now confined to odd tight grunts and sustained whimpers.

"He looks different," Theresa said.

"Of course he does," said Larry. "We all do."

"She's right," said Helen. "He looks… *more* different."

And Tony did. His arms, his legs, his torso were all changing.

"Oh my goodness," Larry said. "It's like a complete change."

"Full-body job," Don said.

"What the fuck?" said Ricky, looking at Don. "Are you smiling?"

"You bet he is," Scala replied. "This is what he's been waiting for."

"What does that mean?" said Theresa.

Scala bent down. She put a hand on Tony's chest. It seemed to calm him.

"It means it's happening," she said. "Maybe before it was supposed to."

"Way earlier," said Don. "Which is fine."

Scala stood up.

"It means Don lied to us," she said. "All of us."

"I don't know what you're talking about!" cried Larry.

"Oh my God," Helen said. "Look."

On the ground, Tony was unconscious, eyes still open, and he had stopped convulsing. But the skin on his face was rippling, like water when the wind blows over it. His eyes remained still, but the rest of his face seemed to be…

"It's fucking melting!" shouted Larry.

Tony's face was first dissolving, then coming back into focus, then disappearing again. Then with a jolt it resolved itself into another face entirely.

Ricky took a step back. The man lying there was bulky and had a shaved head.

He recognized him at once from the room in the future. It was Will.

"What's *happening*?" Larry cried. He was hysterical now.

"Ask him," Don said. He was looking at Ricky. "Ricky knows, don't you?"

Ricky said, "I just brought it forward."

Scala laughed. "Like that's all there is to it. You just *brought it forward*."

"Brought what forward?" It was Larry this time. "What the fuck are you people talking about?"

"The plan," said Don. "Ricky doesn't know what the plan is, or what it's for, but somehow he knew how to make it happen earlier."

"Same way you did," Ricky said. "I put an ad in the paper."

The rest of the group were silent now, as if they'd just given up asking questions. On the sand, Tony's new body was still.

"Why the fuck did you think that was a good idea?" asked Scala.

"Might as well," said Ricky. "Bring it on and get it done."

Scala shook her head in disgust.

"An ad," Don said. "How did you even know… never mind. It doesn't matter now."

He stepped back.

"Hey, Larry," he said.

"Yes?" said Larry, shakily.

"You OK?" asked Don. "Only you don't seem to be yourself today."

"What—" Larry began, and then doubled over in agony.

Larry's change was much faster than Tony's. He jackknifed a few times, threw out an arm or a leg, and then pitched face forward into the sand, where he lay in silence until Don flipped him over like a pancake so he could breathe.

"Hey, Mig," said Don.

He beamed at the others. "Who's next?" he said.

Theresa was next. She clutched at her throat, she staggered about, she tried to grab hold of Don for support, and when he pushed her away she stood there and cried until Helen took her in her arms.

"It's OK," Helen said.

"It's not," Theresa replied. "But I'm old. And I'm ill. I didn't have much time anyway."

She cried out once, and went limp.

Helen laid Theresa's body on the floor. Its face was changing but nobody bothered looking.

"I wanted this change to happen," said Helen. "I thought it would be good. Better, anyway."

Her hands began to tremble.

"I was wrong, wasn't I?" Helen asked.

"Yes," said Scala gently. "I think you were."

"Nothing you can do about it now," said Don. "You saw the others. In a minute or two, you're going to be somebody else."

"Yes," said Helen. "I know that. But there is a difference."

"What's that?" asked Don.

"They didn't know," Helen replied. "But I do. And I'm going to fight it."

She winced as a spasm struck her. A second made her step backward and almost fall.

"Good luck with that," said Don.

Helen wrapped her arms around herself. Ricky could see her flesh moving under her clothes, her body shape changing. But Helen remained calm, only her face showing pain.

"She's making the effort, I'll say that," Don remarked.

"You're an evil fucker," Scala said.

"How can I be?" Don said. "I'm a time cop, remember."

He laughed a little.

Helen's hands were on her face now.

"I can feel them," she cried. "I can feel them trying to come through."

"You can feel how you like," Don said, "but you can't stop them. Look at your body."

Despite her struggle, Helen's body was no longer her body. Only her face remained the same, as though somehow that was all she could control.

"Few seconds now and they'll be coming through," Don said.

"Not if I have anything to do with it," Helen said.

"Over your dead body, right?" Don said, grinning.

"Stop it!" Scala cried.

"I can't," Don said. "My friends are in charge, not me. And they are very keen to come through."

Helen's eyes were closed in concentration.

Then she opened them.

They were still her eyes.

"Not long now!" Don called.

Helen looked at Scala and Ricky.

"This is what I wanted," she said. "Even now. I wanted to be someone else, and I am."

"They're going to kill you!" Scala said.

"No, they're not," Helen replied. "Not if I kill them first."

"You can't do that," Don said, but there was doubt in his voice.

"I can," said Helen.

She smiled.

"Because this is my body and my mind."

Helen's face tightened in pain. She closed her eyes.

"No!" she shouted.

And she exploded in a burst of light.

They stood there for a moment, blinded. When they were able to see again, there was nothing there but a patch of sand that had become glass from the heat of the explosion.

"What happened?" said Ricky.

"She beat them," Scala said.

"That's annoying," Don said, kicking the burnt sand where Helen had been. "Now we're a man short."

After that, nothing in particular happened. The wave of arrivals seemed to have been halted – *maybe Helen did that*, Ricky thought – and it was just Ricky, Scala, Don, and the three unconscious bodies.

It was evening now and the beach was entirely deserted.

Scala hugged herself against the cold.

"Is that it?" she asked Don. "That was your great plan? Bring three thugs here from the future?"

"There's kind of more to it than that," Don said. "It's like the song says."

"What song?" asked Ricky.

Don smiled.

"You ain't seen nothing yet," he said.

TWENTY-TWO

Don opened the back of the Econoline. In the gathering dusk, Ricky thought he could see a few heavy objects under tarpaulin. Don pulled out a large bag which turned out to be full of wood and kindling.

"Getting cold out," he said, and began to build a fire.

Ricky looked at Scala. She caught his eye for a second, then said to Don:

"What's in the van?"

"The future," said Don. "I mean, not literally, we can't bring anything back except ourselves. But we can bring *ideas*."

He threw something at Ricky. It was a box of matches.

"We need to warm these guys up," he said.

Anyone passing would have seen a small group of people having a beach barbecue and thought, *strange weather for it*. If they'd come closer, they might have seen one of the party dragging two or three bodies nearer the fire.

Don had been trying to prop the bodies up, with little success, and was now just rolling them nearer to the heat.

"Maybe he's dead," Scala said. "Maybe they're all dead."

Don shook his head.

"He'll be fine," he answered. "You have to remember that normally this happens when the subject is asleep. And usually it happens piece by piece, not all in one go."

"Traumatic," said Ricky. "By the way, Don, how's your arm?"

"My…"

"It's funny," Ricky said, "you're the only person nothing's happened to."

Don rolled up his sleeve. The arm was thin and pale still.

"Nothing's happened to you since we met, I mean," said Ricky. "Everybody else, we all got a couple of changes. Pretty visible ones, too. But you – all you got is a thin arm."

Don shrugged.

"Lucky, I guess," he said.

"Lucky or you just bound your arm up for a few months, made it look skinny," Ricky said.

"And why would I do that?" asked Don.

"To make us think you were in the same boat as we were," Ricky answered. "To pass as one of us."

"That's ridiculous," Don said.

Scala made a face like she was remembering something.

"I read about that," she said. "People do that, when they want to fake an illness or—"

"Or when they want to pretend their body is being taken over by another body," Ricky finished.

"Put some more wood on the fire," Don said. He was holding something in his hand.

"Oh great," Scala said. "A gun."

"Well, we are in Florida," Don said, smiling. "Now put some more wood on the fucking fire."

As Don moved the bodies around, Scala sat by Ricky.

"You recognize those people?" she asked.

"Talking to me now?"

"Don't be a jackass," said Scala.

"Yes," Ricky said, exhaling. "I saw all of them. They're the gang, I guess you'd say."

"Is that all of them?"

Ricky shook his head.

"The boss lady. Jane," he said. "She's not there. And the guy with my hand, Joe."

"The guy who's going to take your body," said Scala. "And a woman."

She frowned.

"I think we can see where this is going," she said.

"You're right," Don said. "You got it in one. If this was a movie, I'd be clapping my hands slowly and ironically. Well done."

"Why aren't they here?" asked Scala. "The other two."

"Because you always send the henchmen in first," said Don. "Because if this didn't work, the expendables get fucked instead of the main men. Like Gary did."

"Gary?" asked Scala.

"Helen," Ricky replied.

"So where are they?" Scala repeated.

Don looked at Ricky and Scala and grinned.

"They're going to burst in you, you might say."

They sat there for some time, watching the moon come up.

After some hours, Will came round. Don gave him some water and a blanket.

Andy, who had been Theresa, and Mig, who was Larry, were next. They were groggy but, Ricky felt, not groggy enough. Mostly they were confused by their environment. Ricky guessed people didn't have nice sandy beaches where they came from, or if they did, it wasn't safe to sit on them.

"Where's Gary?" asked Mig.

Don told him.

"Son of a bitch," Mig said. He gave Ricky a furious look.

"Wasn't me," said Ricky.

"It will be soon," Mig replied.

• • •

Don was in the van getting what looked like flasks of soup for the others.

"It's like the fucking Hardy Boys," said Ricky.

"Who?" Scala said. "Don't tell me, I don't care. Listen, we need to do something."

"You think?" asked Ricky. "I am way ahead of you."

"Oh God," Scala said. "Please don't tell me you have a plan."

"I have a plan," said Ricky.

He picked up a large and heavy piece of driftwood.

As Don came out of the van, Ricky slammed him in the back of the head and grabbed him just before he fell.

"Run," he told Scala.

"Great plan," she said. But she ran.

Andy saw what was happening first, but he was too stiff to stand up.

"What the fuck?" he said.

Mig got to his feet.

"Get them," he said.

Scala ran, Ricky behind her with one arm around a mostly unconscious Don. The sand was thick and soft, and she ran as if in a slow dream.

"This way!" Ricky shouted.

Ricky's Aztek was parked at the side of the road.

"Get in," Ricky said to Scala.

"Fucking push!" Mig shouted.

He was in the driver's seat of the Econoline. It started, and with a shove from the men, made its way across the sand.

Andy slammed the rear door shut.

The van stuck in the sand.

Ricky tied Don's wrists together with strips of plastic.

"One more time," said Mig, and gunned the engine.

"They're moving again," Scala said.

"Buckle up," Ricky replied. "We're in for a hell of a ride."

"In a Pontiac Aztek," Scala said, drily. "With its own integral tent."

"You remembered," said Ricky.

The Econoline was out of the sand and nosing across the sidewalk into the road. Ricky could just see it in his rearview mirror.

Don moaned a little.

"And why are we taking him?" asked Scala.

"Insurance," Ricky replied. He grinned. "I always wanted to say that."

"Where are they going?" said Will.

"How do I fucking know?" Mig answered. "Just follow them."

"Do you have a destination in mind?" Scala asked. "Or are we just going to drive until you think of something?"

"I told you," said Ricky. "I have a plan."

He hit the gas.

"Fuck me," Mig said. "This is driving? I love it."

He gunned the engine some more.

"I'm not sure you should keep doing that," Will said.

"Go and see Andy," Mig replied. "Make sure the rifles are loaded."

"I can do that," Will said.

"Take the wheel a second," Ricky said.

"No!" Scala said. "Just drive like a fucking normal person."

Ricky sighed, and pulled his phone from his pocket. The car swerved as he wrote a text with his thumb. He sent it and put the phone away.

"You want music?" he asked.

"Very funny," Scala said, as the intro to her latest single chimed from the Aztek's speakers.

She pulled the cable out of the ancient iPod.

"I have other tunes," said Ricky.

"Not according to this you don't," Scala replied, scrolling through the songs. "I knew you were a stalker."

It was getting dark now. Storm clouds gathered and in the distance they could see flashes.

"Looks like a big one coming," Ricky said.

Scala shook her head.

"There's no hurricanes expected," she said.

Don looked up.

"Things are changing," he said.

In the Econoline, Andy was opening boxes and pulling out rifles just as a truck pulled out of a junction and nearly hit them.

"Lights!" shouted Will from the back.

Mig fumbled around on the dash. The radio came on.

"This storm just got frisky," said a woman's voice. "Which means it could develop into a full-scale—"

"The stick on the wheel!" Will cried.

Mig turned the radio off, and the wipers on.

"Other side," Will said.

"Got it," said Mig a moment later.

The lights of the city began to recede as the road turned from smooth blacktop to something more ragged.

• • •

"Where are we?" asked Don. "If you don't mind me asking."

"He won't tell me," answered Scala. "So he's not going to tell you."

"South," Ricky said.

"South?" Scala repeated. "From Miami Beach?"

"Yep."

"Oh fuck," said Scala. "You're going to drive to Cuba."

Ricky said nothing, just put his foot down.

The road was bounded by scrubland and grit now, the only light from the Aztek's beam.

"The edge of nowhere," said Don.

"That's the idea," Ricky replied.

"You think you can lose them?" asked Don. "These guys have got nothing to lose and nowhere else to go. They'll never give up."

"I don't want them to give up," Ricky said. "I want them to keep going."

Time passed. Sometimes Scala thought she could see the Econoline behind them in the gloom and sometimes she wasn't sure.

She took out her phone. The map had no roads on it to speak of, but there was a compass.

"This isn't south," she said.

"That's right," Ricky answered. "Part of my plan, you see, involves not telling Don anything, in case, you know, he's got a transmitter in his head or something."

"Dude," said Don, "this isn't *The X-Files*."

"Your references are totally fucked up," Scala said.

Don was sitting upright now. He had an eager look on his face, like a dog that knows it's been talked about.

Ricky caught his eye in the rearview mirror.

"Tell her, Don," he said. "Tell her how you did it."

"Did what?" asked Scala. Don's face was a blank now.

"Came here," Ricky said. "How he came *through*."

Don said nothing.

"Not saying, are you?" Ricky said. "I know why. It's because it hurts. Even now, years later. Not in the arm, or the eye, or anywhere physical. But inside you."

"Shut up," said Don.

"I read the reports," Ricky said. "The ones Isinglass found before you killed him. The cuttings he brought back from Alaska."

"That's enough," Don said. He began to twist the cuffs against themselves.

"That's not going to work," Ricky said. "You're less strong than you were when you were seventeen."

"When you were…"

Scala looked at Ricky, then at Don.

"Oh fuck no," she said.

"Oh fuck yes," Ricky said, grim relish in his voice.

"I'm right, aren't I?" Ricky went on. "You came through like we did, but you were the first. After the coins and the cats, I mean. They had to be sure. They had to be certain it would work. So they sent you."

"I volunteered," Don said, coldly. "I was the only one smart enough."

"Except maybe for the boss lady," said Ricky. "Except for Jane, and she sure wasn't going first."

"I volunteered," Don said. "I knew what I was doing."

"What was it you said?" Ricky asked. "There has to be a space. There has to be someone for you to go into. And there was, wasn't there? Someone who you knew where they'd be, someone who was *compatible*. Same blood type, same genes – same everything."

"We had no idea if any of it would work," Don said. "For all I knew, I was going on a suicide mission."

"Well, you were right about that," Ricky said. "Because you killed yourself, Don."

He looked at Don's enraged face in the rearview mirror.

"You didn't send yourself into some stranger's body, not like your pals," said Ricky. "You chose someone you knew, someone you'd *been*. You went back in time, into your own body, and you fucking killed yourself."

Don pounded his tied fists on the seat back. Then he stopped, and slumped back, silent.

"That doesn't make any sense," said Scala. "I mean, what about the grandpa thing?"

Ricky shook his head.

"You tell her, Don," he called out.

"Doesn't work like that," Don said finally. "It's the time planes that are different, not the people. I could… occupy… that body and not be affected because I already existed. Otherwise how could I travel back?"

"What was it like?" Ricky asked. His voice was quieter now, and calm. "Realizing that each part of you was killing a part of you that was there before?"

"It wasn't gradual, it was fast," said Don. "Like what's going to happen to you when they catch up with you."

"OK, so you weren't conscious of what was happening," Ricky said. "I get that."

He turned in his seat.

"But *he* was," said Ricky. "The younger you. He must have felt the whole thing."

Don lunged forward. Ricky pulled out a pistol and grinned.

"Look what I found in your coat," he said. "Now sit back."

"That was a little harsh," said Scala, a few minutes later.

"Taste of his own medicine," Ricky said. "Also," he went on, "I'm not done yet."

He turned to Don, who was slumped on the back seat, looking sullen.

"Maybe you'd like to tell us the whole truth now?"

TWENTY-THREE

"OK," Don said. "The world I'm from," he went on, "it's not so different from this one."

"I hate to say this in the circumstances," Scala said, "but please, cut to the chase."

There was an event (Don said) and those who survived the event called it the Pulse. It changed everything.

After the Pulse, and the immediate effects of the Pulse, and the *after*-effects of the Pulse, life did settle down. There were good guys and bad guys and people in between.

"There's always going to be cops and there's always going to be robbers," Don said.

"And which were you?" Scala asked.

Don grinned. "A robber," he said. "A big, bad robber."

Don was one of the survivors (he went on). There were a lot of people left after the Pulse, which was either a weapon which killed people but left buildings, or which destroyed buildings and killed people, he wasn't sure, but since the Pulse was a mess of a disaster, it didn't really matter. It destroyed enough buildings and it killed enough people to make it academic. But Don lived.

"Out in Alaska there were two things in our favor," he said. "One, we were far from the epicenter of the thing; and two, we were used to a tougher environment. So civilization went on after a fashion, and I survived."

Don made his way south. The world was a little warmer now, except where it was a little colder, and there was nothing for him in Alaska. He was looking for work as he went – helping people rebuild their homes for food and shelter – and if he was honest, he was getting pretty fucking bored with it. Everyone either had a gun and an attitude problem, or they were some sucker and his dumb wife, apologizing for not having more food to give him or not needing any help around the place. Don was a grown man now, intelligent and ambitious, and he was well aware that this new world was not offering him the opportunities he wanted.

Then one morning Don walked up to a tatty-looking farmhouse and there they were. "They were younger than me," Don said. "And they were more than survivors."

The gang – they called themselves that, right from the start – were small at first, and some of them were young, and one or two were old. But Jane was there, and Mig, and Andy. They had taken the farm from some sucker and his dumb wife, and they were stockpiling anything they could lay their hands on – food, booze, guns, even some gold they'd got somehow.

At first, they were just a bunch of local raiders, robbing passers-by and demanding protection from local farmers, but the gang wanted more than that. They were, like Don, intelligent and ambitious, and there was a world out there. A world that was returning to normal. The gang wanted a piece of it.

"Half the country was still fucked," Don said, "and half the country was what you people would call *futuristic*. They had rebuilt the internet, they had machines that could cross the Pacific Ocean in an hour, and they had cured most of the viruses that sprang up after the Pulse, but most of us were still crapping in holes in the ground and growing our own potatoes."

The gang were expanding. They had muscle now, as well as brains, and as time went on they went from being a little gang that lived on a farm to a big gang who were going to take over a city, which happened to be Miami. It was a good time for all concerned. Jane was the boss, and Don was her number two, and they had a thing going on between them.

"Then one day they busted us," Don said.

The gang were based in a nice building in the city now with guards and security checkpoints at each end of the street – none of which were of any use when the cops came with their drones. There were drone copters, and drone missiles, and drone tanks, and the whole operation took about five minutes.

"We were taken into custody," Don said. "Tried, convicted, and sentenced to death."

"Wow," said Scala. "This is a lot different to the story you told me."

She turned and looked at him.

"You'll be telling me you're not a time cop next."

Interlude

The cell was long, and cold. It was long because it wasn't so much a cell as a prefabricated cabin, and it was cold because it was made of metal and had one shatterproof plastic window, which was scraped on the outside by the endless prairie wind and on the inside by years of prisoner graffiti. Inside there were two beds, one table, and one chair. The chair and the table didn't match and neither did the beds, giving the cell the look of an unsuccessful storage unit.

The cell had two occupants. One was a stocky, nervous-looking man with big, untamed eyebrows, and the other was Don. They had been sharing the cell for ten days and neither of them had done more than nod at the other. Silence was common on death row: once you've banged your plastic cup against the wall a few times or shouted at the shatterproof window, there's really nowhere else to go after that except silence, self-harm, or suicide.

Don couldn't speak for the other guy, but he wasn't interested in hurting himself and he wasn't ready to end it all, so he just lay on his bed or sat in the chair, thinking. Sometimes he thought about his life back in Alaska, and the winters that didn't seem much less cold than the ones in the old days, Pulse or no Pulse. Sometimes he thought about his time living the high life, drinking the best drinks and taking the newest drugs. But mostly he thought about the two words Jane had shouted at him as they dragged her away to a waiting van.

Hold on.

And if there was one thing Don was good at, it was holding on.

He'd never been able to figure out how the cops had found them. An inside job seemed the likely answer, but most of the gang were either too smart or too dumb to rat on the others. In his mind, Don was compiling a list of likely suspects, but that's where it stayed: in his mind. He never forgot Jane's words but, sitting here in the stupid cabin that was probably going to be the last room he'd ever sleep in, looking out at the bleak dead prairie with its rows and rows of barbed-wire fences, it seemed impossible that he'd ever see any of the gang again, let alone get to track down and kill the traitor in their midst. Still, it helped with passing the time, to sit there and imagine what he'd do when he found him. Other prisoners, judging by the moans and grunts coming from the other cabins, passed the hours and days in fantasies of a sexual nature; Don kept himself sane with dreams of torture and death. And those two words.

• • •

What Don's cellmate did for an inner life was impossible to know. He just lay on his bed, eyes shut, his eyebrows occasionally twitching like a caterpillar dreaming. When he did open his eyes, to use the pisspot or to collect his food from the slot in the door, it was always with a heavy sigh, and once his task was completed he would get back on his bed and close his eyes again.

It was the kind of thing that might annoy you, if you were the kind of person who got annoyed. Fortunately, Don was an even-tempered man – well, kind of – so he didn't let it get to him. Maybe sometimes he did fantasize about smothering the man with his own pillow, or perhaps beating him to death with the only chair, but generally he just let his cellmate get on with his routine of sleeping and sighing. After all, he had been told to hold on, and that was exactly what he was going to do. No fights, no quarrels, nothing to draw attention to himself. That was the plan.

Until one morning the man with the bushy eyebrows began to cry.

Don hated it when people cried. It affected his concentration, especially when he was trying to hurt them, and it was very much outside his emotional sphere. Don had never patted someone on the shoulder, passed anyone a Kleenex, or said, "There, there." His dad had never been one for displays of emotion (not counting anger, anyway) and Don had followed his father in that at least.

So a man crying just a few feet away from him was not pleasant to Don. He wondered how he could make the noise stop, and after rejecting the easy options – shouting, suffocation – turned in his seat and said:

"What the fuck is wrong with you?"

The man stopped crying for a moment and looked hurt (*like a fucking kid*, thought Don).

"Sorry," he said.

At first, Don thought he was going to leave it there, but then the man started gulping and wiping his face and then said:

"You wanna hear my story?"

Answers flashed into Don's brain, like multiple choice options.

Fuck no.

I'd rather be stabbed.

Fine, if it'll shut you up.

Instead he smiled, with some effort, and said:

"Sure, why not?"

• • •

The man sat up, found something in his sleeve, and blew his nose with it.

"My name," he said, "is Frank."

He threw Don a look. It was a significant look.

"Am I supposed to know who you are?" Don asked.

Frank smiled. It was a wry smile and Don wanted to punch it off his face.

"I guess not," he replied. "But you should."

He sighed deeply.

"Everyone should," he said.

It seemed that Frank had been some kind of scientist, back in the day, doing experiments with time or some weird stuff like that. Don, who was not a stupid man, found it hard to keep up with Frank's rambling monologue, some of which was to do with the science and most of which was to do with how Frank had been set up – by whom, Don wasn't sure, but the government, the secret services, and the cops were all definitely involved.

The whole thing sounded like the highest-grade BS to him, but Frank was adamant about one thing: he had been a scientist, working on the most important project of all time, and when it had gone wrong, Frank's project had been hurriedly shut down, and so, it would appear, had Frank.

"Look at me," said Frank, bitterly. "Sat in here with you, no offense."

"None taken," lied Don.

"They said I was a genius," Frank went on. "They said I was a new Einstein."

He looked around the cabin.

"Do you see Einstein in here?" he asked. "Do you see Newton? Rutherford?"

"No, I don't," Don freely admitted.

"That's right, you don't," Frank said. "And you want to know why?"

Not really. "Tell me," said Don.

Frank blew his nose loudly.

"You ever hear of a woman called Marie Fevrier?" he asked.

Don had never previously heard of Marie Fevrier, but half an hour later he knew all about her and her Method, and how she had managed to project herself, or a version of herself, Frank wasn't entirely clear, back into the past.

"She was there," Frank said. "In some form or other, I still don't know, but she was there. And you know what else?"

"No," Don said, flatly.

"She was in the room with herself," said Frank excitedly. "She was in the room with a baby, and that baby was her. Do you get what that means?"

Don shook his head.

"Marie Fevrier went back in time and did the one thing all the theories, all the books, say you can't do," Frank said. "She met herself. And nothing happened. History didn't change. Nobody ceased to exist, no alternate timelines opened, no one's grandparents failed to be born, none of that. She could have thrown that baby out the window and her world – our world – wouldn't have been affected one jot."

"How—" Don began.

"How do I know?" Frank almost shouted. "Because I ran tests! I replicated her experiment. I sent people back and got them to try and change history. Oh, not in a big way, I didn't shoot Hitler or any of that. But I sent people back and had them make changes here and there. And you know what?"

He smiled. It was not, Don thought, an appealing smile.

"You could go back in time and kill yourself, and it would have no effect whatsoever on history. My history, your history – your life would just carry on."

"I'll bear that in mind," Don said.

After that, Frank wouldn't stop talking. He told Don how he'd sent a tin box back through time and known it had worked when he'd seen the dust of ages on it. He told Don how he'd been taken away by the powers-that-be and put to work in an underground laboratory ("Just like in a James Bond movie," he told Don, who wondered what a James Bond movie was). And he told Don about *replacement*.

Frank was big on replacement. It was like his special subject or something. Once he'd repeated all his other stories until even he was bored with them, he turned his full attention on his new theme.

"You could send someone back like Fevrier did," he said. "And she was there but not there, if you see what I mean."

"Like a projection," said Don, as he always did at this point.

"More like a ghost," Frank said. "So you're in the past but not. And the real trick would be sending someone back who was fully in that world. But to do that…"

He paused, just as he always did at this point.

"…you need to replace someone."

· · ·

The whole deal, as Frank explained it (and wow, could he explain it) was that if you sent someone back in time, it would involve putting them where another living person was. This would of course mean killing that person which – even though that person was in the past and therefore probably already dead – was not just illegal, but could be a vote loser in elections.

"Imagine the fuss," said Frank. "People finding out that their grandpa not only got killed by the government fifty years ago, but worse, got *replaced*. It could make you very unpopular."

"You'd know," Don said, then realized he'd spoken out loud. He looked at Frank to see his reaction, but Frank was still going on about replacements. *He's not even listening*, Don thought. Then something caught his eye.

Something was different. Something outside the window.

"So," Frank continued, oblivious, "the government did what

every government does when it's scared of something. They banned it – officially, that is. Unofficially, they doubled down on research. Which is where I came in."

"Unh-hunh," said Don, one eye on the window. He could see something bright and distant, its light smeared by the scratches on the window.

"My team and I started sending people back," said Frank. "First one was a convict called Steiner. He was harmless enough – nobody wanted to send a murderer back – but he was a tired old lifer and he didn't care if they sent him to the moon so long as he got a change of scenery."

Was the light getting nearer? Or – Don suddenly thought – was there more than one light?

"Anyway," Frank went on. "We sent Steiner back, into the body of some other fellow, and he exploded."

"What?" said Don.

"The guy we sent Steiner into," said Frank. "He blew up. At least, we think he did. When we tried to pull Steiner back, we just got... guts."

Don nodded to show he was still listening and went back to looking at the window. He could definitely see more lights now: two, maybe three.

"It took a while, but eventually we figured out there were two ways to do this without killing anyone," Frank went on. "Send the person back into their younger self – which didn't always work, believe me – or do it bit by bit."

"Bit by—" said Don.

"One piece at a time," Frank said.

"You're kidding."

"I know, right," said Frank. "But it worked. Hard part was the brain. Quite a few messes on the table there. But we figured it out."

The lights were getting nearer.

Don could hear footsteps in the corridor outside.

"So what happened?" he asked Frank.

Frank sighed.

"Fucking democracy happened," he said. "Change of government, clean sweep, we got shut down. And I," he said, with resentment and bitterness in his voice, "ended up in here. For murder, would you believe?"

He looked at Don like a dog seeking approval.

Don adopted a sympathetic expression.

The door of the cell flew open. A guard stepped in, and fell to the ground.

Two masked figures came in, both armed.

"Hey, Frank," said Don. "You want to get out of here?"

• • •

The trucks were armored, but they were surprisingly fast, even on the rough prairie terrain. They were also loud, so Don could hardly hear what Mig was shouting. Then again, he didn't need to: Mig's gestures were pretty clear as he pointed to Frank and mimed slitting a throat.

"He's with me!" Don shouted, pointing to himself. Mig raised an eyebrow and blew a kiss.

"Fuck you," said Don, but quietly, because Mig was, after all, a psychopath entirely devoid of emotion except for his love of cats and murder. Instead he raised a *what is this guy like?* eyebrow at Andy, who was at least sane. Andy responded by turning his head away. Don guessed he wasn't too pleased at being sent out on a rescue mission.

He didn't blame Andy, either: the materiel, the planning, the whole thing must have cost a lot of time and money. And of the gang – Andy, Mig, Will, and the others – nobody understood Don's importance other than the boss herself.

Jane.

Hold on, she had said.

Well, Don thought, as he looked at the endless miles of prairie and the burning prison behind them, *I held on*.

"Where are we going?" asked Frank.

In answer, Mig punched him in the face.

"Shut your fucking mouth," he explained.

Don smiled. It was good to be with his people again.

• • •

It was late at night when the armored trucks finally pulled in outside an abandoned motel on the edge of the desert. Don got out and looked around. In the full light of the moon, he could see a dusty field studded with bent and twisted posts.

"Used to be a drive-in," said Will.

"Huh," Don replied. He looked up. A single light shone from one of the motel bedrooms.

"She's waiting for you," Will said.

• • •

Don knocked on the door and waited in the corridor.

A few seconds later, the door opened and he felt the blunt end of a revolver against his face.

"It's me," he said.

She pulled him into the room.

• • •

Later, when they were sweaty and exhausted, Jane said:

"They all hate your guts, you know."

"Let 'em," said Don. He stroked her hair. "What I've got's going to change everything," he said.

• • •

In the morning, when everyone had slept and eaten and felt a little more human, Don went to see Frank. Mig had tied Frank to a bed and he lay there trussed and scared looking.

"Untie him," Don said.

Mig reluctantly cut the ropes. Frank sat up, a sullen look on his face, and massaged his arms.

"Is there any food left?" asked Don.

"He can have some of mine," said a voice Don hadn't heard before.

"Who are you?"

"His name's Simon," said Mig. "Some kid we found outside Detroit."

"Is he OK?"

Mig gave him a look.

"Are you OK?" he asked, a sneer in his voice.

Don got to his feet. So did Mig.

They were just about to square off when Jane came in.

"Knock it off," she told them.

Don stepped back, winked at Mig.

He nodded at the man on the bed.

"This is Frank," Don told Jane. "Frank, this is Jane. Tell her everything you told me."

Frank told her. When he had finished, Jane whistled.

"Hell of a story," she said. "Is it true?"

"Only one way to find out," said Don. "But first…"

He looked around the motel room.

"…we need to find a new place."

· · ·

They drove for two days before they found it. A compound, five cabins surrounded by chain-link fence with barbed wire on top. Gates, spotlights, security system, even a genny.

Inside there was dust and animal shit. The cupboards were full of canned food and drinks cartons.

"Why is nobody here?" said Andy. He stuck a straw into a carton, took a tentative sip.

"Apple," he said.

Don looked around. There was a door with a keypad.

He turned around, walked into the kitchen, and came out a few seconds later with a piece of card. Don keyed the numbers on the card into the pad and the door opened.

"Oh God," Andy said.

The smell was terrible.

· · ·

After they'd removed the body from the bunker and cleaned with bleach and hot water, they were able to take it all in.

"Was it a meth lab?" asked Will, looking at all the glassware.

"Guess so," said Don. "Looks like the previous owner OD'ed."

"Why?"

Don shrugged.

"Who knows?" he said. "Maybe it was suicide. Maybe he got locked in and went crazy. Either way—" and he smiled, "—we got ourselves a sweet deal."

The gang spent the next few weeks making the compound into even more of a fortress, raiding nearby homesteads for supplies and weapons, while Don helped Frank turn the meth lab into a suitable workspace.

One day it was all ready. Don and Frank stood in the middle of a room that had been designed to make crystal meth but had now been repurposed for a greater task.

"So what do you need?" Don asked Frank.

"Cats," said Frank. "Cats and nickels."

• • •

"He's been down there for weeks."

"I know, I know…"

"The boys are getting antsy."

"The boys are always antsy."

"Don't talk back," Jane said.

"Sorry," Don replied.

They were in the living room. The door to the bunker was closed.

"For all we know, he could be contacting the cops down there. They could be on their way right now."

"He's an escaped fugitive. Mig shot three guards. He's going nowhere."

"I don't even know why we're doing this."

Don grinned.

"Because I can give you the world," he said.

He took her hand.

"Think about it. The past. You've seen the videos. People were soft then, they were lazy. Fat fucking idiots, and each one with a big streak of victim running through them. Before all this happened, before the Pulse, humanity was nothing more than a playpen full of big pink slugs. Before the Pulse, people were complacent, they were soft. Worse than that—" now Don sneered, "—they were *optimistic*."

"I don't know, it seems like a risk."

"Jane, we've lived with risk all our lives. We've been on death row, we've killed cops and judges. We've lived our lives on the run. If we go back to the past, we'll go through that world like a fucking chainsaw through butter. We'll be kings. And queens."

Jane sighed.

"OK," she said, "I was getting tired of being an outlaw anyway. A queen sounds better."

• • •

They told the others. Simon just shook his head.

"This is—"

"This is real," Jane replied. "You better get used to it. All of you."

Mig raised his hand.

"What?" said Jane.

"Does it have to be cats?" asked Mig.

• • •

"The nickel," Frank said, holding up a weathered and blackened coin, "is your link with the past. It is an authentic historical artefact. Concentrate on it and you will feel the moment shift."

"And what's that?" asked Will. He pointed at something on the table.

"This?" asked Frank. "This is a photograph of a cat."

"So long as it's only a photo," Mig muttered.

"This cat is long dead," Frank went on. "But it lived here, same as this nickel, and at the same time too."

"How do you know?" asked Simon.

"Family album," Frank explained. "So we also know it belonged to this man."

He held up a second photograph, a red-haired man in a plaid shirt holding a cat. The same cat.

"The experiment today is to send a man back in time and see if he can return with something living."

"Excuse me?" said Andy. "Send someone back? One of us?"

"No," Jane said. "Not one of us."

She looked at Simon.

"Hold him down," she said.

. . .

Simon screamed throughout the entire process.

"Focus, and it won't hurt so much," Frank told him.

"Maybe give him something?" asked Don.

"Any sedative would reduce his powers of concentration."

Don looked at Simon, who had dug his nails so far into his palms that they were bleeding.

"I'd say his powers of concentration were pretty reduced as it is."

Frank gave Simon a mild dose of sedative. As Simon's breathing became steadier, he told him:

"Hold the nickel in your hand. Think of the man."

"I can't!" Simon shouted. "I—"

And then he was gone.

"Shit," said Will.

They waited, but Simon didn't return. They waited all day and all night, but he didn't return.

And then in the early hours of the morning, Don was woken by crashing sounds from the bunker.

He went downstairs to find Simon, bloody and wild-eyed, standing in a mess of broken glass. He had something in his arms.

"I did it," he said. "It's dead, but I did it."

And he threw a dead ginger tom onto the floor.

• • •

"We can do it," Don said, when the lab had been cleaned up. "This is just the start."

Jane nodded. "OK," she said. "We can send a man to the past and we can bring him back. But now what?"

"What do you mean?" asked Don.

"We can't just barge into the past like a bunch of morons," Jane said. "It would be like running into a bank with no guns shouting, 'give us the money'. We need to be sure of what we're doing. We need a base, we need a direction. We need a plan."

The planning was the hardest part of all. While Frank ran tests – and while Simon became a shadow of himself – Don began to look for the best time, and place, to start up.

"It's tricky," he told Jane. "Too far back and we're living in an age where people shit in their hands, too far forward and we hit the Pulse."

"So what do you suggest?"

"There's a sweet spot. It's pretty civilized and most people are living fairly great lives, but it's also decades before the Pulse. There's some bad stuff, but mostly if you've got guns and money, you can do pretty much what you like. And when the Pulse hits, we'll be ready. We can ride it out, and when things get back to normal, we won't be hiding in the fucking woods, we'll be on top of it all."

Jane nodded, taking it in. "I like the sound of it. Any snags?"

"Just one," said Don. "You guys are OK because you're all pretty young. But I've got some years on you."

"So?"

Don looked troubled. "There's a slight risk I might run into myself," he said.

Jane smiled. "Then you'd better deal with that risk," she said.

• • •

"We're not ready," Frank said. "We still need to find a way to iron out the kinks in this thing."

"What kinks?" asked Don and it seemed to Frank that Don sounded irritable, like something had changed in him.

"For a start, there's the dangers of transference—"

"Which we have reduced immeasurably by working on the single-body-part thing."

"Yes, but then there's the question of what happens to the other person when you come through—"

Don looked so angry that for a moment Frank thought he was going to hit him.

"The other person?" he said. "Since when have you given a fuck about the other person?"

"I'm just saying—"

But Don was gone.

"I need to get out of here," said Frank to no one in particular.

• • •

Will found him a couple of days later, in one of the outbuildings, staring at a nickel and holding a photograph taken from an old local newspaper Frank had found lining a sock drawer. He was crying.

"It's not working," Frank was saying. "Why isn't it working?"

• • •

"We don't need him anymore," Don told Jane.

"You sure about that?"

Don made a face.

"I know how to do this. You know how to do this. Hell, even Mig knows how to do this."

"OK. Make sure you get all his papers first."

• • •

"We're going for a little walk," Mig told Frank.

Frank shook his head.

"Oh no," he said, backing away toward the door, "I'm not going anywhere with you."

"Have it your way," Mig replied, and stabbed him in the throat.

• • •

"We need to move," Jane said one morning as Mig parked the truck in the yard.

"What?" said Mig. "But it's nice here."

"It was a lot nicer before you painted Frank's room with his own fucking blood," Jane answered. "But that's not why we're leaving."

She looked across the yard. Simon was standing out in the cold, looking permanently stunned as he always did lately.

"I think someone's got plans," she said. "Maybe go back to the past, make themselves a new life without us."

Mig frowned.

"Want me to deal with him?"

Jane shook her hand.

"We need a replacement first," she said. "Know anyone?"

"There's a couple of guys I know," Mig said.

"Get a message to him," said Jane. "Tell him to meet us in the new place."

"There's a new place already?"

"This is what I do," said Jane. "I plan ahead."

• • •

"All packed up?" asked Don.

"All packed up," said Will. Andy nodded.

A door opened and Mig jumped into the truck.

"Let's get out of here," he said.

As they drove away, the compound exploded in a *whomph* of flame.

"I like to say goodbye properly," said Mig.

• • •

The new place wasn't as nice as the old place. It was kind of basic, and Will had to share a room with the new guy, who was called Joe, had tattoos on his knuckles, and snored. Not that there was much time for sleep. They worked on the plan, and they kept working on the plan, and when they'd done working on the plan, they started again and worked on it some more.

• • •

Then one day, when Simon had been brought back with a folder of real estate details for office space in the Miami area, Jane said:

"OK, it's time to do this."

And it was. Everyone got their instructions, their tasks, and even their code names ("Why is he Lima and I'm Dogface?" asked Mig, looking askance at Don).

And they did it.

TWENTY-FOUR

"The rest you know," Don said. "Jane said there wasn't time for that."

"And she sent you back to kill yourself," Ricky replied.

"Like I said, you're next," replied Don. "You just got a temporary reprieve is all."

The Aztek made its way down unlit roads, past broken road signs and abandoned farms.

"Long story short," Don said, "there's no Victim Replacement Program, no time cops, and no hope for you. There's just the gang, coming like a fucking hurricane."

"Good to know," said Ricky, and turned left into a narrow road.

"Where exactly the fuck are we?" asked Scala a few minutes later.

"Looks like the ass end of nowhere," said Don.

"That's the idea," Ricky answered.

It was very dark now, and when Ricky slowed and rolled down his window to look more closely at a sign, Scala could hear the chirp and skitter of animals in the night. She looked down at her phone and saw, to her utter lack of surprise, that there was no signal.

"I hope you know what you're doing," she said.

"Me too," Ricky said.

He rolled up his window and drove on.

The Aztek drove on, its driver and passengers silent in the all-encompassing dark.

Later on, Scala looked in the rearview mirror. Behind them she thought she could see a pair of headlights.

"I think they're—" she began.

"Shit!" Ricky shouted.

A pickup truck shot past them, accompanied by a blast from its horn.

"Was that them?" asked Scala.

"Could be," said Don, sounding hopeful.

"Unlikely," Ricky said. "Your guy can hardly drive a van down the highway, let alone race a pickup down a dirt road."

A few minutes passed.

"Ricky," Scala said, "are you *following* that truck?"

"Hey," Ricky replied, "you said my name."

"I can't see the van," Scala said, turning back in her seat. "I think we lost them."

"Don't tell Ricky that," said Don.

"What? Why not?"

"Tell her, Ricky."

"Oh fuck," said Scala. "Is this—"

"All part of the plan," said Ricky.

"We're going to die," Scala said.

"But that was *my* plan," said Don, agreeably.

They came to a turning that only looked like a turning if you squinted so you could tell the dirt that was the entrance from the dirt that was just dirt. Ricky turned into the dirt that was the entrance.

Scala peered at a sign.

"Smart farm," she said. "What the fuck is a smart farm?"

"Not smart farm," Ricky replied. "*Smart's* Farm. As in the Smart family. As in me."

"Oh God," Scala said. "This is the place you told me about."

"My grandpa's farm," Ricky said.

"Your grandpa's alligator farm," Scala remembered. "Is this where we're hiding out?"

"Not so much hiding out," said Ricky, "as making a last stand."

"I love last stands," said Don. "They're so futile."

Ricky drove on about a half mile then stopped, turned on his brights, and honked his horn three times.

Someone honked back, also three times.

TWENTY-FIVE

They drove as far down the track as they could, and when it was all potholes, they got out of the car and began to walk. Ricky had a real flashlight and Scala had one on her phone. Don, whose hands were still tied, stumbled along as best he could, which wasn't very well at all. After he had nearly pitched forward onto his face for the third time, Scala reluctantly took his arm.

"Thanks," Don said, then: "Hey, is this a good place to die pointlessly or what?"

Scala let go of his arm again.

"Are there still alligators here?" she asked Ricky.

He shrugged.

"Hard to say," he answered. "Grandpa sold the ones he had, but there's a good chance there's a few gators around. Just stay away from the water."

"What water?" asked Scala.

"That water," said Ricky, shining his flashlight into a black, solid-looking pool. "These pools connect to the swamps. There used to be gates, but they'll have rotted away by now. So stick to the path."

"This is a path?" Scala said.

"I can see lights," said Don. "Hope there's an old-fashioned farmhouse welcome up ahead."

Scala looked up. Don was right. Ahead of them was... not a farmhouse as such, but a small, low building of some sort, weakly illuminated with a thin, yellow light.

"*Bienvenido a mi hacienda*," said Ricky.

There was someone waiting outside the building. She had a very large gun.

"Hi, sis," Ricky said.

"Hi, asshole," said Katie.

Katie took them inside the house. It was furnished with dead insects and a large table. The table had several guns on it.

Ricky picked up one of the guns.

"Put that down," said Katie. "You want to kill someone?"

"Who are the guns for then?" asked Ricky.

"Me," said Katie. She looked at Scala. "I'm the nervous type," she said. "I like to have my babies with me."

"I like her," said Don.

"Shoot him first," Ricky said.

"Now," said Katie, loading some guns, "would be a really good time to tell me what the fuck is going on here."

Ricky told her.

"Now *you* tell me," she said to Scala. "And please, make it less crazy."

Scala shook her head.

"I can't," she said.

"You mean he's telling the truth?"

"Yep."

Don stood up.

"They're both nuts," he said. "They kidnapped me and now they want to kill me. Call the cops!"

"I am a cop, you prick," Katie said, and kicked him in the crotch. Don collapsed onto the floor.

"Ow," said Scala, appreciatively.

"Thanks for coming," said Ricky to Katie, when she'd stopped loading guns.

She looked at him.

"Is this where I'm supposed to say, 'nobody hurts my little brother except for me'?" she asked. "Because I'm not doing this for you."

"Why are you doing it then?"

Katie shrugged.

"Bored, I guess," she replied. "Also, being a woman cop, I don't get to hurt people as much as I'd like."

"Maybe if you were nicer," Ricky suggested.

"If I was *nicer*," said Katie, "I wouldn't want to hurt people, would I?"

"What's in those tubs?" asked Scala.

"More ammo," Ricky answered, confidently.

"Is there fuck," said Katie. "It's sandwiches."

She gave him something.

"A hammer?" asked Ricky.

"You guard this prick," said Katie. "I need some air."

She went outside.

After a minute, Scala followed.

"You want something?" Katie said.

"Just air, same as you," said Scala. "Oh, no, wait, I also wanted to know why you're such a dick with Ricky."

"Everyone is," Katie replied. She took a bite of her sandwich. Scala nodded.

"I guess you have a point."

"Guess I do."

They ate their sandwiches.

"I know who you are," Katie said. "I saw you on that show."

"Everyone did," said Scala.

"I'm surprised you don't have some sort of private fucking army looking out for you."

"Yeah, that's how being a pop star works."

"You know what I mean," said Katie. "You don't have to be in the middle of nowhere in the dark with me and my asshole brother, waiting for shit knows what to come down on us."

Scala looked at her.

"Yes I do," she said. "When I was a kid, my dad was already dead and my mom was more interested in my bookings than me. But I had a brother. His name was Greg. And when I was getting… *famous*… Greg always looked out for me. I used to get shit at school, you know? Before I got tutors, the big kids would pick on me."

"So sad," said Katie.

"I expect you'd have been with them," Scala replied.

"Maybe."

"Anyway, Greg was pretty bad at fighting but he'd step in. He'd take on the big kids, and he'd generally get the crap beaten out of him."

"These kids," said Katie. "They were girls?"

"Yeah."

Katie snorted.

"And later on, when I was... in difficulties."

"What does that mean?"

"Drinking," said Scala. "When I was drinking, he woke me up in the mornings and he took me to the meetings. Every day, for a year."

"How did he die?"

"Who?"

"Greg. I'm guessing this is all the build-up to Greg dies and Ricky is like a substitute for him."

Scala looked at her.

"Greg's a corporate lawyer in Atlanta," she said. "And he's nothing like Ricky. Ricky's an idiot who's going to get us all killed."

She sighed.

"I just don't want that to happen."

Katie muttered something.

"What?" asked Scala.

"I said, nor do I."

They finished their sandwiches.

"Better get back inside," said Katie.

"Wait," said Scala. "I thought I heard something."

They went back inside. Katie turned the lights off and stood in the doorway, listening.

"About a mile and a half away," she said, and picked up a gun.

Ricky put down his hammer and did the same.

"Put that down, or I'll shoot your cock off," said his sister.

Scala went to look at Don. He was hunched down in the corner of the room and looked pretty happy.

"Why are you so cheerful?" she asked.

"Because it's coming down," he said. "And when it does come down, I'll be living the sweet life. You people won't know what's hit you."

He grinned.

Katie came back in, picked up some guns, and went outside again.

Ricky had another sandwich.

"The thing I don't understand—" Scala began.

"You mean another thing you don't understand," said Don.

"—is this," Scala said, ignoring him. "Why us? Why me and him and the others? What did we even have in common?"

"Nothing," Don said. "Nothing except you all lived in the same city and we just needed a bunch of people to land in."

He grinned at her.

"Why, did you think you were special?"

"Those people were special. Larry and Tony and Theresa and the rest," Scala said. "They were people who'd done nothing. They had lives and they didn't deserve to die."

"Suckers," said Don. "I gotta pee."

Katie had the guns, so she took Don outside.

"You ate my last sandwich," Scala said.

"A time like this and all you can think of is food?" Ricky said. "If we get out of here, I'll buy you an entire Denny's breakfast."

"I don't want an entire Denny's breakfast, I want my sandwich," said Scala.

She sat down on the floor. Ricky did too.

"Don said we were only chosen for this shit because we all lived in the same place," she said. "If we'd lived fifty miles away, we'd be fine."

"Story of my life," Ricky said, then: "Do you think we're going to die?"

"Jesus, blunt," said Scala. "I don't know. There's a van full of bad guys from the future out there and all they have to do is think really hard and we either get taken over by other bad guys or we explode."

"I'll take that as a yes," said Ricky.

He turned to her.

"I'm glad I met you, though," he said.

"Yeah, makes it all worthwhile," Scala replied, but she was smiling.

"You know," she said. "Your sister doesn't really think you're an asshole. And neither do I."

She stood up. "OK," she said. "Let's do whatever it is we're going to, or die trying."

They tied Don to a heavy workbench and carried the big table with all the remaining guns on it outside. Katie loaded everything she hadn't loaded already.

"Is there anything I need to know about these jerks that you haven't told me?" she asked.

"They're pretty much bandits," said Scala. "And if they capture us, we'll die, or at least cease to exist."

"You had me at bandits," Katie said, and picked up the largest gun.

They could see the lights of the Econoline now, and then the van itself, bumping along in the darkness.

"How many?" Katie asked.

"Three," said Scala.

"Three against three," Ricky said.

Katie snorted.

The van parked next to Ricky's Aztek. They couldn't see what was happening, because it was too dark.

Then the Aztek burst into flames and it wasn't dark at all.

"The fuckers!" shouted Ricky. "There was no need for that!"

"Making sure we can't escape," Katie said.

"I loved that car," said Ricky.

"Tent in the back and everything," Scala said.

In the blaze from the Aztek, they could see the three men walking toward them.

"Mig's the big guy," Ricky said. "He's probably the most dangerous. Andy's small and Will—"

"You're just grading them by height," said Katie. "That's kind, but not helpful."

"They're all evil and they've all got guns," Scala said.

"That's more like it," Katie said, and shot the nearest one in the head.

"Shit!" Ricky shouted as the body fell to the floor and the others scattered.

"What?" Katie said. "You said they were bad guys."

"Yeah, but – OK," Ricky replied. "It was sudden, that was all."

"Next time I'll write them, make an appointment," said Katie.

"Who'd you get?" Don called from inside the building.

"Andy," said Ricky.

"Aw, that's a shame," Don said. "He owed me money."

"Where the fuck are they?" said Katie.

"You shouldn't have scattered them," Ricky said.

"Scattered? There's only two of them."

"They still got guns!" Don called.

Scala looked around.

"I wonder if there's any gators about still," she said.

"Gators?" Don shouted. "Is that your plan? Great backup!"

A few minutes passed, silently except for the chorus of night creatures all around them.

"Back inside," Katie said.

They put the workbench against the door, with Don still tied to it, then turned out the lights and crouched under the windows.

"I really hate to do this," said Katie.

She slid a pistol over to Ricky.

"I'll take one," Scala said.

"Ever been on a shooting range?" asked Katie.

"Ever heard of stalkers?" Scala replied. "Of course I've been on a fucking shooting range."

There was a deafening roar and the glass in the window above Ricky's head shattered and smashed.

"Come out!" Mig shouted from somewhere outside. "Come out and we won't kill you!"

Another burst of gunfire took the rest of the window off and spattered the wall behind with gouged bullet holes.

"I don't think he's telling the truth," Scala said.

Katie stood up and fired her enormous rifle through the window. Some bushes lit up and there was a shout. She ducked down, half a second before another barrage of gunfire shot over her head.

"How much ammunition have they got?" she asked.

"There were a lot of boxes in that van," said Ricky.

"OK," Katie replied.

She picked up a grenade and threw it into the night. There was an explosion followed by a weird, guttural roar that was almost a scream.

"Fuck," said Katie. "I think I hit a gator."

Time passed.

"You know this could go easier for you," said Don.

"Shoot him in the tits," Katie said.

"Gross," said Scala.

"I just want you for your bodies," Don said. "Seriously, though," he went on, "I don't need her. The cop. So give up and we'll let her go."

"Katie?" asked Scala. "Do you think he's telling the truth?"

Katie thought for a moment.

"Sorry," she said. "I was just wondering which tit to shoot first."

"So what's the rest of the plan?" Scala asked Ricky.

Ricky smiled.

"This pretty much is it," he said.

"OK," said Scala.

More time passed.

"Why don't they just rush us?" asked Ricky.

"I see you don't watch a lot of cowboy movies," Don replied.

"Nobody watches cowboy movies," Ricky said.

"This here's the fort," Don said. "It's made of brick, and it can be defended. Your lady friends have got weapons so all the injuns can do is wait."

"Nobody says injuns anymore," said Scala.

"I come from a much less politically correct time," Don said.

Something landed in the middle of the room.

It was a grenade, with the pin out.

TWENTY-SIX

"Shit!" shouted Katie and Ricky at once.

Ricky got there first. Fumbling, he managed to grab it, and throw it toward the window.

"No, you dick!" shouted Katie.

At the exact same moment Ricky threw the grenade, there was a burst of gunfire and Ricky fell to the ground.

Scala crawled across to Ricky.

"Is he OK?" Katie said. She sounded scared.

Ricky sat up.

"Ouch," he said, holding up his hand. It had been grazed by a bullet.

"Lucky," said Scala.

"Hey, it's not *my* hand," Ricky replied.

"Assholes," said Don. "They could have damaged the integrity of the receptacle."

"You're talking about me, aren't you?" said Ricky.

"So if they kill us, or maim us," Scala said, "they can't come through?"

"Can't transfer into a corpse," Don replied. "Not that you should—"

Scala stood up.

"Hey boys!" she shouted. "Don says you can't kill me!"

She fired her gun into the night.

A muffled shout came back.

She sat down again.

"Wasn't a gator that time," she said.

"Three of them," Katie said. "One possibly injured."

"Or dead," Ricky said, hopefully.

Katie shook her head. "He'd have yelled more if he was being killed. Three men, three doors."

"And one van," said Scala. She was standing by the window.

Katie said, "What's that got to—"

"It's moving," Scala said.

They looked out the window. The van was moving, but slowly, then faster, as though being pushed.

"What are they doing?" said Ricky.

"I think they're using it as a battering ram," Scala said.

"That's not going to work," Ricky said. "These walls are pretty strong."

"They're not aiming for the walls," said Katie as the van gathered speed. "They're aiming for the garage."

Will, wincing in pain, threw something into the back of the van, something bright.

"Take that, motherfuckers!" Mig shouted as the van rolled out of sight and into the garage doors.

"Why are they doing this?" Ricky asked.

He heard the garage door splinter and break.

"So they can get in here through the door into the garage."

"But we can just shoot them."

Katie's reply was lost as something exploded a few feet from the room they were in.

When Ricky could hear again, he found he was on the floor. There was dust everywhere, and bits of wood.

"Is everyone OK?" Scala asked.

"Yeah," said Katie, coughing.

The dust cleared. Mig was standing there, with Katie's gun in his hand.

"Never better," Mig said. "Van's fucked, though."

"You set fire to the ammo crates?" Don said as Mig cut his cuffs off.

"Not all of it," Mig said. "We're not stupid."

Don gave him a look.

"Says the guy who also set fire to the car."

Mig shrugged.

"I like setting fire to stuff," he said.

"Don't tie them up," said Don.

"Why not?" asked Will. He didn't sound pleased.

"Because we don't want to damage the goods," said Don. "Which also means," he added, looking at Will, "no hurting the goods."

"They owe me for this," Will said, holding his bloody arm.

"Sorry," said Scala.

"Don't worry," Don said. "Payback is on its way."

"What exactly is happening?" Ricky asked.

Don massaged his wrists.

"We need to make a few adjustments," he said.

"Oh, that's right," Ricky said. "Because we messed up your big arrival and Helen killed your pal."

"That," said Don, tight-lipped, "and because the big arrival was meant to happen on the beach, which is a stable location, and not in the middle of fucking nowhere."

Scala showed Katie her hand.

"Wow," said Katie. "That proves nothing."

"Ricky," Scala said, "show her your ears."

Ricky shook his head.

"It won't do any good," he said. "When she doesn't want to believe something, she doesn't believe it."

"That's me," Katie said. She sounded proud of herself.

Don grinned.

"People like you," he told her, "are our greatest weapon. Because when somebody doesn't believe they're going to get hit, it's so much fucking easier to hit them."

He took something from his pocket. It was a handful of change.

"Are we ready to begin?" he asked, then, without waiting for an answer, he threw the coins on the floor.

"Now what?" Katie asked.

"Oh, these?" Don said. "These are coins which exist in this time and also in the future. My friends, who are also in the future, will be using them as a kind of focus so they can come back in time to now."

"You really expect me to believe that?" Katie asked, contemptuously.

"No," said Don. "Isn't it great?"

He looked over at Mig.

"Him first," he said.

Mig dragged Ricky to his feet and pulled him over to the middle of the room.

"What are you doing?" Katie shouted.

"Shut your fucking hole or I will blow your face off," said Don, amiably. "Clothes," he said to Ricky.

"What?" Ricky asked.

"Jesus, do I need an interpreter?" asked Don.

Mig pushed Ricky down onto the floor.

He turned his head. Katie was crying.

"It's OK," Ricky said. "Just let it happen."

"Let what happen?" Katie said. She sounded scared.

Scala moved over to her and held her.

"Maybe don't look," she said, but Katie pushed her away.

Ricky didn't fight them. He just lay still as Mig and Don pulled his arms and legs away from his body, making him vaguely star-shaped.

"Look," said Mig. "A shit angel."

"Joe's coming," said Will. "I can feel it."

They sat there, looking at Ricky's unmoving body.

"He's taking his fucking time," said Mig. "Maybe the move screwed things up."

Don shook his head.

"The move just slowed things up a little," he said. "Will's right. Joe's coming."

He looked down at Ricky.

"And you're going," he said.

At first it was impossible to see, but Ricky felt it. A twitch of the nerves, a spasm of muscles, a small pain in his gut.

Then his limbs began to jerk.

"Hold him down," Don said. Mig and Will took an arm each, and Don leaned on Ricky's legs.

"What's happening to him?" Katie said.

Ricky's body was – there was no other word for it – *rippling*.

His skin looked like shadows were passing over it, rapidly like storm clouds. The color and texture of his flesh changed each second as if some kind of visual signal was being sent through him.

Ricky screamed.

"Stop it!" Katie shouted.

Ricky's body began to leap and shudder, so they held him down more firmly. The muscles under his constantly changing skin twisted and turned like ropes, and his chest swelled and sank.

Scala could see ribs appear, disappear, then return again. She could see his legs lengthen and his shoulders broaden.

Ricky's head turned toward Scala. He clenched his jaw, but his jaw was warping, taking on a different shape. He closed his eyes, but his eyeballs bulged under their lids.

And then, almost as quickly as it had begun, it was over. Ricky lay there, his body silent and unmoving.

Except it wasn't Ricky's body anymore.

"Where is he?" Katie screamed. "What have you done with my *brother*?"

Don grinned.

"Ricky's gone," he said. "Just gone."

Scala went to hold Katie and this time she let her.

"Joe's awful quiet," Mig said, after a while.

"So were you when you arrived," said Don, but he leaned over and grabbed the body's arm.

"Pulse is fine," he said. "He'll come round in a while."

He looked at Scala.

"Her turn," he said to Mig and Will.

"About that," said Scala.

Don stood up. He smiled again.

"Not keen?" he asked. "What is it about you that makes you so special?"

Scala frowned.

"I just don't feel like it is all," she said.

"Oh, OK then," Don said. "Wish you'd told me earlier, would have saved us a lot of hassle."

He turned to Mig.

"Get her," he said.

Scala didn't struggle when Mig and Will grabbed her. She just looked at Don and said:

"Remember Helen?"

"Yeah," said Don, casually but not as casually as he'd hoped.

"I plan to go the way she did."

"Who's Helen?" asked Will.

"Never mind," Don said.

"Don't fucking tell him never mind," Mig said. "Who is she?"

"Just some—" Don began.

"Helen fought back," Scala said. "She knew what was coming, and at first she welcomed it."

"She wanted it?" Katie said. "Who would want that?"

"Helen did," Scala answered. "She wanted to be herself, but

in a different body. And when she realized at the last second that she couldn't control what was happening, that she wouldn't be herself, she fought back."

"She the one who exploded?" Mig said.

"Yep," Scala said. "She was the one who exploded."

She smiled at Don.

"So go ahead," she said. "See how your big scheme goes with your boss's guts all over the room."

"You wouldn't do it," Don said.

"Why not?" Scala said. "I'm going to die anyway. You told me that several times. So I'm just going to fight her when she tries to come in, and she's going to die."

She looked at Mig and Will.

"Go ahead, boys," she said. "Turn me loose."

"OK," Don said, "We need to sedate her."

"Yeah, 'cos disused farmhouses are just filled with sedatives," said Katie.

"Sedatives are a bad idea," Will said. "She needs to be awake. Also, if she changes her mind and struggles, it could damage her. And she needs to be in one piece for the transfer to work."

"Shut up and let me think," Don said.

Mig looked at Will. "You heard the genius," he said. "Shut up and let him think."

"Alright," Don said to Scala. "How's this? You do as we say or we kill her."

"Wow, great plan," Katie said. "You're going to kill me anyway, dumbass."

Mig let go of Scala's arm.

"I've had enough of this," he said. "Boys, it's time for plan B."

"Plan B?" said Don. "What's plan B?"

Will took Don by one arm and Mig took him by the other.

"What the fuck are you doing?" Don shouted.

Mig pushed him down onto the floor.

Don struggled, but he wasn't a match for Mig's bulk. Will, whose arm was still not right, sat on Don's legs.

"This is fucking stupid!" Don said. "I'm Jane's number two! She needs me."

"Which makes her number one," Mig said.

"No!" Don shouted.

"Great argument," Will said.

"The thing is, Don," said Mig, "no fucker likes you. You're an asshole with a big mouth."

"Also a fucking weirdo," Will said. "Killing your own self? What the fuck sick shit is that?"

"Anyway," said Mig. "We agreed we're all expendable except for the boss."

"Why me?" Don said. He was pretty much crying now.

"Firstly, your work is pretty much done here," Will said. "Then there's the asshole thing. And thirdly, logistics. You came through yourself, which means it should be real easy for someone else to come through you."

"Like a wet paper bag," said Mig.

He took a coin from his pocket.

"Is that a silver dollar?" said Scala.

"Nothing but the best for the boss," Mig replied.

He threw it onto the ground.

At first, nothing happened. Don struggled a little but the fight had gone out of him, or maybe he was just tired.

Then Don groaned. His limbs twitched and he cried out. His skin began to change.

"My hands!" he cried out.

And then he was just one long scream.

Scala tried to look, but she couldn't. It was too awful, and besides, she was in pain herself.

She watched in disbelief as her own hands changed in front of her, and cried out because it hurt.

"What the fuck?" Katie said. "I do not understand any of this."

Don screamed, then he was silent, and then he changed. It was more sudden than with Ricky, and more dramatic, because where the body of a middle-aged man had been there was now the unconscious form of a younger woman.

"There she is," Mig said, and smiled.

"What do we do with these two?" said Will, indicating Katie and Scala.

"Wait till the boss comes round, of course," Mig said. "She'll know what to do with them."

TWENTY-SEVEN

Outside, the rain, which had not been light before, was now hammering down.

"What is up with this fucking weather?" Mig said.

"You don't like it," Katie said, "go back where you came from."

"I am so looking forward to killing you," Mig replied.

"Do it now, assfuck," said Katie.

"He can't," Scala said. "He has to wait for his boss to wake up."

"What a fucking mommy's boy," Katie replied.

Jane began to come round.

Will gave her some water.

"Thanks," she said, sitting up. She took off Don's jacket and shoes.

"You OK, boss?" asked Mig.

"Fine. Coming through Don was like punching a wet paper bag," said Jane.

"No regrets, then?" Scala asked. "No second thoughts?"

"I let him inside me," said Jane. "Guess it was his turn."

"Wow, sentimental," Katie said.

Jane got up, with help from Will and Mig.

"Do we have transportation?" she asked.

Mig looked at the ground.

"Your bitch here blew up all the transport," Katie said. "I guess Don was the one with the brains."

"Nice try," Mig said. He turned to Jane.

"I saw a pickup truck down the track a way," he said. "It had branches over it so I guess someone was trying to hide it."

He smiled at Katie, who gave him the finger.

"OK," said Jane. "Wake Joe up, tell him we're leaving in ten."

Mig went over to Joe's body and began to shake it.

"He is *out*," he said.

"Maybe he's dead," suggested Scala.

"Chalk up another one to Team Fucking Asshole," said Katie.

Jane picked up a gun.

"Says the bozo who got me an armory," she said.

There was a flash in the sky, followed by another, then another.

"I thought this was supposed to be the fucking sunshine state," said Mig.

"Should have paid more attention in moron school," Katie replied.

"I think it's a hurricane," Scala said. "Coming on fast, too."

"We need to get out of here," said Jane. "Will, load the truck with all the guns and ammo you can find. I'll come out with you."

"What about me?" asked Mig.

"You stay here and kill those two," said Jane.

The rest of the gang went outside. The lightning was almost constant now, as were the immense thundercrashes.

Mig picked up a gun from the table.

"That one's not loaded, jerkoff," Katie said.

Mig picked up a second gun.

"Better?" he asked.

Katie shrugged.

"Get up against the wall," said Mig.

"Why?" said Scala.

"I don't want to shoot you sitting down," he said.

"Like it makes a difference," Katie said. "I can't even die sitting down."

She stood up. Scala followed her.

"OK," Katie said. "We're ready."

"Any last requests?" Mig said.

"Does 'go fuck yourself' count?" asked Katie.

Scala said nothing. She looked round the room. The table of weapons, the busted-in windows, Joe's body on the floor.

"Hell of a day," she said.

Katie looked at Mig.

"Jesus, do it before we die of old age," she said.

"Fuck you," Mig said. He aimed at her face and pulled the trigger.

Nothing happened.

"The—" said Mig, and pulled again.

"He believed you," said Scala.

"First mistake," Katie said. "Never trust someone who says a gun is loaded."

She pulled a handgun from out of her clothes.

"Second mistake," she said, and shot Mig in the chest.

"Let's get out of here," Katie said.

"With you on that."

Scala picked up a gun.

"Sure you can use that?" Katie asked.

"I told you," Scala said.

"Telling is one thing," Katie said. "Doing is another."

Scala was about to reply when there was a loud noise from outside and a flash.

Katie fell to the ground.

The door opened and Jane came in with Will.

"I fucking knew it," she said. "I'm surrounded by cretins."

Katie moved. Her leg was covered in blood.

"Hand-picked cretins," she said, and passed out.

Jane kicked her in an absent-minded way, then said: "I'm sick of this."

She turned to Will. "Bring the truck around."

"I should stay here," said Will.

"I said bring the truck round," Jane said.

Will went out and Jane closed the door.

"You ever wonder why me?" she asked.

"Lately?" said Scala. "All the time."

Jane laughed. "Don told you, right? You and everyone else, random choices."

"Just because we were in the same place," said Scala.

"Does that sound likely to you?" asked Jane.

"How would I know?" Scala said. "This has never happened to me before."

"You were chosen for two reasons," Jane said. "Mostly because of convenience. Most of Florida had survived the Pulse, which made it unusual, so it was easy to find a place to gather you all. Why look farther than your own doorstep?"

"Except for Don."

"Poor Don," said Jane. "It was almost funny, sending him all the way up to Alaska to kill himself. I tell a lie," she corrected herself, "it *was* funny."

"You said two reasons," said Scala.

"I did, didn't I?" Jane said.

She put down her gun.

"I can't just walk into your world and hold up a bank," she said. "It's too much to learn, and besides, I need something more."

"Let me guess," said Scala. "You need to quit and go legit."

"That's right," said Jane. "I need money, and I need position. I need to look like a good guy and advance my career. Improve my status."

"And to do that…" Scala prompted.

"I need a new identity," Jane said. "Someone who has money and position. Someone who can go where they like and do what they like."

She put her finger on Scala's chest.

"Someone like you," she said.

Scala pried the finger off.

"Don't you have to, you know, time travel to do that?" she said. "Which means you missed your window."

Jane laughed.

"If I can come through into Don from years in the fucking

287

future," she said, "then I can certainly come into you in the present."

"That doesn't make sense."

"Honey," Jane replied, "we're just molecules, right? A big swarm of atoms floating round in a space which is also made of atoms. Me going into you is just a cloud going into another cloud."

"Sorry," Scala said. "Not gonna work. You were too scared to do it before and nothing's changed."

"Scared, no," Jane said. "Getting here was nothing to do with you. All I needed to do was make sure I was in this room, and Don was the easy way to do it. I walked through him like he was a fucking field of wheat."

She looked at Scala with cold, not entirely sane eyes.

"You can't stop me," she said. "All I need to do is dose you up a little, make you more amenable, and you won't even know you're gone."

She smiled.

"You're next," she said. "Better get used to it."

The door opened and Will came in.

"Truck's loaded," he said. "Just a couple more guns in here."

Jane pointed her gun at Scala.

"Time to go," she said.

"Wait," Scala said. "What about Katie?"

"Who's Katie?" said Jane. "Oh, her. She'll bleed out."

"She's a cop," Scala said. "If you leave a cop here, they'll never stop following you."

"Fuck," Jane said. "I don't need this right now. Will, get her in the truck and then we can drop her by the road somewhere."

"Considerate," said Scala.

Will carried Katie's unconscious body out of the room.

"Anything else?" Jane asked, sharply.

"Just this," said Scala. "Don't look behind you."

Jane turned.

Joe punched her in the face and she hit the ground.

"I told you," said Scala.

"What the fuck, Joe?" Jane said, wiping blood from her mouth.

"He's not Joe," said Scala.

"Did you see me wink?" the man said.

"No," Scala said. "You winked?"

"You're joking. I winked at you," he replied. "To say, you know, it's me."

"I didn't see it," Scala said. "Sorry."

"What the shit is going on here?" Jane said.

"Hi, I'm Ricky," said the man.

"It nearly killed me," Ricky said. "Then I thought of Helen, and what she said, and how she nearly did it. But Helen didn't know what was coming, not really, and I did. So I fought. I almost blacked out, it hurt like hell…"

"But you did it," Scala said. She looked at him. "Lot nicer looking, if you don't mind me saying."

"Not at all," Ricky said. "Just need to get these lasered off."

He held up his fists. FUCK and YOU.

"I'd keep 'em," Scala said. "Gives you attitude."

The door opened.

"I got her in back," Will said. Then:

"Joe?"

"That's not Joe," said Jane. "Shoot him."

"What?" Will said.

"Oh, Christ on a cross," Jane said. She picked up her gun from off the floor and aimed it at Ricky.

"No!" Scala said, and leapt at Jane.

The two of them fought for the gun. Then Scala twisted Jane's arm and there was a sharp bang and Will fell to the ground.

Jane pushed Scala aside and ran out of the building.

"Get after her," said Scala.

"In that storm?" Ricky said.

"Your sister's in that truck," Scala said.

Ricky ran out.

Scala bent over Will's body, took something from his pocket, and followed Ricky outside.

Jane was having trouble starting the truck.

"You need the key," Scala shouted over the noise of the storm.

She held it up.

"Give it to me!" Jane shouted.

"Let's get Katie out first," Scala said.

"We're bargaining now?" Ricky asked.

"How far do you think she's going to get in a stolen truck?" asked Scala. "A truck registered to a cop. They'll be on her like fucking piranhas."

"OK," said Ricky.

He opened the passenger door of the pickup.

"Don't shoot me," he told Jane, and pulled Katie from the cab. She was unconscious, but the bleeding had stopped, which he supposed was something.

Ricky could barely move in the wind and the torrential rain

as he took Katie back inside. Scala threw the keys through the open cab window. Jane beckoned Scala closer.

"I'll be back for you," she said. "Maybe not tomorrow, but soon."

"And I'll be waiting," said Scala.

They watched from inside the house as Jane started the engine and began to drive. The wind was battering the truck as it moved off.

Something flew past the window.

"Was that a tree?" Ricky asked.

The truck moved a few yards, then stuck in mud. They saw the driver's door move as Jane tried to open it, but the wind was battering the truck so strongly now she couldn't push it hard enough.

There was an enormous gust of wind, an eruption of soil and branches. The truck was caught up in it, and flew into the air. It wheeled in the rain and lightning for a moment before smashing back into the ground, where it crumpled and broke in half.

"I don't think she's in Kansas anymore," Scala said.

Ricky and Scala watched for an hour, but nobody came out of the truck.

Katie came round slowly. When she saw what looked like Joe bending over her, she tried to blind him with her thumbs, but fortunately for Ricky she was too weak.

"We'll explain later," Scala said.

"Lot to take in," Ricky agreed.

He pulled his pants away from his stomach.

"What are you doing?" Scala asked.

"Just checking," said Ricky.

"Now?"

"Hell yeah," Ricky answered.

Scala rolled her eyes.

"Fucking guys," she said.

They didn't want to sleep, but they did. When they awoke, the sky was clearing. The rain had stopped and the wind had fallen.

Scala stayed with Katie and Ricky went outside.

He looked back at the house and shook his head.

They took the bodies they could find and laid them out around the truck. Then they threw the guns into the water.

Ricky picked his sister up and he and Scala began to walk down the track toward the road.

"I got muscles," he said.

"And if you want to keep them," Scala said, "you'd better start going to the gym."

"Rats," said Ricky.

After a mile or two, an RV pulled over and gave them a ride to a hospital in the city.

TWENTY-EIGHT

"I still don't believe it," Katie said.

The table beside her hospital bed was littered with cards, flowers, and fruit. Next to it, in the least comfortable chairs in the world, were Ricky and Scala. Katie was sitting upright in the bed and staring at the face of the man who had once been Joe but was now her brother.

"Better get used to it," Ricky replied.

"I mean, you always looked like such a sack of shit," she went on. "And now – jeez, if you weren't my brother..."

Ricky choked.

"Don't," he finally managed to say.

"Technically," Scala said, "neither of you share any DNA or genetic similarity, so if you want to jump him, you can."

"Please stop," said Ricky.

Katie grinned.

"Fucking coward," she said. "It's him alright. You're off the hook, little brother."

"I see you've had plenty of visitors," Scala said.

"Cops don't like it when other cops get hurt," said Katie. "But yeah, they're good people."

She took a fistful of grapes.

"They found the truck like I said they would, at Grandpa's farm," she said. "I told them I was driving out that way when the storm began and drove in to take shelter."

"And then what?" asked Scala. "A gang of nameless, ID-less crooks with a load of weapons were using it as their hideout and you engaged with them?"

"Pretty much," said Katie. "Is there a likelier explanation?"

She ate a grape.

"Besides," she said. "This way I'll probably get a medal, and what is significantly more fucking useful, a promotion."

"So everyone's happy," said Ricky.

"Oh, I'm never happy," Katie said.

He looked at her.

"What are you smiling for, then?" he said.

• • •

Ricky and Scala walked down the corridor together.

"Let's get a coffee," she said.

"Fuck that," said Ricky. "There's a Denny's across the street."

• • •

"There's cream on top of the pancake," Scala said, "and there's a cherry on the cream."

"Your point being?" Ricky asked.

"I'm just saying that if you want to go on being buff, maybe you should watch what you eat."

"Maybe I don't want to go on being buff," Ricky said, sucking cream off his fingers.

"Oh God, that's vile," Scala said. "If you stop being buff, you're going to look like a fat fucking busted scarecrow. Just lumps and bulges."

"OK," Ricky said. He was half listening to Scala and half watching a group of women at the next table who were looking at Ricky and giggling.

"Do not lick your finger," said Scala. "Do *not* – oh God."

"I'm just having some fun," Ricky said.

"I can't look," said Scala, covering her eyes. "Are they dialing 911 yet?"

"One of them is writing something on a piece of paper," Ricky said. "I think it's her number."

"Oh God," Scala said.

One of the girls came over. She dropped a scrap of paper on the table.

"He's killed people, you know," Scala said.

"She's joking," Ricky said.

The girl looked at Scala.

"You're her," she said, then: "Are you *dating* him?"

"No," said Scala. "Definitely not. No."

"We're friends," Ricky said.

"Wow," the girl said. "You must be getting plenty to friendzone *that*."

Scala looked at her.

"Actually," she said, "I'm going to ask him to be my new manager."

"Smart move," said the girl, and left.

"You're what?" Ricky said.

"Jonty's gone," Scala replied. "And I need to get back to work."

"I'm a pap," Ricky said. "Also a loser."

"You *were* a pap," said Scala. "And I don't hire losers."

Ricky frowned.

"Do I get a new camera?" he asked. "And a laptop."

Scala shook her head. "Laptop, yes. Camera, no. Not a pap anymore, remember?"

"I'd need a car."

"I'm not buying you a fucking Aztek. Integral tent or not."

Scala looked at him. She was almost smiling.

"Think about it," she said.

Ricky thought about it.

"When do I start?" he asked.

Thanks

This book is named after the song "Ricky's Hand" by Fad Gadget, which – like all of Frank Tovey's work – is unique, remarkable, and brilliant.

And it would not have been possible without the influence of the work of Jack Finney: his astonishing novels *Time and Again* and *From Time To Time* were very much in my mind when I wrote this.

Much gratitude also goes to everyone at Titan but especially Cat Camacho, Julia Lloyd, Lydia Gittins, Michael Beale, Adrian McLaughlin, Dan Coxon, and Andy Hawes.

About the Author

David Quantick is an Emmy Award-winning television writer for such shows as *Avenue 5, Veep, The Thick of It* and *The Day Today*. He is the author of *All My Colors, Night Train, Sparks, The Mule,* and two writing manuals: *How To Write Everything* and *How To Be A Writer*. Find him at davidquantick.com or @quantick on Twitter.

For more fantastic fiction, author events,
exclusive excerpts, competitions, limited editions and more

VISIT OUR WEBSITE
titanbooks.com

LIKE US ON FACEBOOK
facebook.com/titanbooks

FOLLOW US ON TWITTER AND INSTAGRAM
@TitanBooks

EMAIL US
readerfeedback@titanemail.com